The people of Eli and Jenny's generation found themselves both bored and uncertain in a time when old truths had been rendered obsolete and new ones had yet to take their place. The restless energy that had brought the race up from prehistoric savagery, dammed up, sought for an outlet. Finding nothing, it turned on itself, the beast-instinct that was still part of man, blindly recognizing man's unhappiness and blindly seeking a physical cause of that unhappiness to blame and battle.

Thus the world was a loaded bomb for which Sellar's pogrom against the Members provided the arming device . . . .

Time To Teleport/Delusion World

TIME TO TELEPORT/DELUSION WORLD

Other Gordon R. Dickson titles available
  from Ace Science Fiction:

Alien Art/Arcturus Landing
Dorsai!
Home From the Shore
Lost Dorsai
Love Not Human
Masters of Everon
Naked to the Stars
Necromancer
On the Run
Soldier, Ask Not
The Space Swimmers
Spacial Delivery
The Spirit of Dorsai
Tactics of Mistake

Combat SF, edited by Gordon R. Dickson

TIME TO TELEPORT

GORDON R. DICKSON

DELUSION WORLD

SF

ace books

A Division of Charter Communications Inc.
A GROSSET & DUNLAP COMPANY
51 Madison Avenue
New York, New York 10010

TIME TO TELEPORT

copyright © 1960 by Gordon R. Dickson

DELUSION WORLD

copyright © 1961 by Ace Books

An ACE Book

Published Simultaneously in Canada

2 4 6 8 0 9 7 5 3
Manuractured in the United States of America

TIME TO TELEPORT

CHAPTER I

A COURIER air-sub with the coral red of the Underseas Power Group tipping its wing stubs came diving out of the blue south sky at a little after noon. It checked, and for the short space of several minutes hung hovering above the huge floating structure that was Cable Island, seat of government and political neutral ground for the Autonomous Groups, symbolically built and anchored in twelve hundred fathoms of chill sea water above the theoretical midpoint of the old Atlantic cable. Then the Island signaled clearance; and the ship dropped gently to the landing deck. From it stepped a young man of less than twenty. He wore a silver tunic trimmed in red; a sea-green kilt was clipped about his lean waist by a gun-belt and holster from which a handgun with a coral-red butt protruded. And an ebony-black official courier's cloak clung to the magnetic shoulder tabs of his tunic, while a courier's pouch with thumb-lock was clamped to his right forearm.

A lieutenant of the Neutral Guard took charge of him, impounded the gun and checked him through the scanners. These mechanical watchdogs discovered nothing dangerous either on or within the courier. The officer turned him over to two guards with instructions to conduct him to the main council room, and there deliver him to Eli Johnstone, the Spokesman for his Group. The two guards saluted, about faced and set off smartly, marching in step and rather hurrying the brightly dressed young man between them. It was,

1

perhaps, an unnecessary display of military manners; but the five hundred man Neutral Guard were, after all, the only professional soldiers left on Earth.

The main council room of Cable Island occupied the very center of the mammoth structure, being surrounded by committee rooms and these in turn surrounded by the offices of the individual groups. Above all this was the solar deck and the landing deck upon which Poby Richards, the courier, had come down with his air-sub. Below it were the living quarters, recreation centers and such, while the bottom layer of the Island was taken up by kitchens, storerooms and machinery.

The main council room itself was a steep-sided circular amphitheater, the sides of which were arranged in three levels and each level divided into sections to hold the representatives of each individual Group. There were sections for one hundred and twenty-eight Groups, but, in practice, only about thirty Groups bothered to have representatives permanently stationed on the island and it was unusual to find more than twelve Groups at business in the council room at any one time. The truth was that the larger Groups usually each spoke for a number of smaller ones as well; as a result there were at this particular moment only ten Spokesmen present in the amphitheater. One of these ten was from the highly important Communications Group, headed by young Alan Clyde; and another from the Underseas Domes whose Spokesman was that same Eli Johnstone that Poby was seeking.

Eli had built Underseas—and himself along with it—into a political factor to be reckoned with.

The Underseas cities had a unanimity of feeling that the land Groups lacked. Eli had united the small Underseas Groups who needed a strong voice to speak for them on the Island; and for the last five years he had been able to stand forth and match point to point with Anthony Sellars, Spokesman for the overwhelmingly large Transportation Group. Sellars was considered by most to be the most powerful political personage in the world. He was the lion that Eli worried; and, wolflike, fought in the never-ending battle for position among the Groups.

They sat now across the amphitheater from each other, each in their respective sections, Eli nursing the knee of his bad left leg absent-mindedly with both hands beneath the cover of the desk that, with his chair and himself, occupied the front of his section, walled off by waist-high partitions from the sections on either side. He was a slight, dark man in his late thirties, with a thin face early graven in bitter-humorous lines. The lines were deepened now by strain and fatigue; and he sat in a half-daze of numb tiredness, listening with only half an ear to the flexible baritone of Jacques Veillain, Underspokesman for Transportation, as he rehearsed the popular list of indictments against the organization presently under discussion, the Philosophical Researchists. The members of that organization called themselves Members of the Human Race, but to the easily swayed, easily frightened little people of the world they were the "Inhumans."

"—vivisectors and mutators," Veillain was snarling at the assembled Spokesmen and Underspokesmen. "These so-called Philosophical Researchists would write us all off as outmoded ape men to usher in their new era of monstrosities—"

In front of and a little to one side of Veillain, Anthony Sellars sat immovable, his square, flat face without expression as he listened to the words of his Underspokesman. Watching, one would have thought that there was no connection between the two, that Veillain's attack on the Members was as fresh to Sellars as it was to the others in the council room; yet, as everyone present knew, Veillain was merely preparing the ground for his superior, laying down the artillery barrage before Sellars' personal assault.

Eli was the last man present to be deceived by appearances, and he let his attention slip from Veillain entirely and his gaze wander along the first level until he came to the Communications Section and Alan Clyde. The young Spokesman sat listening, his dark, narrow-featured face propped on his right fist, his expression thoughtful. Eli watched him carefully. Alan was brilliant and elusive. Eli had been wooing Communications for some time now, with little evidence of success.

The rest of the council, thought Eli, as he withdrew his attention from Clyde and let his gaze wander around the rest of the room, was even more badly attended than usual. Besides himself, Sellars, and Clyde, he counted only seven full Spokesmen and a scattering of Underspokesmen and aides. True, the really important representatives like Bornhill of Atomics and Stek Howard of Metals, were where you would expect them to be in their sections. But the great majority of the seats were empty. Some of those present looked frankly bored.

And yet this was at a time when political rivalry among the Groups was at its peak. Paradoxical, thought Eli, nursing his knee, but not so paradoxical at that, when you came to think of it. The Groups had outlived their usefulness, the political setup had frozen and was now beginning to mortify. Which was one of the reasons he, at least, was getting out of it.

With the swiftness of a lifetime of practice, he buried the thought before it had time to linger in his mind. *Sellars,* he thought, *Tony. Yes, I'm sure Tony sees it too that the Groups can't last. Eighty years ago they were a good idea. Organize the world along mutually interdependent lines and end all possibility of war.* The barriers to be not geographical but occupational. How could Transportation declare war on Meteorology, or Meteorology on Communications? No one cuts the rope he hangs by. But that was eighty years ago when the old hates and prejudices still held. *Now,* thought Eli, *the world is ready to act as a single unit and Tony wants to be on top of it. That's the reason for this witch hunt against the Members he's been pushing. Well, let him. People aren't that primitive any more . . .*

"—and when our police broke into the laboratory, all the equipment within it was found to have been melted down with thermite and to be practically unidentifiable," Veillain was saying. "By careful reconstruction, however, it was

possible to ascertain that some of it had been radiation devices. . . .''

Eli felt a sudden tap on his shoulder. He turned his head
and looked back and up into the serious, healthy face of Kurt
Anders, his Underspokesman.

"Courier, Eli," said Kurt.

"All right," replied Eli. "Thanks, Kurt. Bring him in."

Kurt moved back and a scintillating combination of silver,
red, green and black slipped into his place. Eli smiled.

"All right, Poby," he said. "What've you got?"

"A sealed cube relayed through Dome One, Eli," whispered Poby. "Here . . ." and he held out the arm to which
the pouch was attached.

Eli fitted his thumb into the aperture of the thumb-lock and
it, recognizing his print as the one it had been set for, snapped
open. Not one, but two cubes came rolling out.

Poby Richards blinked foolishly at them.

Eli looked down at the cubes and then back up at Poby
curiously. He juggled the little objects in the palm of his
hand.

"But there was only one!" Poby protested, his face tragic.
"I know—I mean, I watched the pouch sealed myself in
Dome One and it's been locked on my arm ever since." And
he held out arm and pouch for verification.

Eli looked back at the cubes. They looked identical, but of
course they would not be. For a moment he rolled them back
and forth in his palm and then his hand closed over them.

"Let it go, Poby," he said. "But go back and wait for me
in the office. I'm going to want you later."

"Yes, Eli," and the young courier slipped away. Kurt
moved back into the vacated space.

Eli turned to the desk in front of him. In the polished black
surface that winked back at him there was a slot. He turned
the cubes over in his fingers until he found on one of them a
mark he was expecting. He slipped this one into the slot.

There was a moment's pause and then from the high
headrest of the chair a voice seemed to murmur in Eli's ear.

"Eli: Everything is ready. Arthur Howell."

Eli nodded. He turned his attention back to the mysterious extra cube. For several seconds he sat, turning it over before his eyes and thinking. Then he put it, also, into the slot.

Again the pause. Then, this time, a deeper, familiar voice.

"Eli: You—"

Swiftly, but with decision, Eli stabbed at the disposal button on the desk. Before his eyes a little panel flashed back and the new voice in his ears cut off as he watched, through a shielded transparency, the two cubes tumble into a little recess where the flash of an electric arc consumed them. The small panel snapped back again. Eli drew a deep breath and released the button, before turning his attention back once more to the orating Veillain.

But Veillain had nearly finished. He was winding up now on a graceful note and turning the floor over to Sellars. Eli sat up; and by an effort of will forced the tiredness from him so that the council room seemed to suddenly stand out sharp and bright, and the people within it to take on a new solidity, as if the illumination of the amphitheater had suddenly been upped a notch. Veillain was sitting down and Tony Sellars was rising.

He was a large man but his impressiveness did not lie in his size. He was, in fact, slab-bodied, with wide shoulders, but a wide waist also—wide, but flat, for there was no fat on him. And he held himself stiffly erect, so that he seemed to move all in one piece and bend, with difficulty, only at the waist, when he bent at all. His body was the big-boned, serviceable carcass of the manual laborer—what would have been called a peasant's body at one time in history. His tunic, kilt, and long, official cape of Transportation blue, seemed to square him off, rather than lend him grace and dignity. He was in his late forties, with hair untouched by gray and face unlined.

"All right," he said, laying his large, capable hands palm down on the desk before him. "My Underspokesman has given you the background. Now I'll give you the rest of it."

He paused, sweeping them all with his eyes; and his gaze, like his rough-hewn body and his dominant voice, broadcast to them a sense of power and conviction that his way was right and his conclusions true.

"The Groups," he said, "have always prided themselves on a high degree of tolerance. And for over half a century this tolerance hasn't been abused."

With Sellars' eyes straight upon him, Eli permitted himself the luxury of a small ironic smile. But if the Spokesman for Transportation noticed, he gave no sign of it.

"There is, however," he went on, "a point at which tolerance must give way to the dictates of common sense. Such is the present time.

"In the last twenty years we've seen the emergence of a secret society masquerading as a philosophical association. The members of this society have taken to themselves the notion that the human race is obsolete. They have taken it on themselves to decide we're all due to become extinct to make way for the next generation, which will be something entirely different."

Sellars paused and let his slow, impressive gaze sweep the room once more.

"Now that," he went on, "is a fine theory. And as long as it stays a theory I don't mind who holds it. But these crackpots who call themselves *Members* of the *Human Race*—as if only they were, and nobody else was—have gone ahead to try and give evolution a helping hand. Their notion of this is to try hard radiation on themselves and anyone else they can get their hands on, to dabble in every sort of dirty occult business they can dig up, and to practice gene experimentation on their own children.

"This, alone, to my mind, is reason enough for us to get together and clean up the situation they've caused. But there's more to it than just that. I've had Veillain list you off some accounts of what's been discovered lately about these so-called "foundations" and "research centers" they put up, and if you listened to him carefully, you heard only one thing—and that is simply this. These Members—these *In-humans* as people rightly call them—are succeeding."

He stopped to let this sink in. The council room remained silent about him; and, after a second, he went on.

"I tell you they *are* succeeding. The fact that I cannot at this moment produce a specimen of their 'next step in evolution' should not blind you to the fact that we have abundant indirect evidence that such specimens do exist. Fiddle a bit more and you'll get some dangerous freaks. Want an example?

"For two hundred years now the human race has been playing with the idea of possessing the so-called psi faculties—telepathy, telekinesis, etc. And for thirty years the Members have been telling us that our next evolutionary step would be not a physical, but a mental one, which would enable us to possess these faculties. But for the first twenty-five of these years they were publishing regular reports about their experimentation in this field, and had so often repeated their belief in the existence of such faculties that the general public had become almost tone deaf to that particular portion of their propaganda scale.

"Suddenly, during this last five years, the reports dwindle. The propaganda ceases, references to the psi faculties become general and vague. Why? And now that we, at least, within the Transportation Group, have to root them out of their dark corners, there are inexplicable instances of Members being warned of our raids ahead of time, of Members disappearing from the equivalent of locked rooms. How?"

Sellars paused once more.

"Both these things," he said slowly, "as well as a growing body of popular legend that sounds as if it might have come from the darkest of the Dark Ages, confirm me in my belief that the Members have succeeded in developing something or things, or being or beings, that are actively dangerous to the whole race as we know it today. In my mind the only solution is for us, for once, to set aside the autonomy of our individual groups and form a single united, supreme authority to deal with this present emergency. I leave it to you."

And with that Sellars sat down, yielding the floor.

Glancing swiftly around the room, Eli was aware of the shrewdness of Sellars' appeal that had particular force with this particular audience. The fight among the Groups had always been to narrow the fight—for the leaders of larger Groups to crowd out the Spokesmen of smaller Groups. And this would be a step forward. For such a supreme authority, to be successful, would have to be restricted to a few members, and where would those members be found except among the few top-ranking representatives here at this moment? Stek Howard's face was frankly interested, Kurachi of Plastics had a half-dreamy, half-expectant smile on his face, and even old Bornhill's eyes were veiled and thoughtful under his gray brows.

"Idiots," growled Eli to himself.

For a moment he struggled with his conscience against the knowledge that this was, strictly speaking, no longer any of his business. Then, abruptly, he gave in. "Ahoy, ahoy, check!" he muttered to himself and, getting to his feet, raised his voice. "Mr Chairman!"

Stek Howard, Chairman of the Day, came out of his pleasant abstraction and banged the gravel on his desk before him.

"Underseas," he acknowledged.

"Thank you," said Eli. All eyes in the council room were on him now and he smiled pleasantly back at them, but especially at Sellars.

They all looked back at him; and not, he noticed, particularly with approval. The wealth and size of Transportation so overshadowed all of them individually, that usually their attitude was distrust of Sellars and a bias toward Eli. Today, however, Sellars had dangled a juicy plum before their eyes and they did not want Eli coming along and pointing out that it really belonged to somebody else.

"Spokesmen and Gentlemen," said Eli. "I am surprised—in fact I'm astonished at your reaction to what you've just heard. I've sat here and listened in horror to what Transportation had just had to say. I was assured that you had listened with horror too. At the close of his words I could hardly restrain myself from jumping to my feet, and only held myself back because of the conviction that you, all of you would be jumping to your feet, to say, as I am saying''—Eli turned to look Sellars blandly in the face— ''that Transportation has set forward the only possible method of dealing with this situation. And furthermore I can conceive of no man more worthy or capable to head such a supreme authority than Spokesman Sellars.'' He sat down.

The council sat back, shocked, as Eli took his seat. He leaned back and whispered to Kurt.

''Come on, Kurt,'' he said, ''Back to the office.''

Slowly and with dignity he got up, inclined his head to the chairman, and led the way back and out of his section. As he went up the ramp and passed out through the exit at the top of the amphitheater, a low muttering of representative to representative across the low walls between sections broke out behind him; and he smiled to himself. He had thrown his weight in the wrong direction at the wrong time for Sellars. Now the natural suspicions of the others would fight against their cupidity. A more powerful Sellars might be risked for the increase of power they themselves would gain. But a possible Sellars-Eli combination? Not if they knew it.

So Eli smiled. But abruptly the smile faded, to be replaced by a scowl.

''You're a damn quixotic fool,'' he murmured to himself. ''Why the hell didn't you keep out of it?''

CHAPTER II

THE OFFICES belonging to Underseas formed one of the smaller suites and were well removed from even the large committee rooms. This, combined with the fact that business was still theoretically in process in the main council room, led to their being deserted at this particular hour, with the single exception of a secretary at work in the outer office.

"See that we aren't disturbed, Kara," Eli told her, as he and Kurt entered the outer office and he led the way, with his swift limp across to the half-open door that led to the inner office that was his own.

"Yes, Eli." She looked up, her dark, somewhat angular features important with a message. "Poby Richards—"

"That's all right," said Eli. "I've spoken to him, Kara."

He led the way on into the private office and shut the door. Leading the way past the half-open aperture of a sliding panel that opened on a little adjoining room fitted with couch and lavatory, he came to the large, impressively paneled desk that was standard Spokesman furniture. The desk was equipped to do everything but measure him for a new suit of clothes; and during all the seven years of his residence in this office, he had scarcely used a tenth of the gadgets installed in it. Now, as he came up to it, he punched buttons with recklessness.

A piny scent swept through the office, a murmur of woodland music crept out on the air and the desk, like a dutiful patient sticking out his tongue for a physician, thoughtfully protruded a small but complete bar from one end of itself.

"How about a drink, Kurt?" asked Eli.

"Why I suppose so," said Kurt, a little surprised. It was the first time such an invitation had ever been extended to him by Eli. "I almost never . . ."

Eli sighed a little.

"Neither do I any more," he said. "There was a time when I never expected to run out of thirst. But it's odd, somewhere along the way I seem to have lost it. Well"— he turned brisk—"we'll have one anyway. The occasion calls for it."

And he proceeded to make himself busy with the materials in the bar.

Kurt chuckled.

"You did a nice job."

"Nice job?" echoed Eli, looking up.

"On Tony," said Kurt.

"Oh, that," Eli frowned. "Kurt, you're going to have to watch out on that. I've just spiked this business temporarily." He checked himself abruptly, and rose with two glasses in his hands, one of which he handed to Kurt. "I'm getting ahead of myself. Here, take this."

Kurt accepted it, a little unskillfully.

"Well now," said Eli. "Here's to you, Kurt."

"To me?" said Kurt, surprised.

"Yes," said Eli, and took a small drink. "How'd you like to be Spokesman for Underseas?"

Kurt grinned. But Eli did not. And gradually Kurt's grin faded. He put his glass down on the edge of the desk.

"You aren't getting out, Eli?" he said, incredulously.

"That's right," said Eli, cheerfully. "Only I call it retiring." Kurt's face was a little pale.

"You're joking."

"No, I'm not," said Eli sharply.

"But—" Kurt stumbled. "You must be. Why, you *are* Underseas, Eli. The only reason our coalition groups stick with us is because of you."

"That's nonsense," said Eli, setting his own drink down

on the desk. "They stick because of the advantages of being combined with us."

"But I couldn't handle them!" burst out Kurt in desperation.

"How do you know until you've tried?" asked Eli. "Besides, if you want, it won't have to be more than temporary—until the Domes appoint someone officially to replace me. I think they'd give it to you without a question if you wanted it. But if you don't, they'll be able to find someone else." He looked at the stunned Underspokesman with sympathy. "But you don't know until you've tried whether you'll want it or not."

"But you, Eli," said Kurt, looking up at him. "I can't understand why *you* want to get out!"

Eli sighed gustily, and the bitter lines in his face sharpened momentarily.

"I suppose you thought the Spokesmanship was something I wanted," he said.

"But, my God, Eli," protested Kurt stupidly. "You went after it like a house afire. No one knew you eight years ago!"

"Well, it wasn't," said Eli, watching him. "I suddenly woke up to realize that I was getting older and not doing anything. Everybody my own age fitted into the world. I felt I had to catch up, so I went gunning for the biggest job I could find."

"And now that there's no place else to go, you're getting out?" There was accusation in Kurt's voice.

"No," said Eli. He half turned from the Underspokesman, staring at the wall of the office, but not seeing it. "I went into politics because I thought I was wasting my time doing nothing. How, I think I'm wasting my time in politics. All my life I've been hunting for what I really want to do; and I've just decided to keep after it." He flicked a glance at Kurt. "Or do you think that at nearly forty I'm too old?"

"No," said Kurt, quickly. "No but . . ." he hesitated, then suddenly burst out. "But it's a selfish thing to do, then."

"Agreed," said Eli cheerfully. It was the kind of merciless admission that he liked to make; and it restored his good humor. He became conscious, suddenly, of his aching knee and sat down.

"If that's the only reason you're getting out," amended Kurt. Having uncovered feet of clay in his idol, Kurt was in a hurry to cover them up.

"Another reason is that I think the world is headed for hell in a handbasket," said Eli. "But that needn't concern you."

"I don't understand," said Kurt.

"It doesn't take understanding," said Eli. "The most casual observation shows the Groups disintegrating as a governmental system; there's no place to go but toward a completely single-unit world and in spite of the experience of the past two thousand years we don't seem to be ready for that yet. What would *you* guess the immediate future is going to be like?"

Kurt stared at him.

"Do you really believe that?" he asked. "I know times are tense, now, with all this superstition about the Members—"

"Tense!" echoed Eli. "Times are always tense. People are always—"

He had swung about in a half turn as he spoke and now he suddenly halted.

"Poby!" he said.

Looking very embarrassed indeed, the young courier was standing in the panel entrance to the little side room of the office. Now, with Eli's and Kurt's eyes full upon him, he faltered out into the main room.

"You asked me to wait for you in your office, Eli."

"You've been listening to all this?" demanded Eli.

"I fell asleep on your couch in there." Poby was suffering, and at once the state of his feeling jumped the gap between him and Eli as if it had been a static spark.

"Well, in that case," Eli said, turning back to the bar and smiling, "I imagine you rate a final drink, too. What'll it be?"

Poby stared at him for a moment in bewilderment. Then Eli's words penetrated through to him.

"No, Eli," he cried. "Why, I couldn't drink to that!"

Eli straightened up above the bottles and looked at him in slight astonishment.

"Couldn't drink to what?" he asked.

"Couldn't drink to your leaving," said Poby.

Eli stared at him. Poby stared back defiantly.

"It's not a thing for celebrating," said Poby. "It's a tragedy. Millions of people count on you. If they don't have you, who're they going to trust? If you leave—"

"Poby," interrupted Eli, dryly.

Poby stopped speaking.

"That's better," said Eli. "Now, I am not King Arthur and you are not Sir Bedivere. Thank you for your high opinion of me, though, all the same."

"But it's true," said Poby.

"Well, and if it were," said Eli, "have you ever heard of the right to individual happiness?"

"All right. You can answer me—" said Poby, "because you're a master statesman. I can't talk! All I can do is tell you."

"That," said Eli, wearily, "is what is wrong with most of the people in the world at any time. We'll leave the matter at that, Poby, before you and I run aground on the shoals of our mutual argument." He turned to Kurt. "It's still early. I'm going to leave right away. I'll give you a recording of my resignation and you can release it whenever you feel ready. You know all there is to know about the situation and the position at the present time. Poby"—he swung back to the courier— "get that ship of yours ready. I want you to deliver me to a place about two hours from here."

Poby turned and went, to follow his instructions and think of all the arguments he might have used on Eli if they had only come to mind at the proper time. Eli waited until the youngster was out of the room. Then he turned back to Kurt.

"I'll be at the University of Miami's Calayo Banks Shallow Water Research Station," he said.

"I didn't know they had one," said Kurt.

"Let's hope nobody else does," answered Eli. "Keep that address to yourself." He looked around the office. "Well, I guess that does it—except for the resignation.'' He moved over to the desk and its recorder.

"You know," said Kurt abruptly, following him, "the boy was right."

Reaching over to press the record button, Eli lifted his head from the desk and looked at the Underspokesman oddly.

The air-sub thrummed through the skies. He looked out the window at the blue Mediterranean below, thinking his own wry thoughts.

He and Poby were alone in the small craft. They were flashing now over the Mediterranean at some sixteen hundred miles an hour, headed for a certain point of the Turkish coast.

"Do you see it yet, Poby?" asked Eli.

"Just a minute," the pilot scannerset in front of Poby chimed suddenly, a single dulcet note. "There! Locked on," said Poby. "We'll be down in ten minutes." He set the automatic pilot.

The plane dropped swiftly through the still air. Eli shook himself suddenly out of his mood. He gazed out the window and saw the surface of the world rushing up to meet him. Minutes later they were on the water and taxiing up to a small stone jetty sticking out in the ocean below a large resort home that dominated some smaller houses clustered down the beach from it. A fat man in white tunic and blue pantaloons was waiting on the jetty for them.

The ship reached the jetty, Poby opened the door and Eli got out.

"Well, Hassan," said Eli, as he stepped up onto the jetty.

"Well, Eli," responded Hassan Bendhruk. "Come on up to the house. I've got everything ready for you to look at."

Two hours later, they sat at lunch in the pleasant little loggia extending from one end of the house.

"I'm getting too old," said Hassan, "to remain the head of a secret police."

"Then you're glad I'm disbanding this little organization of mine?" said Eli.

"Well, not really," said Hassan, grimacing slightly above the cup of coffee he had just picked up. He put it down untasted. "Perhaps I'm just trying to talk myself into the fact that I could be glad."

"Well, I'm rather glad to hear that," said Eli. "Because there are still a few things I might need done. I thought"—Eli raised one eyebrow in a quizzical expression that gave his face a slightly satanic look—"you might be willing, you alone, to do a little part-time work for me from time to time."

"Oh, that!" said Hassan, spreading his hands eagerly. "Of course!"

"You see," said Eli, "the trouble is, a man who has got to the point in the world's eye that I have, cannot just safely step back down into the anonymous ranks of the private citizens again. I know I'm through. But others may not be so quick to believe that. To some, I won't mention who . . ."

"Our friend whose name begins with an S," murmured Hassan, folding his hands lazily over his stomach.

"Or others," said Eli. "And it may well happen that one or more of these people will decide not to take a chance on a change of heart in my case. You understand?"

"I think," replied Hassan, "that I can fairly well guarantee to let you know of anything planned against you from the sources of danger we know of." He grimaced again, slightly. "News comes daily, to knock at my private door and offer itself for sale. It is one of the sad advantages of having a great deal of wealth to pay for it." He peered keenly at Eli. "But you really are quitting?"

"Yes," said Eli. "I'll give you my address."

"I have it already," sighed Hassan. Eli grinned, a trifle sourly. "What you're going to need there," went on Hassan, "is some foolproof means of communication with me that doesn't attract too much attention."

"I suppose," answered Eli ironically, "you've already got that figured out?"

"As a matter of fact, I have," replied Hassan. "If you

want to come along, I'll show you what I mean.''

He rose; and Eli rose with him. Together, they went out of the loggia onto the lawn, and down a winding gravel path to the sea's edge. Here they stepped into a little water skimmer, and Hassan sent them sliding over the waves down the coastline.

A few miles down the beach, they came upon a section of limestone cliffs. Here the gentle surf broke raggedly along a rocky shore. Hassan maneuvered the skimmer in among the rocks and over the surf, with such aplomb that for a moment Eli suspected him of wanting to wreck them both, and the little skimmer with them. But then, suddenly, they made a sharp turn; came upon a sudden opening in the rock, and shot through into a watery cave at the far end of which light glowed.

They slid back through the cave and around a corner. The little skimmer approached and popped through a wall of pure light. And, without warning, they found themselves in a sort of brilliant underground world.

It was an enormous cavern, glittering with illumination. An artificial sun burned overhead, so brightly that human eyes could not look up and see against its glare the ceiling of the cave. For the rest, the vast expanse of the cave was planted and laid out with grass and paths almost like a formal garden aboveground.

Hassan tied up to a small jetty. They stepped ashore onto rock. And around a dwarf fir tree, a small bent man, wearing old-fashioned spectacles, came to meet them.

"This," said Hassan, "is Johann Schoner, Eli."

"Honored," said Eli.

Johann Schoner bobbed his head in acknowledgement of the greeting. But he looked almost agitatedly at Hassan.

"But I'm not ready!" he said. "You know I'm not ready. I told you yesterday, I couldn't possibly—"

"All right, all right!" said Hassan with humorous exasperation. "We don't need any messengers yet. I just wanted to show Eli what they were like."

"Well . . . well, in that case"—Karl turned back toward his fir tree, casting a glance back over his shoulders—"this way, then. Come along, Johnstone.''

Eli followed, and Hassan along with him, between some small trees, and back into a section of the cave, that had been walled off into compartments, by tall barriers of light. As they stepped through one of these barriers, he found himself surrounded by tiny darting birds small enough to nest, it seemed, in the palm of his hand.

"Become a bird fancier, have you?'' said Eli, smiling at Hassan. Hassan shook his head seriously, his heavy face ajoggle with the movement.

"Show him,'' he said to Johann.

Johann reached into a heavy pocket hanging from his tunic belt. From the tunic pocket, he took out a small chamois leather bag, with a draw-string. He opened the draw-string, and extracted a small white metal ring, which he handed to Eli.

"Put it on, put it on,'' he said.

Eli slipped the ring onto the fourth finger of his right hand. It fitted perfectly.

"Now what—'' he began, and, with an almost soundless flutter of tiny wings one of the small birds about him—a drab brown morsel scarcely larger than a mandarin orange, with wings outstretched—perched like a piece of thistle-down upon that same ring.

Eli stared at it. It threw back its miniscule head and abruptly, without warning, poured forth a stream of silver notes, astonishing in their loudness for one so small.

"Now,'' said the voice of Hassan in his ear, "squeeze the ring.''

Eli did. From the ring came a tiny sound. It spoke in human language. "Pleased to meet you, Eli,'' it said.

Eli turned his head to stare at Hassan and Johann.

"Quite a gadget,'' he said dryly.

"You wear that ring,'' said Hassan. "These birds can fly halfway around the world, if necessary. However, it won't be necessary for them to do quite that much to reach you. We'll have some of them based on the mainland, not more than eighty or a hundred miles from where you'll be. Just wear your ring, and get out in the open, at least once a day if possible.''

"The birds are trained to come to this ring?" said Eli, glancing at it curiously.

"Not trained, *sensitized!*" put in Johann eagerly. "A process akin to the instincts that used to cause them to migrate."

Eli shook his head briefly in admiration.

"And the song can be made to carry any message?" he asked.

"Any at all," responded Johann. "Even a fairly long one. You see, the translator in your ring takes into account frequency, modulation, pitch and a number of other things about each note in extracting information. Oh, it's quite complicated, I give you my word." And he rubbed his nose, juggling his glasses, in obvious delight.

"I see," said Eli.

"Well then," put in Hassan, "you keep the ring, Eli. We'd better be getting back. I'll talk to you later about this more, Johann."

Johann tenderly captured the little bird that had continued to roost this while upon Eli's finger and carried it off through another wall of light. Hassan led Eli back out to the skimmer.

The ride back to the house was a quiet one. But when they were once more ensconced in the loggia, sipping coffee, Eli spoke—a little bitterly, and as much to himself as to Hassan.

"And I thought I was getting away from all of this," he said, looking out over the sea.

"You know better than that, Eli," said Hassan. Eli turned his head to look at him; and saw that the other man was coldly serious. "People like us must always know it. For instance, I've heard ground rumors already, just since you resignation, that something or other is being hatched against you."

Eli continued to look at Hassan for a long moment. And then slowly, wearily, he nodded.

"It would be," he said.

CHAPTER III

THEY DROPPED down out of the bright sky toward the blue water.

"That's the spot, then," said Eli, peering out the window on his side of the ship.

"Yes," said Poby.

Poby was handling the air-sub as if he loved it, bringing it in a wide sweep, gently, gently, yet swiftly into the ocean. Below them Eli picked out a glinting dot on the azure expanse of the Florida waters around the tiny sterile sandspit of Calayo Banks Cay, lost and lonely in the sea. Like a tiny bright coin dancing on the waves when he saw it first, it steadied and swelled to the transparent hemisphere of a solar roof over the top of an underwater station. Then they were landing in a fume of spray and it swelled bubblelike above them, with the brown sea-resistant concrete of the jetty pushing out from it, lifting toward them over the chop of the waves as they taxied up to it.

When they bumped the magnetic mooring rim of the jetty and locked there, Eli stood up. Poby, reaching over him, threw back the hatch and stepped past him to turn and give him a hand from heaving air-sub to the immobile jetty. Eli

21

had one quick glimpse down through the clear water as he stepped across, a momentary picture of sixty feet of station reaching away and down through the fantastic clearness of the water to the white sand far below. Then he found his feet on the jetty; and turned back to Poby.

"Well, that's that, Poby," he said.

"Yes, Eli," the young courier looked at him rather helplessly. Eli rubbed his narrow jaw thoughtfully.

"What's your home Dome?" he asked. "You told me once, but I've forgotten."

"Number Three, Pacific," said Poby.

"That's right," said Eli. "Well, I want you to go there for the next few weeks; or at least until Kurt makes public my resignation. If he does that, go directly to him and put yourself under his orders. You understand why I'm doing this, Poby?"

"I think so," Poby answered.

"I've had this planned for a long time. I've set things up so I can step out quickly and without fuss. But for the general public it can't be that sudden. Kurt is going to announce that I've gone into a surgical hospital to have my knee worked on. Only he or you know that I'm actually, as of now, no longer spokesman. I trust you to keep the information to yourself."

"Yes, Eli."

"All right. Get me an order blank from the ship and I'll write you a predated order for a month's leave."

Poby leaned back into the air-sub and produced a small pad of order blanks, on one of which Eli scribbled the instructions he had just given. He signed it and pressed his thumb on the sensitized signature area, tore off the order and handed it back to Poby.

"There you are," he said and held out his hand. Something in the other's eyes made him add, "Look me up in about a year if you still feel like it."

"I will. I'll find you," said Poby.

They shook hands, and slowly Poby re-entered the air-sub, pulling the hatch closed behind him. The airboat sparked as its motors thrust it away from the magnetic pull of the mooring ring. Then it had surged away from the jetty and was gone, leaping into the air. Eli stood looking after it a little sadly. Nostalgia was not one of his usual indulgences, but he let it touch him now, momentarily.

The sound of footsteps on the jetty behind him brought him around. A young woman in her early twenties and a young man scarcely older were coming from the solar deck of the station, through a watertight, stormtight door flung wide, to meet him. He turned a little awkwardly, favoring his one bad leg, and took them in at a glance, the tall dark man and the small, blond woman.

The man was big-boned and young, with a large nose set a little crooked, which, however, did not spoil the general effect of his good looks. There was scarcely half a dozen years difference in age between him and Poby, but this one could almost have passed as Poby's father. He did not so much look old, as mature; and he had probably looked mature since he was sixteen, with rectangular, solid jaw and a stiff bristle that required shaving twice a day. But his eyes were the clear, uncynical eyes of his proper age, and a little wondering and a little kind.

With the woman it was different. About the same chronological age as the young man, she had an ageless quality about her. Small and light-boned, with hair so light and fluffy of texture that it seemed she had despaired of bringing it to any discipline of form, so that it floated like a loose cloud about her head. Her face was pointed and fragile, with such a clearness of skin, that although she was not conventionally pretty, she struck at any moment a memorable picture for any man to carry with him afterwards. Her lips and eyes molded the visible expression of everything she said; so that from that first moment on until a long time afterward, until he knew her very well (and even then) Eli was to find himself watching one of these two features of hers, as she spoke.

She spoke now, half-running forward to keep up with the long steps of the man beside her.

"Eli! You were quick! I'm Jenny Wina."

"Hello, Jenny" he said, smiling, and taking the hand she gave him. She held it and turned him toward the man. "And this is Dr. Mel Bruger."

In a period in which first names were almost universally used, even on first acquaintances, Eli caught the hint of an inferiority complex in the tall man and responded accordingly.

"Hello, Doctor," he said, and was rewarded by a smile flashed by Jenny from behind Mel Bruger's back.

"Hello," answered Mel, shaking hands. His voice was slow and deep. "Arthur Howell and Ntoane are downstairs."

"Both doctors also," said Jenny—and the slyness of the remark, Eli could see, was lost on Mel.

They turned and went into the station, dogging the weather door shut behind them. The still air of the solar under the brilliant sun was hothouse warm. They walked across the plastic floor like polished white marble between tables and deck chairs, and entered an elevator capsule whose tube projected like a transparent sleeve up through the floor of the solar deck to about eight feet. The capsule held them all easily and they dropped with a rush of released air to the fifth level of the station, a scant dozen feet above the ocean bed.

Down the hall was the lab and the two men in it looked up as they entered. One was Arthur Howell, a thin, angular man in his fifties. The other was a sensitive-featured, black-skinned man who at first glance appeared to loom beside Howell like a giant.

"Dr. Ntoane," said Jenny, as they came up. "And you know Arthur Howell."

At second glance, as he shook hands with the dark man with the Basuto name, Eli perceived that appearances had deceived him, for Ntoane was scarcely taller than himself. A trick of ideal body proportioning, however, made him appear much larger, so that he was in fact, like a giant in miniature, with a calm face and intelligent, but rather unhappy eyes.

"Happy to meet you, Eli," he said, quietly. His hand, as it

grasped Eli's in handshake, had a strong, sudden pressure behind it.

"Don't embarrass me," said Eli, with a smile. He turned to Howell. "Well, Arthur!" he said, extending his hand.

"Hello," said Howell, giving Eli's hand one quick pump and them dropping it. "You made good time. That's good. What do you think of the station?"

"I think it looks excellent," said Eli.

"Yes. I do too," said Howell. "Well, now that you've met everybody, come on back to my office with me. I want to talk to you. You can finish up here, Ntoane?"

"Of course, Arthur."

"Fine. This way, Eli." And, without waiting for any further parleying, Howell turned and began to lead the way back between the cluttered benches, sinks, and equipment of the lab. Eli, with a humourously apologetic smile at the rest, followed him.

Howell led him to an office opening off the far end of the lab. A little square cubicle had been fitted with desk, chair, and filing cabinet. Howell, himself, perched on the edge of the desk and waved Eli to the chair.

The man who had sent Eli the message cubes and now sat opposite him with one toe of one narrow foot on the ground and the other foot beating nervous time back and forth in the air, was well into his fifties. Howell was skinny. His elbows were knobby, his hair mostly gone, and his bony face cut with lines, but the violent energy of the undergraduate was still with him. That he was abrupt and intolerant was natural, it was part of him.

"How much time have you got?" he said without preamble as Eli sat down.

"As much as you need," said Eli. "I've resigned the Spokesmanship."

"Fine. Excellent," said Howell. "Well, I'm pretty sure we can do it."

"Only pretty sure?" Eli said.

"There are no hundred percents in medicine," said Howell, didactically. "You came to me five years ago with a question as to whether the human body couldn't be rebuilt with new parts in pretty much the way an engine is. I'm now prepared to try and answer that question."

"With me as the subject," said Eli wryly.

"Precisely," replied Howell. "However, that needn't concern you. There were some other things I wanted to talk to you about. First, you asked me to look into the matter of your lame knee. I have. There's nothing wrong with it."

In spite of himself, Eli was nettled.

"I happen to know there is," he retorted.

"Well, you're wrong," said Howell. "If it bothers you, it must be psychosomatic. See Mel. He's got his degree—"

"Is that why he's here?" demanded Eli.

"No. I need him for the operating. I'm a research man, pure and simple. I don't operate myself."

"That's good," said Eli. "Because I don't intend to see anyone in that line professionally, now or ever."

"Why not?" Howell was looking at him curiously.

"Because it's a waste of time," said Eli.

"Well," Howell shrugged. "It's not my department. Suit yourself. Now the first thing we need are some tests on you."

"You've had nothing but tests!" said Eli.

"Certain data has to be brought up to date. Nothing extensive." Howell glanced at the watch on his wrist. "When did you eat last?"

Eli had to stop and think.

"This morning."

"All right," said Howell. "I'll give you a short, timed dose to put you under. From there you should go into a natural sleep and we can start taking checks on you. Come along."

He led the way out through the lab, stopping on the way to take a tiny green capsule from a refrigerator and pass it over to Eli. The three other people in the station had gone about their business and were nowhere to be seen. Howell led Eli out of the lab and up a level and down a hallway to a spacious room dim-lit by the sunlight filtering down through thirty-odd feet of water and the two-foot thick pane of treated window glass. A wide, white bed sat on the polished floor, surrounded by banked instruments. But the rest of the room, with its couch, viewing screen, table and chairs, was like any good hotel room. Eli took the green capsule Howell had given him; and, after the other man had gone, lay down on the bed and let sleep claim him.

At some time later, he woke in the darkness. For a moment he thought that only a matter of minutes had passed and he was still alone, waiting for the drugged sleep to pull him under the surface of consciousness. Then, a soft, all-pervasive humming and the shielded glow of little signal lights from the now-operating machines about his bed disillusioned him. He lifted his head and caught a shadowy glimpse of a figure clad in a white tunic that moved about the machines.

"Doctor?" he said uncertainly.

The white-clad figure approached him. A cool hand touched his forehead.

"Lie back," said Jenny's voice. "Sleep, Eli."

He lay back, drowsily becoming aware of a pressure, like that of soft hands encircling wrist, bicep, thigh and throat. There was something familiar and pleasant about Jenny's voice that he could not be troubled to investigate right now but which made him want to hear it again.

"What are you doing?" he asked.

"Analyzing you," her soft tones answered him. "Pulse, pressure, metabolic rate, and a lot of other things. Don't talk. Just lie back and close your eyes. Try to sleep."

He closed his eyes and mouth. The bed was warm and he was aware of an all-encompassing comfort in the knowledge of her presence moving about him.

"Will you take care of everything?" he asked dreamily, out of the returning billows of slumber.

"I'll take care of it," she whispered. "Just leave everything to me. And sleep, Eli, sleep."

Reassured, he lost his troubled hold on consciousness. The darkness closed in again. He slept.

CHAPTER IV

ELI DREAMED he was running through a huge and empty city. The buildings were tall, gray and empty; and the streets were at first deserted and gray. But finally the people who lived there came in a group and surrounded him.

"You'll have to go to the city hall at once," said a man with an earnest, weary face.

"Why me?" Eli asked.

"Because you've got a mark upon you," said the man. And they all crowded about Eli, insisting that he go.

"All right, I'll go," he said. And he started walking off by himself in the direction of the city hall. But when he was a safe distance away from them, he shouted back, "I've changed my mind!" and took to his heels again.

He lost them in the maze of streets and descended to the vehicle levels. On these he continued to wander until he came to the edge of the city. And there, on the gray, open plain, he saw that there was a camp set up, like the camp of a Roman legion on the march. But when he wandered into it, he discovered that the soldiers were all a strange alien species, neither animal nor human. And as he walked through their camp one of the officers came up to him.

"Get back to your post, soldier," the officer said.

"Oh, I'm not one of you," said Eli. "See, I'm just like your enemies, the people in the city. I even have a mark on me."

"That mark does not matter," said the officer. "It is merely the surface manifestation of another, different mark that makes you one of us. Look at it, now."

"I don't believe in marks," said Eli, and he began to walk off swiftly. As he went he expected every minute to feel the officer's hand on his shoulder; but when he looked back, he saw the other still standing, staring after him. He started to run and ran until he came out the other side of the camp into open country which was wide and gray and covered with mist. He ran through this for a while until he realized he was lost. He sat down for a moment to rest, but then it struck him that he must keep going and find some kind of shelter. He got up and continued on through the mist until suddenly he came face to face with Mel Bruger.

"What are you doing here?" Mel asked.

"I'm looking for something," answered Eli.

"That's a common type of evasion that we often run into in psychiatry," said Mel. "What you really mean is that you're running away from something. Now, what are you running from?"

Eli woke up. For a moment he continued to lie where he was, remembering the dream. The bedroom was still about him, once more dimlit with sunlight through the water beyond the window, but the machines were pushed back from his bed and the tapes gone from arms and legs. He groped for the headboard of the bed and with his finger set the artificial illumination of the room up to daylight. I ought to remember that dream, he thought. But already the insubstantial substance of it was evaporating like morning fog in the day's brightness.

He rose and dressed in the fresh tunic and kilt that somebody—probably Jenny—had laid out for him, popping the sealed, transparent packaging with a feeling of pleasure, and shoving his discarded outfit down the incinerator slot in the far wall of the room. The colors were a new combination, rust and gold, which made it almost certain that Jenny was responsible. None of the others here would ever have presumed on so bright a choice for him. However, Eli found he did not mind. He was feeling a new and cheerful sense of freedom from the obligations that had held him these past years; and he went out to breakfast in the rust-shot gold of his tunic and the gold-flecked rust of his kilt without qualms.

Howell caught him at the entrance to the automat and had coffee with him while he breakfasted. They had the little room to themselves, everybody else having eaten several hours previously; and while Eli dug into his chicken pie, Howell outlined the procedures for the morning, which was to consist of some more tests of Eli in the lab.

"And what about the afternoon?" asked Eli with a grin. "Or do I have that to myself?"

"More or less," said Howell, looking a trifle sour, for what reasons Eli could not at that moment understand.

He found out just before lunch, when the last of the prodding, picture taking, sticking, and slicing was finally finished up.

"All through?" said Howell, popping into the lab, where Ntoane and Jenny had been doing most of the work. "I suppose you can see him now, then."

"See who?" asked Eli, putting his tunic back on.

"I don't know," said Howell somewhat brusquely. "He flew in this morning in his own private flyer. His name's Seth Maguin."

Eli stopped moving, suddenly. Then, conscious that his reaction was noticeable to the rest, he continued mechanically putting on his tunic.

"Oh, yes," he said. "Why didn't you tell me before?"

"I didn't want anything interrupting the rest of the work." Howell glared at him.

"I'll see he doesn't get in the way," Eli assured him. "Where is he now?"

"Up on the solar deck," said Howell.

"Thanks," said Eli. "I'll go there."

As Eli rode up on the elevator, he was conscious of a tiny sore spot on his left forearm, from which tissue had been removed, and another on the inside of his mouth on the left cheek from which a section of the mucous membrane had been clipped by a small, gleaming instrument in Jenny's capable fingers: He touched the sore spot in his mouth with the tip of his tongue; exploring like a child; and thought of the clean smell of Jenny's hands as she worked close to him. The same haunting familiarity which had touched him the night before at the sound of her voice, came to him again.

The capsule rose above the solar floor; and he caught sight of a lean, fine-featured man who stood awaiting him, apparently having just risen from a deck chair near the transparent wall of the dome. The mark of Berber blood was strong upon this other, in his dark skin and shiny brown hair. A dark-colored, all-weather cape was clipped to his shoulders and he stood with his hands on the back of one of the chairs and smiled at Eli.

Eli went toward him.

"You're a damn fool, Seth," he said without preamble, as he got within speaking distance. "Sooner or later Sellars checks up on everyone who sees me. Do you want to be found out?"

"You're my brother," said Seth. "And I think you're in trouble." He held out his hand, and Eli took it. They sat down together.

"What gives you that idea?" asked Eli.

"That's a foolish question," answered Seth Maguin. "You might as well ask me how I found you here, or how I know you didn't listen to the cube I sent you yesterday at Cable Island. As soon as you recognized my voice you destroyed it. I know these things; and you could know the equivalent of me, if you'd only tear down the walls you've built up to block off that section of your mind."

"We won't go into that, again," said Eli, "After all, we're only half-brothers."

"What of it?" countered Seth. "We still had the same father; even if he didn't know that one hot night in Ankhara had given him a son. But we both knew who we were the day you and I looked at each other across the playground at the special aptitude school in Bermuda where we'd been sent because of our ratings on the tests. We looked at each other and knew. Not only I knew—you knew."

"I don't remember that far back," said Eli.

"Then why do you admit the relationship now?"

"I don't in public," replied Eli. "And in private . . . what's the difference? There's nothing to blood relationship but an accident, lucky or not, depending on how you look at it."

"It matters when there are special mental abilities carried through blood relationship from the same source. Our father had it."

"Did he?"

"I have it."

"And you—"

"No," said Eli, definitely. He shook his head with sudden weariness. "I won't talk about this, Seth. You're a Member and wedded to the notion. I'm not and I don't believe in it. Now let's drop it and get to the reason you risked being brought to Sellars' attention by coming to see me."

Seth looked at him, a faint, upright line between the fine shadows of his dark brows.

"It *is* the reason I came," he said quietly. "What are you here for?"

"That's my business," answered Eli, meeting him eye to eye.

"Forgive me," said Seth sadly. "But there's so much I know about you. You're free of ordinary politics now—I know that—and I'd hoped to bring you in with us."

"No!" exploded Eli violently. "I sold my freedom for a mess of politics these last eight years and I'll never sell again—on any terms. For all my life I've tried to find the solutions of my problems in the ways other people find theirs. From now on I want to be left alone to do as I want."

Seth shook his head.

"That's impossible for you, Eli."

"Suppose you tell me why."

An electric tension—high voltage—crackled suddenly between them.

"Because," said Seth, "the world doesn't go that way. History won't allow it. I don't mean past history, but present history, this moment, in the way it determines the future. This moment, which is not just this moment in this one little area, but this moment the world over, with all its present, momentary happening and potentialities that those happenings imply. That is how history builds, not on a few but on an unimaginable multitude of casual incidents."

"I don't see it interfering with me," said Eli grimly.

"It can't help but interfere," replied Seth. "Conflict's inevitable, and you're one of the factors in the conflict, along with us, the Members, with our belief in a great future for the race; and Anthony Sellars, with his armbanded group of people who are theoretically merely qualified first-aiders who can be called upon in any public emergency, but which we know are the core of the army he is raising against us."

Eli moved his head restlessly against the back of the deck chair.

"Words," he said. "Suppositions. Rumors."

"Are they?" demanded Seth. "We happen to know at the moment that Sellars is planning to uncover living proof of the popular rumor that credits us with having used hard radiation and gene experimentation on humans."

"I would have thought he had more brains than that. Anyone with sense knows that couldn't be true."

"But Eli," said Seth. "It *is* true."

Eli turned and looked at him as if he had never seen him before.

"It was a possible solution," said Seth, his dark eyes unhappy. "It had to be tried. Somewhere along the line, someone had to try it. It was before my time, back twenty or thirty years ago, and the experiments that survived are all grown up now. I could not have made such a decision myself, I think; but that is perhaps because I, today, know that such tactics are not the answer. But I cannot blame them. Like we who are the present Members, they believed that the future of the race was at stake—at stake as definitely as if a plague was sweeping the world and threatening to exterminate everyone.''

"Where in God's name do you get such a notion?'' burst out Eli.

"What is characteristic of a species which has reached a point where further upward evolution is necessary?'' countered Seth. "The species has reached its limits of adaptation within its present stage. It must evolve, or else.''

"What is there we can't adapt to?''

"Atomic energy,'' said Seth. He looked at Eli. "Do you really want me to explain this?''

"Yes,'' said Eli.

"All right,'' replied Seth. He sat for a minute as if sorting out his thoughts. "All right,'' he went on. "It goes like this:

"I say atomic energy and you laugh; because we've had atomic energy for two hundred years now and it's done nothing but make the world a very pleasant place to live in and an easy life available to all. But this is a very superficial view.'' He leaned forward earnestly.

"I would like to remind you, Eli, of something that had its beginning at the same time as Atomic Theory, and that was the physics of which it was a part. There were men to be found, even in the mid-twentieth century who said that their present physics had opened up a very large room, but that its further walls could be seen; and that, barring some startling new discovery and the plugging of gaps here and there, that particular aspect of science was complete.

"For two hundred years that room has been completely explored—as far as human beings can explore it. What kind of situation does this leave us with?

"Among other things it leaves us without a shield against atomic energy. Down the long history of Man's development the progression has been—first a new weapon, then a defense against it, then a weapon to crack that defense, and a stronger shield, and so on. Now, for two hundred years we have been possessed of an ultimate weapon, which is the end of the line. No defense is possible—there is no more science from which to build a defense. And for two hundred years we have lived in uneasy truce, one with another. Our solution has been to be careful not to play with the fires that might burn us; but this is contrary to man's very nature. What has made him what he is, has been his insistence *on* playing with the fires that might burn him. For two hundred years we have exercised a miracle of restraint. But it is no more than that. As long as the weapon remains, the problem of using it remains also.

"It must be handled and it can't be handled. What's the answer? One—the classic response of physical evolution would be to adapt physically so that a human being could walk through the heart of an atomic explosion without damage. Physics denies us this, as it denies us a defense as well. Two—Man's solution would be to think up something new in physics that would enable him to find a defense. But it seems there is nothing new. Well?"

Seth finished and sat looking at Eli. Eli rubbed his chin thoughtfully.

"You say," said Eli, finally, "that we're at the end of the line but that we can't stop traveling. So the only thing we can do is crash?"

"Yes."

"A little late in the day to be thinking of evolution, if that is true, don't you think?"

"I'll tell you," said Seth slowly. "I think that evolution actually began farther back than we will ever know—before the first bomb fell. And I think that it has already taken place."

"Oh?" replied Eli. "That must be a comforting conclusion for these cripples of your experimentation."

"Eli!" said Seth. "Be shocked if you want to by what I told you, but don't let it affect the fairness of your judgment!"

"The floor," Eli told him, "is all yours, Seth."

"You didn't give me a chance to finish. We—the Members—have reached the conclusion on the basis of forty years of work and what evidence we can and have observed, that the psi faculties bear the same relation to the human race that human intelligence does—though not necessarily in direct ratio to intelligence. In short, everybody has them, with some people having them more than others. We know they exist—''

"I don't," interrupted Eli. Seth stared at him.

"Now, Eli . . ."

"That's what I said."

"Eli," said Seth sternly, "unless you've been willfully blinding yourself, you couldn't have lived thirty-eight years in this day and age without seeing examples of the ordinary psi qualities in action."

"I've seen parlor tricks," Eli said. "I've heard rumors. I've never been convinced."

"*You* out of all the world!" said Seth, with a rare note of bitterness in his voice. "The man on the street doesn't share your disbelief. Even Anthony Sellars makes no bones about believing."

"I say merely I've never been convinced."

"The message cube I sent you, for example."

"I can think," said Eli, "of more than one way that could have been gotten into Poby's pouch without any non-physical means being involved. They range all the way from illegal hypnotic conditioning of Poby to accept a second cube while denying its existence, to some simple sleight of hand with the diplomatic pouch somewhere along the line."

"I assure you," said Seth, "that that cube was teleported directly from the instrument on which I recorded it to the pouch on your courier's wrist."

Eli turned and smiled at him.

"If that's true," he said, "why bother with me? Go on and take the world."

"Because in two hundred years we have never succeeded in making any single such faculty reliable. We have men who can telepath, who can teleport, who can transmute—but not one of them can be relied on to do it to order."

"It worked with me," said Eli, with a casual wave of his hand.

"Things usually work with you," replied Seth, a shade grimly. "That's what I 've tried to tell you for thirty years.

We think, and I believe, that you may have the very thing we need.''

''And what's that?''

Seth threw his arms our hopelessly.

''Who knows?'' he said. Then he calmed somewhat, slipping back into his normal quietness and self-possession. His slim face stared earnestly into Eli's. ''The psi faculties don't seem to show up as a single extra talent, but as a field of extra talents, among them many we can't conceive of. For example—myself.''

''For example, you,'' agreed Eli, good-humoredly.

''My talent, if you want to call it that,'' said Seth, ''seems to lie mainly along the line of something like intuition or insight into people and things.'' He rose from the desk chair suddenly and began to pace back and forth in the sunlight pouring through the transparency of the solar roof. ''Every so often, something will present itself to me in a flash. And from then on my certainty is so fixed that I can't even doubt that thing to myself.''

''And I suppose,'' replied Eli, watching him move, ''that you've some such intuition about me.''

''Yes,'' said Seth, halting and looking at him. ''I *know*—I don't think, Eli—I *know* that at this present moment in history you are the kingpin on which we all have to turn, Members, Sellars, Underseas, and all the people of the Groups anywhere.''

''It's too late now, Seth,'' said Eli. ''I've given up the Spokesmanship.''

''I know.''

''Damn it, don't give me that!'' shouted Eli, suddenly starting up from his chair. ''You can't know.''

''I tell you I know!'' Seth faced him; and for a moment his eyes lit up and his brown face was transfigured with a wild, prophetic glint. ''I know because it is my function to know—everything about you that is necessary at this time. I am bound to you by blood and affection. I am tied to you by chance and time. In the hour approaching there is nothing that can separate us, neither space, nor time nor death!"

For a few seconds after these last words rang out, the two of them stood silent, staring at each other. Then Eli spoke, and his voice was hard.

"Another of your intuitions?" he asked, the sarcasm heavy in his voice. Seth's face gentled and smoothed. He smiled softly at Eli.

"Yes," he said.

Eli sighed and turned away. He crossed back to his deck chair and dropped down into it again.

"You see why I can't accept anything you say, Seth," he said wearily. "It's too wild."

Seth smiled and answered nothing. Abruptly Eli turned to the small table beside his deck chair. There was a small figurine there in snowy plastic, a Grecian maiden with a water jar on her shoulder. He picked it up and threw it suddenly on the floor, so that it bounced and rolled a dozen feet from them.

"All right!" he said tightly. "Let's see you put that back without touching it."

Seth turned his eyes on the fallen figurine. For a moment his face tightened. Then it relaxed.

"I'm sorry," he said, turning back to Eli. "I can't."

Eli let a long breath sigh from him.

"You see?" his voice was almost helpless. He looked up at Seth. "Not that it makes any difference. Even if you were right—even if what you say was true and real, I'd still say no. What you can't understand . . ." he hesitated. "What nobody can seem to understand is that I'm through with all the big questions. Seth, do you know what I want to do?"

"What haven't you done?" smiled Seth. "During your twenties I remember you tried your hand at just about everything. Certainly, all of the arts; and where sciences were concerned—"

"The point was, I was looking for what I wanted to do," interrupted Eli.

"I thought you found it in politics."

"No!" said Eli sharply. "And I haven't found it yet. But

I've found a way to find it.''

Seth said nothing, but watched him.

"I'm going to tell you why I'm here," said Eli. He rubbed the back of his hand in momentary weariness across his forehead. "I've always been running after something—you know that. This same something. And I haven't found it, but now I've started to run out of time.''

He looked at Seth and then away again.

"Well, I've found a way to gain time. If I tell you about it, I want you to keep it a secret.''

"If you wish," said Seth.

"About five years ago," Eli went on, taking a deep breath, "I began worrying about time. I didn't care about my chronological age. What I cared about was that I still hadn't started whatever it was I was going to do. And my body was getting steadily closer to its end—its time getting shorter every day. I got a notion and I dug up Howell, the man in charge here.''

"I've heard of him somewhere before," said Seth.

"He's a good medical research man, one of the best," said Eli. "A little violent, but not bad. I talked my idea over with him, and using my authority as Spokesman got our captive University of Miami to award him a research grant, this station and facilities. The grant was for the development of new techniques in underwater surgery.''

"The Undersea Domes would be interested in that, of course," nodded Seth.

"But that isn't what he's been doing," said Eli grimly. "What he's been doing is working out a technique to rebuild and replace the worn down parts of my body. In these few years he's worked out something. If it works, my body should regenerate on a twenty-five-year-old level.''

He looked at Seth.

"It could mean, practically, immortality," he said.

Seth frowned in astonishment.

"So you see," said Eli "I—" he hesitated. "I have my own life to lead. A man has a right—"

The large three-dimensional screen that rose like a bubble

in the center of the solar floor, chimed suddenly, four dulcet notes, and the head of Jenny appeared in it, several times life-size.

"Oh, there you are," she said, swiveling to face them. "We're knocking off for the cocktail break downstairs. Why don't you two come down and join us."

She smiled and disappeared, Eli got up from his chair.

"Coming, Seth?" he asked.

Seth smiled.

"I'll come for the company," he said.

They moved across the floor to the elevator capsule, the subject between them, by mutual silent agreement, laid aside for the moment. They stepped inside; and Eli thumbed the stud for fourth level.

"A pleasant station," said Seth, as the capsule began to slip downward.

"Yes," said Eli. "I—"

He broke off suddenly. Seth looked at him. "Nothing!" said Eli. And when he saw Seth still staring, he repeated, fiercely. "*Nothing,* I tell you!"

Seth let it go; and the walls of the elevator tube slipped swiftly upward, opaquely about them as they dropped. But Eli was looking through and beyond them, seeing still the momentary picture of the solar deck, seen over Seth's shoulder in the minute before the capsule deopped below its floor level. For a moment the solar had stood out before him, with deck chairs, screen and tables.

The figurine, the little Grecian maiden with the water jar in white plastic, was no longer on the floor where Eli had thrown it. It was once more standing upright in its usual position on the table.

CHAPTER V

THE COCKTAIL break, Eli discovered, was in this instance something more than just a pleasant afternoon interlude. It was, in fact, a sort of combination celebration and send-off party, to mark not only the conclusion of years of preparatory work, but the beginning of the operations, since they would start getting Eli ready for the first of these directly after it.

Eli found himself welcoming the opportunity to sit back and take a good look at the people whom he was counting on to do a number of rather drastic things to him and get away with it successfully. In this moment he thought, as he watched them and listened to the chatter, that Howell's single-minded egocentricity was reassuring rather than otherwise. The man was so certain of himself. Jenny, also, he shifted his eyes to the girl, was reassuring, for a different, almost opposed reason. She seemed the kind of person who would think of him, even when stretched out unconscious on the operating table, as another person, and not as so much flesh and bone to be tinkered with. There was comfort in Jenny, as he had noticed during the testing of the night before. A feeling of concern for him seemed to flow out from her and lap around him.

As for Mel and Ntoane—they were the unknown quantities. Of the two, Eli thought he preferred the Basuto. There was an echo of wisdom to him that seemed to be lacking in the younger man. *Perhaps,* thought Eli, *that's what I have against Mel, the fact that he's young. But usually I like people for that reason.*

He shook his head. There was something about Mel that puzzled and disturbed Eli, a hint of deep-buried, repudiated resentment against Eli for which there could be no reason. Eli thought about it; then gave up as Howell dropped unexpectedly down beside him.

"How d'you feel?" demanded Howell.

"Fine," Eli considered. "A little frightened, I suppose."

"Of the operation. Naturally," said Howell. "Atavistic fear of being hurt, of being helpless. Not afraid of dying, are you?"

"Is there any danger?" countered Eli.

"None," said Howell. "We'll put you under with a lytic mixture this evening. Then take twenty-four hours to get your body temperature down. By that time we'll be able to keep you on the operating table until all of the major organs are out and replaced."

"I suppose you've got the—er—substitutes ready?" asked Eli, feeling a little queasy at the notion.

"My God!" said Howell. "We've had two years to culture them. They ought to be ready."

"Oh? They're all cultures?"

"Of course." Howell peered at him. "You don't think we'd take a chance on anything out of an accident bank?"

Eli did not answer immediately. He was thinking at the moment that it might somehow perhaps be a little more friendly to think of his new heart and liver, or whatever they were going to replace, being natural-grown accessories, so to speak, than the impersonal offsprings of a culture bath.

"No telling what factors we might introduce if we did that," Howell went on.

"It seems to me," protested Eli, mildly, "that even recently I've heard of cultured body parts being refused by the body so that—"

"Nonsense!" said Howell. "In the beginning they had a few cases due to incomplete knowledge of body typing. Not for twenty years now. No, no, it's perfectly simple. Cut, attach mechanical standby, remove, replace, detach mechanical, and there you are.''

Eli winced. Howell, in his attempts to reassure his patient was being markedly unsuccessful.

''If you want, I can take you down to the operating room now,'' said Howell, ''and show you the complete procedure.''

''No thanks,'' said Eli. And as promptly as if he had run up a distress signal, Jenny and Seth both came swooping down at once to break up the conversation.

As soon as he was free, Eli slipped away from the party and went up to the solar roof to be by himself. The sun was just dipping toward the horizon. It had already stained a path of reddish gold across the restless waters of the ocean, from out of the west. The sky was luminous; but in the east the waters were dark. Eli took a turn limping around the deck of the solar.

He had not thought that he would be afraid of anything. But now, whether triggered either by Seth's unexpected visit, or by the imminence of the operation itself, fear was gnawing at him internally. Not a great fear, of the kind that chills the body and stiffens the muscles, but a little rat's tooth of gnawing uneasiness that worked at the back of his mind like an ulcer might have worked at his stomach lining. Deny it to Seth as much as he could, he could not hide from himself the fact that he operated largely with what appeared to be instinct. And at this moment, that instinct was warning him of . . . what? Coming up against that question mark, Eli grinned a little sourly to himself. There was no lack, he thought, of things to make him uneasy.

The world was quivering on the edge of an explosion that would tear it apart, like a balloon at the bursting point. There were hints, through Hassan, of those who might have designs upon his life. And, if this were not enough, he faced an ordeal rather like that of a guinea pig who goes first under the knife in the discovery of a new technique of an experimental laboratory. But more than this—Eli halted his pacing and leaned with one arm upon the back of a chair to gaze som-

berly at the ceaselessly moving ocean—there was the matter
of his own deep unhappiness and out-of-placeness in the
world. He knew what he was about to do, and what he had
done; but there was no way in which he could tell whether
these things which he had done and was about to do, would
bring him peace.

He shook off these morbid thoughts. The sun was even
closer to the horizon now; and he reminded himself that there
were things to be done.

He sat down on the chair, and pushed the key on the
communicator in the middle of the table before him. He had
not pressed the vision key, only the audio. The bubble itself,
in which the head of the operator should have appeared,
remained milky. But her voice came from it.

"Calling?"

"Scrambler," replied Eli. He was referring to the mechanical device at World Central which mixed up its incoming
messages on a random basis, so as to make them completely
untraceable; and then sent them forth from its own location in
one of the basements of Cable Island.

There was a moment's pause, and then a single silvery
chime came from the clouded half-bubble.

"Scrambler on. Go ahead, sir," said the voice of the
operator. There was another chime and Eli knew that even
the operator was now out of the circuit.

"Number two-nine-four, Cable Island," said Eli. Again,
there was an almost imperceptional pause. Then Kurt Anders' voice spoke from the bubble.

"Anders here," it said.

"Kurt," said Eli. "It's me." He reached out and pressed
the picture button. Immediately before him, the bubble
cleared; he stared into the face of his former Underspokesman for the Underseas Domes.

Kurt's slim face looked up at him in astonishment, which
as Eli watched, slowly began to mix itself with gladness.

"Eli—" Kurt was beginning. Eli cut him short.

"No, I haven't changed my mind," Eli said. "I just called

up to tell you that you could announce my resignation now, Kurt. That is, if you haven't done so already.''

The excitement in Kurt's face faded slowly as Eli watched. The face became hard and, Eli was amazed to see, how bitter.

"You can't do this, Eli," said Kurt, at last.

"Oh, but I can," said Eli, smiling, but looking at him closely.

"Tell me, Kurt. I always thought you'd be the sort of a man to welcome the position of Spokesman. But you really don't want it, do you?"

"No," said Kurt flatly, his eyes meeting Eli's. "I don't.''

"Mind telling me why?"

"No, I don't mind telling you why," retorted Kurt. "Under ordinary situations it would have come about naturally, and it would have been just what I would have wanted. But you handed it to me to hold just when it started to fall apart.''

Eli held his face steady; but the shock struck home internally. He had not seen himself before this in the light of a man who hands over a bankrupt company with all the airs and graces of making a valuable present to one who had long wanted it.

"If you feel that way, Kurt," Eli said calmly, "you don't have to take the job, of course.''

"Don't I?" flared Kurt. "Who else is there?"

"Why, I imagine the Domes can find somebody," said Eli evenly.

"Oh, sure, they can find somebody!" said Kurt. "They can find somebody to prop up behind the desk here. But that's not what's needed, Eli, and you know it.''

Eli sighed.

"Kurt," he said, "that's the same old argument that has kept men in positions of responsibility against their will since civilization began. I'm not indispensable. No one is. And you, and to a lesser extent several hundred other men, are as capable of handling the job of Spokesman for Underseas as well as I ever could.''

Kurt looked him squarely in the eye.

"That's not true, Eli" he said.

"It is, whether you believe it, or not," said Eli "I took up politics the way anybody might take up a job as a salesman. I might have easily gone into deep-sea diving. And if I had, Underseas would have gotten along just as well without me. So I can't be all that indispensable and valuabe now."

"And I tell you you are!" Kurt desperately. "Underseas is falling apart without you, Eli—" he hesitated. "The whole world is falling apart without you."

Eli burst into loud laughter. "Don't be a damn fool, Kurt," he said harshly. "I called not only to tell you about publishing my resignation now, but to ask if there was anything I could do to help. But I can see now that if I even twitched a finger you'd have me back carrying the whole load again." He shook his head, grinning a little savagely. "No, no, Kurt, you're going to have to struggle through this on your own. So long, and good luck!" he reached for the cutoff switch.

"Wait!" called Kurt. "I'll come see you, talk to you—"

"No, Kurt," said Eli, shaking his head. "That would make it harder for both of us." He pressed the cutoff switch and the screen went blank.

Eli drew a deep breath. He shook his head and punched another number on the set.

"Scramble," he said, without waiting for the operator to speak to him. There was the customary pause, voice and chime, and then the screen cleared and he saw Hassan looking at him.

"Are you calling direct?" asked the fat man, without preamble.

"Of course not," replied Eli sharply.

Hassan shrugged and breathed out.

"It might have been an emergency you were calling about, and no time or chance to scramble," he said. "How's it going where you are?"

"Pretty much as expected," said Eli. "But what I called about was that I'd like some information from you."

"Always glad to oblige," said Hassan. "Who on, this time?"

"My former Underspokesman, Kurt Anders," said Eli. "Is he in some personal trouble, or something of that order?"

"Anders?" said Hassan. "Nothing political, in any case. He's got a health problem, though."

Eli's eyebrows jerked up.

"Health problem?" he said.

Hassan looked at him ironically.

"He's quivering on the edge of a nervous breakdown, according to his physician," Hassan said. "That job you wished on him is just a little too much for the boy."

Eli frowned.

"Well, keep an eye on him," Eli said. "If something serious happens to him, I'd like to know about it."

Hassan shrugged.

"If that's what you want." His eyes narrowed a little as they rested on Eli. "I'd say you had other things to occupy your mind, myself." Eli raised his eyebrows, ironically.

"Oh?" he said. Hassan did not smile.

"That's right," he said. "A whisper's come in to me here that your assassin's already been picked out."

"But you don't know who he is," said Eli, smiling a little grimly.

"No," replied Hassan. "But according to the word I got, he's at the station with you there, right now."

Eli stiffened suddenly.

"*He*—you said?" he inquired sharply.

"Or she." Hassan spread his hands. "Sex wasn't specified." He gazed curiously at Eli. "You could duck out right now."

Eli shook his head, slowly; his eyes abstracted and thoughtful.

"Up to you, then'" said Hassan. "Keep your eye open for the little birds. If I get something definite, I'll ship the information on to you." Eli nodded. Hassan stretched his hand out over the controls of his own phone, and then hesitated. "Was there something more you wanted from me?"

"No," said Eli, rousing himself. "No. Thanks, that's all for now." He reached out his own hand to the communication set and broke the connection. A voice broke suddenly on his ears. He whirled around.

"Oh, there you are," cried Jenny cheerfully, advancing on him. "I've been looking all over for you. Dr. Howell's already down on the operating level of the station. You're to come down and I'll start getting you ready."

Eli was conducted by Jenny to a room adjoining the operating room and put to bed in what looked like a large quilted stretcher, with an equally thick cover of the same design that covered him completely up to his chin. Only one arm protruded, and into this, at the junction of the medium basilic and median cephalic veins inside the right elbow, Jenny pushed and taped a hollow needle. From the needle a light tube ran up to a bottle hanging head downwards from a T-shaped rack beside the stretcher.

Eli looked at the straw-colored liquid in the bottle.

"That's what Arthur called the lytic mixture, isn't it?" he asked.

"That's right," Jenny smiled down at him, fastening the magnetic strip that held the edges of the top covering to the stretcher and enclosed Eli, by the simple expedient of pressing them together at the bottom and then running her pinched fingers along until their full lengths were in contact.

"What's it made of?" asked Eli. "The lytic mixture, I mean."

"Chlorpromazine, mainly," she answered.

"What's that?" Eli wanted to know. "Something new?"

"It's been used like this for over a hundred and fifty years. You relax now," said Jenny.

Eli wriggled uncomfortably in his cocoon. The material that enclosed him enclosed heaviness and coolness. He was aware of the needle through which the lytic mixture was dripping into his arm, not as a pain, for a small amount of local anesthetic had been used, but as a somewhat improper weight and pressure within his flesh.

"I wish this stuff would hurry up and take effect," he growled.

"It will," said Jenny.

Eli yawned and woke. Jenny had vanished and he looked up into the face of Ntoane. Eli blinked.

"Is—it all over?" he asked. His voice sounded a little croaky and unused. He cleared his throat.

"All over," said Ntoane. "How do you feel?"

"Feel?" echoed Eli.

He became conscious now, of the fact that his cocoon was no longer cool, but warm. Inside it his body felt pretty much as it had always felt.

"I feel all right," he answered.

"Good," said Ntoane. He slipped the end of his thumb between the top ends of the magnetic fastening strips and ran it back along their length to separate them. "Take my hand and I'll help you get up now."

"Get up?" repeated Eli. He felt ridiculous to be parroting every word Ntoane said, but the words seemed to come out by themselves, without any authority from him.

"That's right," said Ntoane. "Here, I'll give you a hand." He slid an arm behind Eli's shoulders and helped him lever himself into a sitting position on the edge of the stretcher-affair. As Eli bent at the waist he felt suddenly as if he had been stabbed in the body, not merely in one spot, but in several places at once.

"Help!" he gasped, grabbing at Ntoane.

"What's the matter?" asked Ntoane.

"Something's wrong inside me," said Eli.

"Merely the incisions. In two days you won't even know they're there. Come on, up now."

Eli looked up to see that Howell had come striding into the room, answering as he came.

"What do you mean, up now?" demanded Eli indignantly. "I feel like I'm coming apart."

"Nonsense" said Howell. "Ignore it."

"You *will* feel better after you've moved around a bit," put in Ntoane sympathetically.

So encouraged, Eli allowed Ntoane to help him to his feet and support him while he took a number of unsteady steps about the room. By the time he had completed a couple of circuits, he was sweating freely.

"That's enough," said Howell, at last. "I'll take him, Ntoane, while you get a wheel chair." And he put his hands firmly under Eli's armpits, holding him until Ntoane brought back the wheel chair from the corridor outside the room.

Once in the wheel chair, Eli relaxed.

"Whew!" he said, wiping his forehead.

"A little difficult at first," admitted Howell dryly. "Come along, Eli and I'll pick out something safe for you to eat. After that you can see your new visitor."

"New visitor?"

Howell was already moving off down the corridor.

"The Spokesman for Communications," he answered. "Alan Clyde, I think his name is."

Eli's eyes narrowed. He pressed the motor button set in one arm of his wheel chair and rolled after the thin man.

After a lunch consisting mainly of liquids, Eli went hunting Clyde. He found him seated with Seth up in the solar, leaning forward with his slim, handsome face politely attentive to the words of the Member. Both men turned and rose and Eli rolled from the elevator and approached them.

"You two know each other?" he said, smiling up at them.

"We do now," said Alan cheerfully.

"How do you feel, Eli?" asked Seth.

"A little sore about the midsection, otherwise fine," said Eli.

"Good, I'm glad," said Seth. He glanced from Eli to the younger Communications Spokesman. "I'll leave you to your own conversation, now. Excuse me."

The other two nodded and watched his lean figure as he went to the elevator and down out of sight. Then they turned back to each other.

"Sit down," said Eli.

"Thanks," Alan took a deck chair, pulling it around to face Eli. "I got your address out of Kurt. He didn't want to let me have it at first. I explained that it was something of an emergency."

"That's all right," said Eli. "You're the one man I don't mind Kurt letting know. I'll ask you to keep the information to yourself, though, if you don't mind. Did he tell you anything except where I was?"

"No," answered Alan. "I couldn't get another word out of him. He seemed worried." And he looked at Eli keenly as if he hoped this statement would surprise a reaction out of the older man that would be more informative. Eli's expression, however, remained unaltered.

"What's on your mind, Alan?" he said.

"Frankly," the younger man leaned forward with his elbows on the arms of his deck chair and folded long, sinewy hands together, "I'm out horsetrading."

"That sounds interesting," said Eli.

"I hope so," said Alan, bluntly. "Because I'm not going to pussyfoot around the business. It boils down to this: Tony Sellars has made Communications an offer."

"Communications, or you?" asked Eli.

"Myself as communications," replied Alan. "Naturally, I can't tell you anything more about it than that it's a proposition for combining forces from now on. But you're capable of reading what you need between the lines on that."

"Well? Why come to me?"

"I haven't accepted yet. As I say, I'm out horsetrading. I thought I'd see what you had to offer."

"Officially," said Eli cautiously, "I couldn't, of course, offer anything. Underseas, of course, would be glad to have Communications on her side."

"That's not what I'm talking about," said Alan. He leaned back in his deck chair. "Understand me, now, Eli. I'm not a cherisher of personal ambition. I'm a representative of a small, but vitally important Group who can't afford to make the wrong decision. If things were to go on as they have for the last half century, with the Groups balancing the world power between them, I'd never abandon our traditional stand of remaining unconnected with any power association of Groups. But you and I know that we're in for a change, and quite bluntly, I want to be on the winning side."

"I see," Eli looked down and rubbed his bad knee thoughtfully, from long habit. "I see I'm going to have to trust you with some further information—if you'll promise to keep this under your hat also until the official announcement is made."

"Certainly," said Alan.

Eli looked up at him. "I've given up the Spokesmanship," he said.

Alan sat perfectly still for a long moment, looking at him. Finally he spoke.

"I don't understand."

"I've quit—retired—gotten out of the job," amplified Eli. "Kurt has my resignation. It should, in fact, have been made public before this. Officially, I haven't even the right now to be discussing Underseas business with you."

Alan's chiseled face showed bewilderment.

"I still don't understand," he said.

Eli sighed.

"I never really wanted the Spokesmanship," he said. "No, I quit. Kurt is temporarily in charge and there's a very good chance the various Domes will confirm him in the position. I suggest you go back and talk to him."

Alan frowned.

"No," he said slowly. "I don't believe I will."

"Why not?" said Eli. "You wanted Underseas on your side. And Underseas is Kurt, now."

Alan shook his head.

"You evidently don't understand, Eli," he said. "It wasn't Underseas I wanted. It's you. Without you, Underseas is just another little two-bit Group—and with even less than ordinary influence because it has no mainland connections."

"Now hold on," said Eli. "Underseas has eighteen other small groups in coalition!"

"And how many will it have once your resignation is announced?" asked Alan. "Be honest, Eli. We all know Kurt on the Island, and he's a nice fellow, but he's not even average Spokesman material. Expecting him to step into your shoes is sheer fantasy."

Mentally, Eli bit his lip. Alan's serving of unpalatable facts was undeniable. And worse than that, it was merely a reflection of the reactions all the group Spokesmen would be showing when the news broke.

"What I don't understand is this retirement business of yours," Alan went on. He glanced at the wheel chair. "What is it Eli? Health?"

"No, no," said Eli wearily. "It's what I told you. I just want out."

There was a slight pause. Then Alan spoke again, with meaning. "I thought I recognized Seth Maguin," he said. "He's a Member, isn't he?"

"And I'm not conducting secret negotiations with the Members, either," said Eli. "Believe me or not, Alan. But it's simply what I tell you."

Alan shrugged and rose.

"Not much point in my wasting your time further if that's the case," he said and smiled. Then the smile vanished. "You realize what this is going to mean, don't you Eli?"

"What?" said Eli.

"It means that Tony is going to have what he wants handed to him on a platter."

"Are you sure you understand him right?" asked Eli.

"Who understands him?" Alan shrugged. "But I know something about what he wants, because he told me in making his offer."

Behind them at that moment, there was the slight rushing sound of displaced air as the elevator capsule rose to the top of the tube; and they turned to see Seth step from it and stride across the floor to the bubble of the three-dimentional screen.

"What is it, Seth?" asked Eli, driving his chair toward the screen. Alan turned and walked over behind him.

"You'll remember, Eli," answered Seth, without turning

around, ''that I mentioned something about living proof that
was to be dug up . . .'' Under his fingers a stud snapped and
a pinpoint of color in the heart of the bubble screen ballooned
suddenly into full representation. The three men found themselves looking down at three bodies with their faces covered,
laid out on adjoining tables in what seemed to be either a
hospital or a morgue. The voice of an announcer came to
them with startling clarity.

''—at approximately ten-twenty this morning. The mob
had been aroused by a rumor of an illegal Member gathering
in a sub-basement of the Geneva City Library. By ten o'clock
mob excitement had reached such a pitch that they moved in a
body into the library in search of the sub-basement. It was
just a few minutes after then that the explosion occurred.
Aside from the three bodies you are now looking at, no one
was injured. Autopsies will be held, however, on these to
determine if they show any physical abnormalities such as it
has been suggested would be the result of illegal experimentation with gene control or hard radiation. Unofficial opin-
ions by local medicians who have viewed the bodies hint that
such physical abnormalities are probably present in all three.
If this is true then the long standing accusation that the
Members engage in . . .''

As if in a dream Eli watched the slow movements of Seth
and Clyde as they turned to look at him. The solar shimmered
and their faces seemed to float slowly toward him, growing
enormously as they came. Their mouths moved but no sound
came out. And in their eyes was a knowledge and a question
. . .

''No!'' shouted Eli, thrusting himself out of the chair onto
his feet. ''No! I can't.''

And he flung an arm up in front of his face to shut out the
sight of their faces. The solar swirled about him and he fell
forward—forward into blackness.

He opened his eyes out of drowsy druggedness to find
himself lying on the bed in his original room, in the half-light
of the sunlit water. Jenny was moving around quietly.

"Jenny," he said.

She turned from what she was doing and came over to his bed. She looked down at him strangely.

"How do you feel?" she asked softly. Her voice was cool and soothing in the hushed room, like a grateful compress on the feverish sickness within him.

"I don't know," he told her honestly. Then added, "Yes, I do. I feel miserable."

"Oh, Eli!"

The abrupt pain in her cry jolted him, so that he looked up in astonishment, to see tears in her eyes.

"Why, Jenny," he stumbled.

She did not answer. And he looked at her, seeing her really now for the first time—the smooth planes of her face, the delicate, turning line of her chin, the mobile mouth and speaking eyes, all at this moment tightened and touched with the pain of a love he had not suspected.

The helplessness of her went through him sharply; he held out his arms to her. She came to them; and he drew her down on the bed beside him. He felt the slim weight of her body pressed against him and the warm wetness of her tears against his neck. Clumsily, he reached over his one arm and gripped her gently by the shoulder, holding her to him. She cried softly, but with relief, and he lay silent, staring at the ceiling.

"How did this happen?" he said finally.

She turned her head upon the pillow, so that her face was toward him. The soft warmth of her breath came and went with her words, tickling at his ear.

"I always loved you," she said. "Even when I was a little girl."

"But you didn't know me," he protested.

"Yes. Oh yes," she said. "I did. Twelve years ago, when you were in Acapulco. You were living in one of the beach additions at the Monteferrato. And we were in the addition two doors down. You remember."

Eli let his mind roll back through time to the years of his purposeless wandering, to his twenties. There had been interludes at many places; and yes—there had been a time at

Acapulco. It was when he had been dabbling with painting and he had gone down there for the sunlight and the ocean. He remembered now the beach additions to the sprawling Hotel Monteferrato, the morning sunlight bright upon their solar roofs. And there had been a Dr. Wina, a short, round, bearded man whose hobby was marine biology. Dr. Wina, his wife, a tall placid woman, blond like Jenny. And a twelve-year-old daughter.

"Was that you?" he asked incredulously.

"You do remember me," she answered.

The little girl had hiked with him on Hornos Beach in the early mornings, before the crowd arrived. He remembered the long, narrowing curve of the wet sand arcing away ahead of them. Sand so white and water so blue that they looked like the over-coloring of a travel advertisment. There had been two months or so of that before his restlessness drove him on.

"I remember," he said now, lying on the bed. "Twelve years, though. And all the time you were growing up."

"I didn't forget," she said. "And when you went into politics, I followed everything you did. I kept waiting for you to marry and settle down. But you never did. Why didn't you, Eli?"

"I don't know," he frowned at the ceiling. "There were so many other things."

"I watched you on the screens," she said. "I never missed a time that you spoke. Dad knew Howell, and when you planned this—"

"Yes," said Eli gently.

They fell silent together. After a while she kissed him; and then left him. But Eli did not move. He stayed where he was, lying on his back, staring at the ceiling and thinking.

CHAPTER VI

"NO," SAID Eli. "No reflection on you, Mel. And I'm sorry, Arthur. But we'll stick to the physical side alone, and that's final."

"What if you fold up like that again?" demanded Howell. He turned to the young man beside him. "Talk some sense into him, Mel."

The big young man looked helpless.

"Eli—" he began without a great deal of optimism.

"No," said Eli. He pushed himself upright, wincing at the soreness of his still-painful incisions, and swung his legs over the edge of the bed. "I'm sorry, gentlemen, but no psychiatry. And now I'd like to get up. Unless"—he looked at Howell—"you've got some reasons against it?"

"No," scowled Howell. "I want you to get up. But I want you to take care of yourself, too, dammit!"

"Then that's settled," said Eli, reaching for his clothes. "What's next on the schedule for me?"

"Trigger chemicals," Howell was looking hard at him. "Come on down to the lab and Ntoane'll fill you up with the ones for today. Can you walk?"

"I'll try."

It was not easy. The incisions still hurt him; but Eli found that by going slowly and hanging on to things, he could travel all right. Mel left him at the entrance to his room, but Howell followed along and stood over him as Ntoane made the injections.

"I wonder," said Howell, when these were over, "if you realize, Eli, just how drastic and important the changes are we've made in you."

"Tell me," answered Eli, humoring him.

"No point to it," said Howell. "I doubt if a single listing of changes would impress you. But the point I want to make is that you probably still consider yourself to be the same man you've always been. And you're not."

"I hope not," grinned Eli.

"It's nothing to joke about!" Howell flared. "You're in a medical no man's land now. Any sort of development can be expected."

"I read you loud and clear," said Eli. It was the bitter, jibing sort of humor that came on him occasionally, when he was being pushed too far. "And now I think I'll go up to the solar."

He turned away. Howell, his eyes glittering with anger, took a step after him.

"Arthur," said Ntoane pleadingly.

Howell stopped.

On his way up in the elevator, Eli felt uneasiness once more stirring inside him. Hassan had said that one of the other three in the station—or had he meant to include Seth in that as well?—was an assassin, with orders to take Eli's life when the proper time arrived. Hassan was not the sort of man to be wrong. Sliding up the elevator tube in the capsule, Eli ran his mind lightly over the four who shared the station with him; not Howell, he thought, not Ntoane, and never Jenny. His mind recoiled from the suggestion that Jenny might be the one. That left Mel.

With sudden decision, Eli punched the stop button in the elevator and sent it back down to the level of Mel's private working quarters.

When he walked into Mel's office, the tall, young man was there. He was seated behind his desk, with a pile of

papers. And he looked up rather sharply, and laid the papers
down as Eli came in.

"Busy?" said Eli. Mel shook his head.

Eli pressed the button that closed the door behind him.

"I thought maybe I better have a little private talk with
you," said Eli.

"Sit down," said Mel, gesturing to a chair beside his
desk. Eli limped over to it and sat down, feeling the stab of
the unhealed incisions in his middle as he did so. He was
aware of Mel watching him with combined curiosity and
wariness.

"I suppose you wonder about the fact I won't let you work
on my mind," said Eli without further preamble.

"I can't help but wonder," answered Mel. "The old
fashioned fear of the psychiatrist belongs back in the last
century."

"Possibly," said Eli, non-committally. "Tell me, just
what do you think you would do for me? And just how would
you go about doing it?"

Mel shrugged slightly.

"I'd explore first," he said, "to find out what possible
psychological basis there is for that limp of yours." He
glanced at Eli's leg. "The reason you're doing something
like that to yourself may have deeper and more troublesome
roots than you expect."

"I know what the roots are, thank you," said Eli dryly. He
met Mel's eye squarely across the desk.

"Are you sure?" the young man said with a slight smile.
"It's almost an axiom, you know, in fact I could say it *was* an
axiom that no person can really know himself, or the reasons
that cause him to act as he does. Any more than a microscope
can be used—"

"To examine itself. I know," interrupted Eli brusquely.
"That's not what I mean. The fact of the matter is, I know of
something connected with my limp, which for purely practical reasons, I prefer to keep to myself."

"But you have no idea what harm you might be doing

yourself.'' Mel leaned forward earnestly across his desk toward Eli. "I still think that there is a certain amount of actual fear of psychiatry at the basis of your refusal to cooperate about this."

"You do, do you?" grunted Eli.

"I promise you," said Mel eagerly. "You will be running no danger. Whatever it is you think you wish to hide, it will be safe with me, as it would be with any other physician."

Eli continued to look him in the eye; and a slow smile grew on his lips. It was a smile that was more than a trifle sardonic.

"Even if you discovered some relationship between Jenny and myself?" he said dryly.

Mel flushed and straightened up abruptly in his chair. Then, with an effort he sat back again.

"Eli," he said, "you have a certain amount of hostility toward me. To answer you, frankly, yes I would just as soon not discover anything in your mind connected with Jenny. On the other hand, I *am* a medical man. With a medical man's ethics and sense of responsibility toward my patient."

"I see," replied Eli in a level tone of voice. "You still haven't told me just how you would go about it."

"Hypnotherapy, to start off with," said Mel, looking levelly across the table at him. "We would have to try and bring to your conscious mind, of course, whatever painful thing your unconscious is repressing."

"And can you be so sure," Eli said, "that there is something I am repressing?" Mel shook his head with almost an air of annoyance.

"All human beings repress things," he said. "If these repressions cause no trouble, there is no need to disturb them. If they do, then we have to go after them."

"By hypnotherapy, and other techniques which put the patient completely at the mercy of his doctor," said Eli.

"Yes. If that's the way you want to put it," said Mel.

"That's the way I want to put it," said Eli. "And that is exactly what I wanted to get straight with you." He stood up from his chair. "I haven't lived this long, in the world of politics and outside it, without knowing when to make myself vulnerable and when not. In this case, I don't think I should take the risk.''

Mel shook his head slowly, with a stubborn but oddly defeated air.

"I can't force you," he said.

"That's right," said Eli. "You can't. But it's interesting to wonder why you might even wish you could.''

Mel looked up at him oddly.

"It would be for your own good," he said. Eli considered him for a moment.

"So," he said, "you're one of those. That's what I wanted to find out." He turned about and left the room.

He went thoughtfully down the hall of the level; and then, suddenly recognized he was passing the entrance to Ntoane's laboratory. He checked himself at the door, hesitated a second, and then pushed inside. Ntoane, a laboratory apron on, was busy washing some glass vessels in a sink. He turned about and dried his hands, as Eli approached.

"Eli!" he said. "Sit down. Sit down! How are you feeling?''

Eli found himself a seat upon a tall four-legged stool.

"As well as can be expected," he answered cheerfully. "How's yourself?''

"Oh, I'm fine," replied Ntoane, laying the towel aside. "Well, if you feel as fine as that, what brings you in here?''

Eli smiled.

"Nothing to do with my state of health," he answered. "Or perhaps it has. I've just been having another little talk with Mel about his tinkering with the inside of my brain.''

"I take it you still haven't agreed," said Ntoane.

"No. And I won't." Eli looked keenly at the dark-skinned man. "Mel seems to be something of the fanatic." Ntoane frowned, and glanced aside at the equipment he had been washing, before answering.

"He's a very good physician," Ntoane said, "as young as he is.''

"If it was your mind, your ego," said Eli, bluntly, "would you trust him with it?''

"Unreservedly," replied Ntoane.

"Even if you suspected that his interest was not all a doctor's might be, in that part of your existence that was concerned with the person of a young lady?" said Eli, grinning twistedly. Ntoane eyes went noncommittally blank.

"That's something I can't judge," he said.

"You see," said Eli, "why I consider it important that he's a fanatic. Fanatics are liable to make judgements in terms of their own values of right and wrong—not only for themselves but for others as well. And act upon those decisions, where others are concerned." Ntoane shook his head. His voice was soft and a little gentle.

"We're all fanatics, in one way or another, Eli," he said. "You. I . . ." he spread his hands, in a yielding gesture.

"I can see it for myself," said Eli, watching him. "That's—or it was—part of my business. But don't tell me you're a fanatic."

"I consider myself one," said Ntoane. "I also have my own standards of right and wrong. And I would like to see those standards imposed on more people than they are."

"And just what is it you'd like to impose?" queried Eli.

"The principles of peace and progress," said Ntoane, looking back at him. "Progress toward peace, and peaceful progress thereafter."

"I would say," retorted Eli dryly, "that, far from being a fanatic, you're simply a somewhat impractical man, Ntoane."

Ntoane spread his hands again, without answering.

"So you don't think I should worry about Mel?" said Eli.

"You might do better," said Ntoane, "to worry about me."

Eli shook his head.

"I might do best of all," he said soberly, "to worry about myself. Where did Howell go to, do you know?"

"I think he's getting some sleep," said Ntoane. "He works all hours, you know." His glance at Eli just then had something almost of a pleading quality. "That's one reason he was somewhat short-tempered just a little bit ago. He hadn't had any sleep for quite some time. It's the way he is."

"Ah? I hadn't realized that. Well, I can see him any other time," said Eli. He got up from the stool. "I guess I'll run up to the solar and rest a bit in the sun." He turned and went off toward the door.

"Eli," Ntoane's voice turned him around. "Eli, you have to start opening up to the world somewhere along the line."

Eli smiled a little lopsidedly, shook his head, and went out the door.

Going once more up in the elevator, Eli found himself experiencing an unusual regret, a regret concerned with his unfairness to Howell.

The fault might lie with the older man, but that did not excuse Eli to himself. He knew what Howell's nature was before he committed himself to this business of bodily reconstruction. It was not in Howell to yield the importance of his work to any other thing or person. Eli, who could adapt, told himself that it was therefore up to him to take the initiative.

But no poking around in his mind. No, not now or ever. This was no casual psychosis which had walled off one whole section of himself; but one consciously won by hard dint of agony and long effort. It was over twenty years ago that he had slipped the last block into place, *resquiescat in pace*, but there was no resting in peace, for it—*for the love of God, Montressor!*—it was part of him and would not die, though buried and forgotten. Yes, forgotten; and he could not remember now what it truly was; but he could remember that he must not remember, for hell is this: to be conscious of suffering and helpless before it.

"Eli."

He looked. Jenny.

"Eli," she came toward him, with a gentle smile, "you came out of the elevator as if you didn't even see me."

"With my head in the clouds," said Eli, smiling at her. "I was making plans for the future."

She looked shy and changed the subject.

"How do you feel?"

"Fine," he told her. "Except for the incisions." He reached a deck chair halfway across the solar and sank into it gratefully. "Where's Alan Clyde?"

She sat down opposite him.

"He left, Eli."

"And Seth?"

She sobered, looking at him. "He left, too, Eli."

"Well, that's too bad," he said. "I haven't seen him for some years. I was looking forward to having some more time to talk to him."

She looked down at the floor.

"Does it make much difference?" she asked in a low voice.

He peered at her, with puzzlement. "Does what make much difference?" he asked.

"That you didn't have more chance to talk to him."

"Oh?" said Eli. "Well, I suppose it doesn't make too much difference. Why?"

"Then you didn't turn on the screen in your room!" Jenny looked up with sudden gladness on her face. "I thought you'd heard but you were pretending to ignore it."

"Ignore what?"

Instead of answering, she jumped to her feet and pulled his chair around so that he faced the solar's screen, just a few feet away in the center of the floor. Then she stepped across and turned the screen on. The image of an announcer at his desk took form in the bubble.

"It started yesterday," Jenny said.

The announcer's voice came clearly to them.

"—and in other large cities the story remains the same. All known centers of Member activity, all hospitals, Foundations, and laboratories have been raided by impromptu citizens' associations. In some cases the civil or local group authority has attempted to give sanctuary to known Members and this has resulted in fighting between local people—"

"What's this?" snapped Eli, turning on Jenny.

"That first raid on the Members in Geneva City," said Jenny. "That was the beginning. All at once it began to happen in other cities. Clyde left right away."

"Spokesmen of all Groups are attempting to restore order. Some cities have been blacked out so that we do not know what is taking place there now. Indications are that full scale riots are in progress in these localities. Among those on which we have no information are the cities of Paris, Rio de Janeiro, Prague, Belfast, and most of the Atlantic seaboard cities in North America. In other localities provisional local governments are being set up to prevent looting and other criminal disorder; and various organizations, in particular the Transportation people qualified for first-aid and assistance armbands, have been particularly helpful. At present—"

"Turn it off!" said Eli, speaking through tight-clenched teeth. He was frozen in his chair, as rigid as if he had been suddenly paralyzed. Only when Jenny jumped to obey and the picture dwindled and disappeared, did he let go of himself, almost collapsing in his seat.

"Oh, Eli, Eli!" She was on her knees beside the chair, crying against the top of the chair back. "I didn't know. I didn't know!"

Sweat was pouring down his face.

"I'll be all right," he gasped. "Get—get me a drink."

Sleekly humped against the floor, a tiny modernistic bar squatted beside the elevator shaft. Jenny ran to it and returned with a glass half full of a non-alcoholic tingler. He choked on it but got it down; and then slumped back, letting the tumbler fall from his hand.

Slowly his face relaxed; the lines of twisted pain smoothed and a little color came back to his skin. He began to breathe easier. Tenderly, Jenny wiped the perspiration from his face and waited.

Finally he heaved a great sigh.

"That's all right," he said. "I'm all right now."

"I'm sorry, Eli," said Jenny. "Oh, I'm so sorry."

"Not your fault," he said. "How were you to know anything about me? Took me by surprise, too."

"But what was it?" she asked, sinking down on a hassock beside his chair and taking his cold hand in hers. He did not look at her.

"Nothing," he said. "Nothing. Sometimes things bother me." He was silent for a moment; then he spoke again. "Seth went, you say?"

"As soon as the news reports began to get bad," she answered. "He—he told me you two were related, Eli."

Eli looked at her with such sudden horror that she shrunk back.

"Eli!" her voice shook. "What kind of a secret is it?"

On the arm of his chair Eli's hand curled into a fist and he fought himself back into self-possession.

"No one," he said, "ever knew but the two of us, before."

"But I don't understand."

Eli drew a deep breath.

"I'll tell you," he said. He looked away from her. "My father, himself, never knew Seth was his son. I never suspected that I had a brother. I thought I was an only child.

"I was an odd child," he went on painfully. "Things bothered me, and I couldn't seem to make anybody understand why. Ordinary things that didn't bother other people. Once, for example, when I was very young, I remember I'd picked up the notion that if I tried hard enough, I could talk to animals. And I tried hard for a long time without getting any place, so finally I asked my father about it. If I remember correctly, I asked him to send me to a man who'd teach me how to speak to animals, like the man who was teaching me to play the violin. And he told me" —Eli smiled a little bleakly—"in a very kindly way, of course, that no one knew how to talk to animals. And when he told me I never could or never would be able to talk to a single creature except another human, I thought I couldn't stand it. All the living things that moved and felt would never be able to tell me how it was."

Jenny laid her cheek against the back of his hand where it rested on the arm of the chair. Eli went on talking.

"And as I grew older," he said, "it got worse. Because I couldn't explain to other people. Everything that lived had some power to touch me. When the growing things budded in the spring, I woke with them, and during the long summer as they grew, I grew with them, and in the fall the pride of their maturity was my pride, so that the onset of winter was like one last flaming great and glorious battle with honorable death. My longing went down with the salmon to the ocean; and never got free again, for whale and diatom held it tight to them. In the end, there was nothing with life in it that I wasn't compelled to feel my kinship with."

Eli stopped and sighed.

"And then, as I grew up," he went on. "I began to be aware of people."

He stopped. Jenny lifted her face and looked at him.

"This," he said, "is the part I cannot explain, never explain, to anyone. I can say I started to feel for them, too, and that's all I can say. From this point on, there are no words."

He stopped again, and was silent for so long, that Jenny spoke up, gently.

"But what about Seth?"

"Oh, yes, Seth," he took up his story again. "You see I didn't have any person I could get this across to—all this that bothered me. So, when I was very young, I first started to make up an imaginary friend, who would understand, without my telling him. I got to know my imaginary friend very well, and he grew in my mind until he had a personality of his own, until he was a real person, with his own problems, that only *I* understood."

He paused and looked at Jenny.

"And then when I was fourteen, my high aptitude rating on the General Tests allowed me to be sent to the School for Special Intelligences on Bermuda. And there my imaginary friend and I came face to face; and he was Seth."

"And had he—" said Jenny.

Eli nodded.

"I had been his, too. When we put our minds together at last, we discovered a great many things, among them that we were half-brothers."

"But how did you find that out?"

"It became obvious to us," answered Eli. "I can't explain."

"And then—" prompted Jenny.

"And then?" said Eli.

"What happened to the two of you after that?"

"Oh," said Eli. "We went different ways."

Jenny looked up at him; but with that one flat statement, his face was set in unyielding lines.

"He thinks a lot of you, Eli," she said finally. Eli looked away, out through the transparency of the solar roof, out over the blue waves to the horizon.

"When he left," Jenny went on, "he left a letter for you."

Eli's head came around suddenly, surprise on his face.

"A letter?"

"Yes," Jenny looked troubled and uncertain. "He said to give it to you when I thought it was the right time. I don't know if it's the right time now, or not. Is it, Eli?"

"I don't know," he answered. "Let me see it."

She got up and went over to a table in the solar. From a drawer beneath its polished top she took a single sheet of folded plastic which she handed to him. At the touch of his fingers, it unfolded. He sat, staring blankly at it.

"I'll go downstairs," said Jenny softly. "I'll see you later." She touched his shoulder lightly and went.

Left alone, Eli looked at the letter and read it.

Dear Eli:

I had hoped to talk to you once more before I left, but there's no time. I write these words instead of leaving my message otherwise, because I would like to leave you something lasting and concrete of myself, and this is all there is to leave.

I'm sorry that our paths of life have differed. Had we been born in a different time, you and I, there might have

been a job where we could have worked shoulder to shoulder.
But there is no point to regret where greater things persist.
For a moment, a few days back, my faith in you wavered. It
no longer does. I cannot see the future, but I trust in it—and
you.

                                                              Seth

   Eli carefully refolded the letter; and laid it on the small
round coffee table next to his chair, as if it was something
precious.

CHAPTER VII

DURING the busy days that followed, the station, with its four men and one woman, went about its business of Eli's body rebuilding in the same atmosphere of spurious peace that characterized a small chip bobbing in the sheltered back-eddy while the main torrent of a river at full floor smashes by just a few feet away. It was, in fact, a moment of historical upheaval and revolution, a convulsion of the race such as had never been possible before, because never before had all people on the face of the globe been interconnected and interrelated in what was, for practical purposes, a single society.

The reasons for this were twofold. First the establishment of the Groups, with their announced purpose of destroying the old sectionalism that had given rise to so much conflict, had inevitably had a much greater effect on the minds of men and women than their founders had originally intended. The intention was to replace an outmoded system with a new and more practical one. The reality was that the death-knell of all systems that attempted to divide the race arbitrarily, was sounded.

For the eyes of the average human were thereby opened to the fact that the world was not naturally in bits and parts which could be assembled to make a whole; but rather an original whole which could be divided to suit, as you would cut up a pie. And almost at once the foolishness of cutting it up at all became apparent.

Yet the Groups endured for eighty years from the first moment of their establishment and mutual recognition. And the reasons for this formed the secondary reasons for the present chaos. First, people were used to some kind of organization. Fear of the stranger still remained a historical habit in a little back corner of many minds and, like most habits, it sought its own justification by demanding a classification into which strangers could be placed. Secondly, though the dynamics of historical progress had been accelerating steadily through the passage of all known time, some years were still required for any universal change to gather enough momentum to overcome the natural inertia of things-as-they-are.

For the Group it took eighty years, which is very good time indeed, when compared with the parallel period of the Dark Ages.

But there was the other, second, reason of major importance. And this was a social and emotional one. The society that emerged from the twenty-first century can be compared to the bloom of a plant that finally stops growing and directs its energy to flowering. With the peaceful harnessing of atomic energy and the refinements and developments built upon the sturdy sub-structure of scientific and other discoveries of the previous centuries, there emerged an everyday existence for the average person that can only be described as free and easy. Population was stabilized, power was unlimited, and necessity had almost ceased to be a driving factor in life.

The result was that, once the second and third generations had accustomed themselves to the novelty of a practical utopia, the lack of a progressive drive began to be felt. The people of Eli and Jenny's generation found themselves both bored and uncertain in a time when old truths had been rendered obsolete and new ones had yet to take their place. The restless energy that had brought the race up from prehistoric primitive savagery, dammed up, sought for an outlet.

Finding nothing, it turned on itself, the beast-instinct that was still a part of man, blindly recognizing man's unhappiness and blindly seeking a physical cause of that unhappiness to blame and battle.

Thus the world was a loaded bomb to which Sellars' pogrom against the Members provided the arming device.

Starting first in the crowded cities and then spreading like fire in dry grass to the smaller towns and countrysides, fanned by the discontent and soul-sickness of man, the last and greatest witch hunt of the human race wrapped the globe in flame and violence. From the few simple original indictments against the Members sprang a veritable Pandora's box of accusations and superstitions. All the ancient monsters of folk-tale and legend came alive again in the name of Members. They were warlocks, hagwives, vampires. They were satanists, voodoo-workers, Frankensteins. Does your neighbor act strangely? Perhaps he is a Member, or a Member changeling. Or perhaps his mind, his soul has been possessed by the Members. Or still and yet, perhaps he is no man at all, but a clever mechanical imitation.

And where were the men of sense? They were there. They were many. They were in the majority. But how many individuals does it take to cause a panic in a crowded theater? How many to start an army retreating on the battlefield? If one man runs amok on a crowded street, how many others flee, how many reach for weapons?

Only in the backwaters like the station containing Eli was there sanity and peace. And while Paris burned and Calcutta mobs tore suspects limb from limb, Eli underwent another operation.

The first operation had been concerned with large body repairs and the replacement of a few major organs. This second was a relatively minor affair which can perhaps best be described as a tinkering with several of the more obscure glands. It was neither as extensive, nor as difficult—though possibly a shade more delicate—than the first. Eli came out of it in short order to find himself feeling very close to normal.

He spent his days recuperating up in the solar, in Jenny's company. Between the two of them an unspoken agreement of intention seemed to have established itself; and Eli found himself, to his amusement and his own quietly intense surprise, literally falling in love. He found also, in this new emotion that he had come to disbelieve in many years before, and now rediscovered with curiosity, a welcome excuse to ignore what was presently taking place in the outside world and to concentrate on such relatively minor things as his own recovery from the operations and the reactions of Mel Bruger.

This unfortunate young man, it became finally apparent, had fallen hopelessly in love with Jenny at the moment at which she had first appeared at the station, some eight months before. And, in spite of the fact that she had then, as now, been completely dedicated to the worship of Eli, Mel had continued to torture himself by remaining at the station and working himself foolish on the behalf of his elder rival. It was a sort of romantic casting of himself upon the spearpoint that appealed to a type of young and gloomy temperament; and Eli was faintly appalled to find that he, himself, had a good deal more sympathy for Mel, than did Jenny who was inclined to laugh at the young man.

The other two men that made up the station's complement seemed both aware of and unconcerned with the situation, Ntoane's reaction being one of polite acceptance, and Howell's one of somewhat grim amusement. Altogether, Eli floated at the midpoint of four points of view concerning himself; and examined and reacted to these emotional vectors with the same sort of minute sensitivity with which he had formerly held his position among the political heads of the globe.

So he occupied himself, while his body mended and changed. But deeply as he buried himself, it was not possible for him to ignore a general knowledge of how outside affairs were progressing. A certain little portion of his consciousness remained sandpapered-sensitive to the world he had withdrawn from; and, although he never listened to news broadcasts himself, he could not keep himself from picking up stray remarks of the others concerning it and building from these, against his will, the overall picture of what was happening.

He knew, for example, that the Underseas Domes, alone of the world, had held aloof from the general hysteria, evidently protected by their submarine insularity, and that they were at the present, jammed and overcrowded by refugees from the disordered cities of the land. He knew that the rioting was generally being brought under control; that the Groups were, for all practical purposes, dead as effective organizations; and that the people controlled by Sellars, spearheaded by his armbanded Transportation members who moved under the guise of relief organizations and temporary local authorities were gradually taking over the reins of government in all important centers. Finally, it was becoming apparent that the news broadcasts were being slanted in Sellars' favor, which was clear indication that Clyde and the Communications Group had, indeed, gone over to the winning side.

Such a state of affairs could, of course, have only one end. It was reached on the morning that Eli walked into the automat for breakfast and found the others violently in discussion—a discussion that cut off abruptly at his entrance.

"What's this?" asked Eli.

He looked from Howell, to Jenny, to Mel. For a moment nobody answered anything and then Howell spoke.

"They're setting up a central headquarters to replace Group authority," he said, a little sardonically. "There was a broadcast by Spokesman Sellars asking Group authorities to meet at Cable Island to arrange it."

"Ah," said Eli. For a minute he stood silent, looking at them. Then he turned toward the coffee dispenser. "Looks like I got out of the job just in time."

He took his coffee over to the table and sat down.

"Did you?" asked Howell.

"Did I what?"

"Did you actually get out?"

Eli looked at him.

"I don't think I'll bother to answer that," he said a little coldly.

Howell waved his hand, no whit abashed.

"There's been no announcement from the Domes," he said. "I thought I'd make sure. I don't want you dashing off to Cable Island just yet."

"Rest easy," said Eli, and drank from his coffee cup.

"When you get through here," Howell went on, "come back to the lab. I want to check you over again."

Eli nodded and the conversation once more became general. As he followed his coffee with breakfast, eating and listening, he learned that the broadcast by Sellars had come in the small hours of the morning from Cable Island, timed as nearly as possible to hit the whole of the globe during daylight hours. The meeting was scheduled for the soonest possible moment after the necessary representatives of the now non-functioning Groups could be gathered together.

Eli finished his breakfast, nodded to Ntoane and Mel, smiled at Jenny, and went off with Howell to the lab. There, the lean medician took samples and went over the surface of Eli's body with an epithelioscope.

"All right," he said, flipping back his head screen at last. "There's no doubt about it now. You're regenerating."

"Regenerating?" echoed Eli blankly, and stared at the older man for a second before the word penetrated. "Oh, regenerating."

It was the moment of climax, the second of triumph for both of them; and yet, somehow, almost it seemed, unfairly, the occasion had crept up on them so naturally that they could not at first react.

"Well that's fine," said Eli, finally, reaching for his tunic. "I suppose this calls for a celebration."

"I suppose so," said Howell. He looked at Eli and abruptly he began to smile. The smile broadened, as Eli, catching on to the humor of the situation began to smile back, until finally it broke into a rare bellow of laughter in which Eli found himself joining.

"The trouble with us," said Howell finally, when they had done laughing, "is that we're getting old. Come on. Let's break the news to the ones who're young enough to appreciate it."

And he led the way out of the lab. Eli followed, wondering a little uncomfortably if his age had really atrophied him to the extent Howell had implied.

This was the second party centering around Eli at the station. It differed from the first mainly in that Seth was not present and that Eli was now allowed alcohol. And of course he discovered, as he had been discovering for the past half-dozen years, that once it was available he didn't want it anyway. He drank several mixed drinks, in spite of that, so as not to spoil the spirit of the occasion.

The chiming tones of the station's message center, coming over the lounge's annunciator, broke in on their hubub. Howell leaned across the bar and flipped the stud on the room screen.

"Yes?" he said.

The voice of the mechanical operator came dulcetly through to them.

"Person to person for Eli Johnstone from Dome One."

"Oh," said Eli, putting down his glass. "I'll be right there." He saw Jenny looking at him, with apprehension, and smiled at her.

"Be right back," he said, and walked out into the hall.

As the soundproof baffles of the lounge entrance cut off the noise behind him, it came home to him that he was really more than a little under the influence of the drinks he had had. He stopped for a second and leaned against the wall to collect himself. Then he went on to the message center, a little room on the same floor with a two-way, three-quarter size screen.

He sat down in the operator's chair and snapped his call-stud. Kurt swelled from a pin-point on the screen before him. The young Underspokesman was haggard and thin-looking. His eyes were staring and dark with strain.

"Eli!" he said.

"Hello, Kurt," Eli answered, keeping his voice carefully even. "What's on your mind?"

"Eli," said Kurt again. There was a despair in his voice that touched Eli in spite of himself. He steeled himself against the weakness. "Eli, you've got to come back!"

"No," the word came automatically from his lips, the long-thought-out response that was the victory note of many self-battles.

"Eli. Don't say 'no' like that. Listen!"

"All right," he said. "I'll listen." And he leaned forward with his elbows on the control board, gazing into Kurt's face on the screen and wishing he had not the drinks inside him that he had, so that his mind could move swiftly and un-clogged.

"Sellars is wrecking the Groups," said Kurt.

"I know," Eli nodded.

"We've held out"—the younger man's voice almost broke—"here at the Domes, because the people were all expecting you to come back."

"That's your fault," said Eli quietly. There was an un-pleasant, metallic taste in his mouth from the drinks. "You should have published my resignation earlier."

"But there's been no chance!" protested Kurt. "It's been one crisis after another."

Eli looked at him, remembering what Clyde had said about the Underspokesman: *we all like him . . . but not Spokes-man material . . . let alone fill your shoes, Eli . . .*

"You know that's what politics is, Kurt," he said. "One crisis after another. The only difference is in the order of magnitude of the crisis." Abruptly he was tired of this fencing around. "You know why you didn't publish the resignation, Kurt," he said. "You were hoping I'd be back."

Kurt's face sagged. "Yes," he said.

"You should know by this time that when I do something I stick to it," said Eli. He sat looking into the hopeless face in front of him, feeling sorry for Kurt, and wondering what to say. "Look," he went on, finally, "you think that if I came back I could pull a rabbit out of the hat for you. Well, I couldn't. You can do anything you want with history but turn the clock back. Remember I told you the world was going to hell in a handbasket? Well, this is it. It's just come along a little faster than I expected."

"Has it?" said Kurt. "Has it?"

"What do you mean by that?" asked Eli.

Kurt's face was tight. "You didn't by chance know this was going to happen, did you?" demanded Kurt. "You didn't by any chance sell out to Sellars, and that's the reason for your resignation?"

Eli looked at him and drew a deep breath. "Kurt," he said. "I'm sorry for you."

And he cut off the connection. For a moment he sat gazing at the blank screen. Then the chime of the operator calling rang once more through the station and he reached over to shut the sound off. There was left nothing but a signal calling-light winking whitely and mutely on the control panel.

He got up and headed back for the party.

In the elevator, however, as his finger was hovering above the button that would send him to join those below again, he suddenly changed his mind. He jabbed instead at the button that would send him to the solar, and felt the elevator shoot him upward. A couple of seconds later he stepped out into the peace and silence of that glassed-in area.

The call from Kurt had disturbed him; and as usual when he was disturbed he woke suddenly into instinctive struggle with anything that acted as a clog upon his thinking processes. The liquor he had just been drinking was just such a clog. Eli was far from drunk, but he felt his wits slowed and mired by the depressing effect of the drinks. He wanted room and air, to rid himself of their effect.

He stepped over to the center table of the solar and pressed the button that caused the large sections of the transparent dome to sink down into the walls of the station. They slid from view and he felt the sea air fresh on his face. He

breathed deeply of it, pacing around the circumference of the
solar as he did so, like a man at exercise on an ocean liner.

What was bothering him, and what had bothered him from
the start of this whole business, from the moment he announced his resignation to Kurt on Cable Island, was the fact
that there had always been something hidden at work in the
action of this project of his. Something he had been unable to
put his finger on, but which he sensed as certainly as he might
have sensed some vague but persistent pain.

He was not used to anything about him remaining elusive
for long. Once he had become conscious of anything affect-
ing him, it was his normal habit to track it down in a hurry and
bring it out in the open where he could handle it. But this time
. . .

He wondered for a second, with a sort of cold shock, if Mel
was right, and that there was something about himself he was
deliberately refusing to face. And maybe it was this that was
taking the control of the present situation out of his hands. He
punched his right fist into the palm of his left hand, cursing
softly as he limped around the circle of the solar. Whatever it
was, it was making him merely one of the pawns of the
present situation, instead of leaving him master of it —as he
had always been master of any situation.

Now, it was exactly as if he was being used by some mind,
some force greater than himself. And that was intolerable.
Intolerable! The very structure of Eli's nature rebelled
against it. He was, and life had taught him to recognize the
fact, one of those few who were simply incapable of being a
servant, let alone a slave to any person or thing. He could
not—*could* not—any more than dynamite could be used to
make firecrackers. In the days of galleys, Eli would not have
survived his first day of being chained to an oar. He would
have died—died fighting. It was the one thing about himself
over which he knew he had no control; and, for that reason,
feared. It was the one piece of knowledge which an enemy
could use to force Eli to destroy himself. And it frightened
him now to think that perhaps at the present moment Anthony
Sellars or someone else did know it.

He broke the circle of his pacing and limped over to the communicator on the center table. He looked at its blank bubble screen and paused irresolute. He had been on the verge of calling Hassan. But before he could touch a button, the thought had come: What could he ask the man? He could not even formulate a question or a demand for information. He could only say, *I feel uneasy. Find out why.*

And to that, Hassan would only return his customary shrug. *And I wouldn't blame him, either,* thought Eli, wryly. He turned away from the set, defeated.

The fumes of the drinks were all but gone from his brain. Sheer body adrenalin had counteracted the dullness he had felt after talking to Kurt. He remembered suddenly that the party was still going on downstairs; and if he did not return soon, they were liable to start wondering about him. And someone—it would probably be Jenny—would be coming up to find out what was keeping him.

He turned once more and headed toward the elevator to go back down. Before he reached it, however, there was a movement through the fresh, salt air about him, and out of nowhere, a small brown body sailed to light with no more pressure than an autumn leaf, on the index finger of his right hand.

He stared at it. It was one of Johann's little birds. It cocked an eye at him, then threw back its head and poured forth a short, sweet trill of sound.

Then it pecked idly at his fingernail, once—Eli felt the tiny beak like the touch of a toothpick, faintly against the nail— and flew off. Eli looked around for it, but its smallness had immediately become lost in the immensity of sky and seascape.

Bemused, his fingers went to the ring Johann had given him. He pressed it. The miniscule voice he had heard once before, spoke to him.

"The order for your death has been given. The assassin is someone you know. You are to die tomorrow."

Eli stood for a long moment, not moving, after the voice had ceased, his fingers still on the ring. Then, with an abrupt

movement, he let go, stepped briskly into the elevator capsule and punched for the level of the gathering downstairs.
The elevator dropped.

Jenny slipped to his side the moment he came back through
the lounge entrance.

"What was it?" she whispered.

"Just Kurt wanting me back," he said. "I told him no."
He slipped an arm around her. "Let's get me another drink."

CHAPTER VIII

ELI WOKE suddenly and without warning, sitting bolt upright in his bed.

"What happened?" he said aloud.

Nobody answered; there was nobody in the room.

For a moment he continued to sit there. What had happened? What was he doing in bed? There had been the party yesterday and it had lasted until evening and he had drunk a good deal and then . . .

"Did I get drunk?" he asked himself; and realized immediately that that was not what was troubling him. It was not just that he had drunk too much and could not remember how the evening had ended—something had happened last night that he could not remember. And something else had awakened him suddenly, just now.

What was the matter with him? He was not drunk now. In fact he was oddly clear-headed—almost feverishly bright and awake. His mind seemed to be working at a tremendous pace on something he could not understand. He jumped out of the bed and began throwing on his clothes. Even before he was fully clothed, he was limping rapidly out of his room and down the corridor.

He saw no one. A wall clock told him it was near noon. He turned and hurried in the direction of the automat.

The others were all there. They looked up from their

lunch, staring at him as if he was a ghost as he came into the room.

"Eli!" cried Jenny. And Howell jumped to his feet.

"What are you doing up?" he demanded. He came swiftly around the table in front of him and steered Eli to a chair.

"Why shouldn't I be up?" asked Eli. "What's wrong with all of you?"

"For one reason," said Howell grimly, "because you're full of nembutalline. You should be dead to the world for ten hours yet. And why ask us?" he checked himself, staring narrowly at Eli. "Don't you remember?"

"Remember what?" asked Eli.

"Mel," said Howell, turning his head.

The tall young medician got up from his table and came over to Eli, peering into his eyes.

"Look at that, Arthur," he said. "His pupils are normal."

"They couldn't be!" said Howell, stopping forward.

"Look for yourself."

"With that drug in him—"

"Never mind that," interrupted Eli, speaking slowly and clearly, and with a strange, furious calmness. "I don't remember what happened last night, or why you should give me nembutalline, and I want you to tell me."

They looked at each other. Howell spoke.

"About ten o'clock last night," he said, "we turned on a news broadcast. There was a report among other things that a number of leading Members had been arrested and would be tried for genocide. They read off some names and one of them was Seth Maguin."

"Seth . . ." white-faced, Eli swayed on his chair. The big hands of Mel caught him.

"Arthur," the young man turned on Howell, "I don't think you ought to tell him now."

"I'll handle this," said Howell, relentlessly, towering over Eli in the chair. "You collapsed, Eli. And when you came to, you were out of your head. You wanted to leave for Cable Island right away. Do you remember now?"

Eli shook his head.

"No," he said faintly.

Jenny brought him a glass of water. He drank gratefully, and a little color came back to his face. He straightened up in the chair.

"I gave you enough nembutalline to keep you out for twenty-four hours," said Howell. "And here you are, bright and awake without any signs of the drug on you."

"Something woke me," said Eli.

"What?" asked Ntoane. His dark face leaned forward between the shoulders of Howell and Mel Bruger. Eli stared back at him as if fascinated.

"I don't know," he said. "Do you?"

"What are you talking about?" broke in Howell sharply. "What could wake you? We were all in here."

Almost with an effort, Eli wrenched his gaze away from Ntoane. He looked over at the worried face of Jenny and smiled at her.

"It's all right," he said.

"All right, hell!" said Howell. "You couldn't come out from under the nembutalline unless somebody pumped an antiactant into you. And none of us here could do it. Is there somebody else in the station?"

"No," said Eli. He got up, suddenly. "What's the news?" he asked.

"Oh, no you don't," spoke up Howell. "You aren't going to listen to any news until we get to the bottom of this. I don't want you going off again the way you did last night."

"They're meeting this afternoon on Cable Island to dissolve the Groups and set up Central Headquarters," said Jenny suddenly. "Is that what you wanted to know, Eli?"

"I don't know," answered Eli. "Thanks, Jenny." He sat down again suddenly. "Something's happened to me and I don't know what it is." He got up abruptly and began to walk around the room. The rest of them watched him. He stopped in front of Ntoane.

"You're a Member," he said calmly.

"Yes," said Ntoane.

"Why didn't you tell me?"

"You had to find out for youself," answered Ntoane. "So Seth said."

"What woke me?"

A look of pain crossed Ntoane's sensitive, dark face.

"I'm sorry," he said. "You still have to find out for yourself."

"What is this?" interrupted Howell. He looked at Ntoane, incredulously. "You're one of those crackpots?"

Ntoane smiled sadly. Jenny went to Eli and took hold of one of his hands with both of hers. He looked down at her and patted her comfortingly on the shoulder.

"I'm not going to leave you," he said. "But right now I'm going to have to work this out by myself." He raised his head and included the others in his gaze. "I'm going up to the solar. Please, don't any of you disturb me for a while."

He turned and went out of the room, feeling Jenny's hand slip despairingly from his. But he did not turn and look back.

He walked down the corridor and rose alone in the elevator. The solar, under the high, bright sun of noon, was still and hot. He walked across it and stood staring away across the level, rolling ocean, toward Cable Island.

—And now it was time to remember. It was time to bring back what he had buried and forgotten, what he had locked away by exercise of his own will. A point in time had been passed, a peak to which he had climbed, and now it was downhill, and the only way was forward. There was no alternate. And now that he had reached this point it was inevitable, so that while once he had known that it might not be and always he had struggled against it, now he knew that it had always had to be and therefore there was a sense of relief at last in facing it.

Remember, he said to himself. Do you remember? A man has eyes and he sees, a man has ears and he hears. And once a man—no, a boy—had something and he somethinged, and he could not bear it. And so he denied it, as a man will say, I will not see, I cannot see. I will not hear, I cannot hear. I will not . . .

For the anguish of it was very great. Day by day, from the time that the world was small, it had grown. For as the world grew, he saw more, he heard more. So, day by day, the load became more heavy in beauty and in pain. And he was only a boy, a young boy, alone. You cannot blame him. There was the world of which his widening perceptions showed him more and more every day. And there was this faculty of his which more and more revealed to him; until he could not bear it.

Was it my fault? O, cry in agony! I did not make the world. The boy alone and the night sky above Bermuda as he walked, a child, lonely and different. I did not make myself. Blessed are the blind for they shall not see tears. Blessed are the deaf, for they shall not hear the sound of weeping. And blessed are they who do not understand.

And he was a child, a child—a boy who should have played and fought and studied and struggled and grew. Instead he walked the level island by the sea in the dark night, under the many stars, hunting for peace. Peace, peace, in the name of mercy, a grown man is little enough and weak enough to face the hunt for peace! And even there, it followed him, the knowing and the feeling, until he could bear it no longer.

And so he denied it. By function of sharp will he amputated this greater-knowing section of himself, denied it utterly and put it from him, walled off the channel to it in his brain.

And now it was time to remember. For something terrible had wakened him from his sleep, something that left him no choice but to remember, and something that he would not know with clarity until he did remember. And now it was time. And now it was time. And now it was time . . . .

He stood facing the ocean with his arms stiff at his sides, his fists clenched and the sweat streaming down his face.

And now it is time. Now is the the time. Now. Now.

No.

Now!

Mentally, he reached out his strong hands to tear down the

long-held barrier walls. And emotionally the weakling spirit within him cringed and cowered and the hands faltered.

You have no choice.

I can't!

You can handle it now.

I can't!

You are older. You are ready now.

I can't. I can't . . . I can't I can't I can't I can't . . .

Out of swirling darkness he came back, a failure, wondering what had roused him. And then, looking out through the glass with seeing eyes once more, he saw an airboat landing in a furious cloud of spray dashed high against the jetty. The hatch swung back, a figure leaped out, came sprinting toward the solar. Moving automatically, Eli went to meet him and opened the transparent door in the dome wall.

It was Clyde.

Haggard face to haggard face, they stared at each other.

"Downstairs," said Clyde. "Downstairs quick and block the shaft. There're ships behind me."

Eli turned and together they ran for the elevator. The capsule was waiting for them and once in it, they plummeted down the shaft to the fourth level. Howell, passing down the corridor, saw them explode from the capsule and swung about on his heel to face them.

"Arthur!" said Eli. "Where's the switch for the storm blocks?"

Howell stared. From the lounge entrance behind him, Ntoane came hurrying out, followed by Jenny and Mel.

"What's this?" cried Howell, annoyed.

Eli swung on Ntoane.

"The storm blocks!"

But the other man was already moving off down the corridor. At the midpoint of one corridor wall, he pressed an unobtrusive stud and a panel swung back. Within was a heavy, single-handled switch, and he pulled it, over and down.

In the silence that held them all, a faint metallic grating

sound came from distant parts of the station and down the elevator shaft. The heavy blocks that scaled the station's weaker spots from anything an angry sea could do were now in place. They were sealed in now, by metal and concrete, nowhere less than half a foot in thickness.

"What *is* this?" Howell shouted again. Clyde answered.

"I'll show you," he said.

He looked around him, and Eli pointed toward the entrance of the lounge. Quickly, the younger man led the way to and into the room where the viewing screen sat, a bubble of blankness. He set it for exterior scan and switched it on.

The ocean above them ballooned into miniature reproduction within it, the solar as its central point.

"Look," said Clyde, pointing to the sky to the station's northeast.

They looked and saw, high and distant, dots approaching swiftly, dots dropping and swelling into flattened, individual shapes, five of them. Quickly they could be recognized as multi-place airboats, wearing the Transportation Group colors.

"They're after me," said Clyde. He swung on Eli. "And after you. And the rest of you because you're connected with Eli. They didn't expect me to come here."

"Why did you?" asked Ntoane.

Clyde grinned, a weary, but cheerful grin.

"They've got nothing but small arms," he said. "And they're all air and surface craft. While they sit around up there and wait for another boat to answer their call for heavy arms or explosives, we can get away in your underwater tender."

"Good work," said Eli, approvingly.

"Look here," said Howell, breaking in suddenly. "I don't understand this at all. Whose ships are those? Why should I run away? Perhaps this man's a criminal of some sort." he looked at Clyde unfavorably.

"Don't be a fool, Arthur!" said Eli.

"Don't call me a fool!" Howell turned on him. "I've got nothing to do with politics!"

"That's beside the point," broke in Clyde. "We're wasting precious time," he pointed to the screen in which they could see the ships now coming in for a landing at the jetty. "Let's get into the tender and out of range before they can trace us."

"You just sit tight," said Howell, "until we thresh this out. In the first place, you can't get away from here by tender. There isn't any tender."

Clyde stared at him.

"Are you crazy?" he demanded. "Nobody builds in the ocean without some kind of submersible for general use."

"Well there was one," said Howell. "But it developed some kind of warp in the hull so that its lock leaked. I told the university to haul it to the mainland for repairs."

"Good God, Arthur!" said Mel. "Didn't you requisition a replacement?"

"What am I supposed to be, a submarine polo enthusiast?" snapped Howell. "Of course I didn't requisition a replacement. What did we want an underwater runabout for?"

"Are you asking me that now?" asked Mel meaningfully.

Clyde let out a heavy breath and sat down suddenly on the arm of one of the big chairs.

"Sorry," he said, heavily, looking at all of them. "If I'd had any idea of this, of course I'd never have led them here."

"I still don't see what all the fuss is about," fumed Howell. "If those are Transportation ships up there, they've got no authority over the rest of us. We're Medical Group and Eli's Underseas."

Clyde stared at him.

"Where have you been these last few weeks?" he asked. "Jupiter?"

"Forgive him," put in Ntoane. "Arthur never has paid much attention to anything outside medicine." He turned to the older man. "Arthur," he said. "The Groups are gone. Remember how we've been talking about it? That means the Group rights are gone too."

"It's Tony Sellars' world," added Clyde. "Those are his

ships up there; and they'll take whatever he wants them to take, which in this case is us.''

For a moment Howell glared around at the grim faces of the others. Then, gradually, the fire began to go out of him and be replaced by uncertainty. He shook his head and sat down without saying anything further. Suddenly he looked tired and very old.

Above them, the sudden slam of an explosion came echoing through the material of which the station was made, down to them. They listened but it was not repeated. In the silence Eli spoke to Clyde.

''What happened?''

''I woke up,'' answered Clyde. He looked at Eli. ''Sit down,'' he said gently. ''I've got some bad news for you.''

''Bad news?'' echoed Eli.

He stared at the younger man and his own words seemed to buzz in his ears. Abruptly he seemed to go away from Clyde and all the others, as if he was standing at the end of a long tunnel and they were at the far end, shouting at him.

''At first I thought I could work with Tony,'' Clyde's distant voice came to him. ''Then something happened to make me realize that the way he was going was a road I couldn't follow . . .''

The tunnel was whirling about Eli. Thunder rolled in the back of his mind.

''I didn't think he would scrap all justice—''

The thunder was growing louder . . .

''—when they arrested the Member leaders and brought them to Cable Island . . .''.

Eli could no longer see and the thunder drowned out the voice of Clyde.

''You needn't go on,'' he felt himself saying. ''You needn't tell me any more now, because I know.''

And out of the elemental fury that beat about him, out of the storm that tore and tossed him, came a pitch, a climax, a point beyond which nothing could endure—from the thunder, lightning, a single jagged streak that struck and split and broke and utterly destroyed that which had stood so long.

And then there was knowledge and an end. He came back to the land of the living and the room in the station where they stood about him.

"I remember now," he said. "Seth is dead. They shot him and the other Member leaders without a trial early this morning. I was with him; and it woke me.

"I know it all now," he said. He looked at the faces of those about him and smiled. "There are no more barriers between us."

CHAPTER IX

ELI LOOKED at them all; and it was as if he had never seen them before—had never seen any people before with such bright clarity. He was like a man who, after years of poor eyesight, had suddenly been fitted with glasses. And the room, and the people within it seemed suddenly shrunken, but hard and clear with a shocking minuteness of detail, like a picture seen through an artist's reducing glass that makes a scene smaller but more intense.

"Yes," he said, softly, "I understand you all, now."

"Eli!" Jenny ran to him, but stopped, suddenly uncertain, an arm's length from him. "Eli?" she said.

"It's all right," said Eli. "I'm all right," He turned slowly until he faced Ntoane. "It's all right, Ntoane," he said. "I know now. I know you've been guarding me for the Members. But it's all right, now."

Ntoane shook his head slowly. His eyes went past Eli. "I'm not so sure," he said.

Eli faced around to find himself facing Howell. Howell had a gun in his hand. It looked incongruous there, as out-of-place as a bongo drum or a paper hat. But the thin physician held it firmly enough.

"I can't believe it," said Eli softly.

"Back up, all of you," ordered Howell. He gestured with the gun and they retreated across the room before him. When they were well back, he walked to the communicator in the center of the room and punched buttons. There was a moment's hesitation and then the bubble screen cleared to show the figure of Hassan.

"And *you!*" said Eli to the image.

Hassan shrugged.

"You should know that much about me, Eli," he said. "Money I have and most things. But intrigue, that's my life. While you were in a position to use me, I played the game for you. But now there's only one man to play for—Sellars."

Eli glanced at the man with the gun.

"And Howell?" he said.

"Intrigue is my line." Hassan shrugged again. "Research is Howell's, isn't that right, Howell?"

Howell flushed, but said nothing.

"Sellars threatened to cut him off from his work, for life," said Hassan. "Everybody's for sale, one way or another."

"Shut your mouth!" said Howell, suddenly and viciously, but holding the gun steady on Eli. "My work will benefit millions in the long run."

"Arthur—" began Ntoane, and bit his lip.

"Kind of unnecessary, isn't it?" said Eli dryly, "with Sellars' armed men knocking on the door?"

"Oh, they don't have authority to do anything but arrest you," said Hassan. "Dr. Howell here is really just acting the part of a good citizen in holding you until they can be let in."

"Except that gun is just liable to go off accidentally, isn't it, before the men get in?" said Eli. He had been watching Howell, and there was sweat on the other's forehead, glistening there.

"*No!*" it was Jenny, crying out. She ran to Eli. The gun in Howell's hand wavered for a moment at her action and then centered once more on Eli's chest.

"Of course not! How can you think such a thing, Eli?" said Hassan smoothly. "Dr. Howell *is* a little nervous, it's true, but . . ."

"Arthur, for the love of God!" cried Ntoane, stepping forward.

"Stand back!" said Howell thickly, lifting the gun.

"Yes," said Eli. "Stand back, Ntoane. Stand back, all of you." He took a step himself toward Howell.

"Stand back," said Howell, sweating. Eli took another step toward him.

"Arthur," said Eli. "You know who I am." He took another step forward. "I'm the man you made over. You constructed me, Arthur. I'm your masterpiece. Are you going to destroy me?"

"Stop," said Howell. "Stop."

"You know me, Arthur," Eli took another step toward him. "Millions of people know me. I tell the truth and I'm as good as my word. Let me tell you something . . ." he made one more step and saw the gun jerk in Howell's hand. "If you shoot me and kill me for Sellars, Tony'll have to get rid of you sometime later on to cover up his own part in it. You know that."

"I've got to have my work." Howell's voice suddenly shot up the scale. *"Stay back, Eli!"*

"No," Eli said, slowly continuing to approach him, "you'll get nothing out of it. And you're not constitutionally fitted to murder a man, Arthur. You don't want to do it. You *can't* do it . . ."

"For the last time, stop!" shouted Howell. The gun lifted, firmed as his arm straightened.

"Look out!" cried Clyde, diving forward. The gun in Howell's hand jerked, wavered and then exploded. Eli twitched backward, stumbled and sat down. Then Clyde and Notane were on Howell. Jenny was all over Eli.

"I'm all right—I'm all right. Let me up!" Eli was saying. "He was pointing clear over my head when he pulled the trigger. I just flinched and lost my balance." He got to his feet and went over to where Ntoane and Clyde were holding Howell. Howell's face was paper-white and his body rigid. He made no attempt to get away from the two men holding him.

"Let him go," said Eli. "It's all right. Let him go."

Slowly Clyde and Ntoane released him. Howell stared wildly at Eli for a moment, then suddenly the stiffness went out of him and he crumpled. Eli caught him and eased him into a chair. Howell was shaking.

"Mel!" said Eli sharply, over his shoulder to the tall young man. "Give him something to calm him down. He'll be all right." He put his hand on Howell's shoulder. "You'll be all right, Arthur."

"God! Oh, God!" said Howell brokenly, his face buried in his hands.

Eli patted him on the shoulder and turned to Ntoane. There was a weary but triumphant smile on his face.

"And now," he said. "I'm ready to go to work. I imagine you can help me?"

Ntoane stared back at him and slowly a smile crept out to erase the strain on his own features and he nodded.

"Yes," he said. "Yes, Eli, I can. Several million of us can."

CHAPTER X

ANTHONY GEORGE SELLARS sat frowning at the desk before him in the Speaker's anteroom of the Main Council Room of Cable Island. Swelling up from the polished desk top a small screen showed him the station on Calayo Banks Cay, from the point of view of one of the airboats at rest beside it. The solar roof was smashed and broken where the door to the jetty had been blasted loose from its hinges, and the furniture of the solar itself was overturned and disordered, but that was all.

The storm blocks that closed the elevator shaft had not yet been cracked.

This was unfortunate—but merely as a matter of timing. An airboat with sufficient explosives to blast an entrance should make its arrival within minutes. No, the station would undoubtedly be opened. That was not what bothered Anthony Sellars at the moment. It was the fact that he had handled the whole business very badly—first by not taking care of Eli the minute his men had taken young Poby Richards and forced the knowledge of Eli's location and of Hassan from him, and secondly by mistakenly putting his trust in Clyde. He had thought he had observed in the young Spokesman for Communications a hardheadedness equal to his own; and, as always when he allowed himself to trust to anyone besides himself, he had been disappointed.

He sighed and rose from the table. In a few moments the remnants of what had been the Council of Group Representatives would be gathering in the amphitheatre beyond the small door to his right that led into the Speaker's Section of the Main Council Room. Some would come from the lower levels of the Island where they had been virtual prisoners since his unobtrusive coup here several days back. Others would have been salvaged from cities around the world where and when his men could find them. In some cases both the Spokesman and the Underspokesman of a Group were dead or unobtainable and a local Group head had been brought in in their place. But, one way or another, there was a respresentative for every Group; and even now they would be entering the Main Council Room, for their last official meeting.

When they were all seated, it would be his job to go in and tell them that the Group system was ready to be abolished and hint that those of them who wished to co-operate would be absorbed into his own governing organization. After that there would be nothing left but the formality of a vote. It was not a prospect to which Tony Sellars looked forward with any particular triumph. Nor could it be said that it affected his emotions adversely, either. It was merely the next step that should be taken in its proper order, one more duty to be performed.

He turned and began to pace the room, not nervously, but with a measured steadiness, as if the occupation was some particularly necessary exercise. There was in his walk the same thing that marked all his action, a studied acknowledgement of duty. Tony Sellars was in fact, in the truest senses, a slave to duty.

Few people understood this man who had been spokesman for Transportation for over twenty years. People did not warm to Anthony George Sellars the way they warmed to Eli Johnstone. Rather they were chilled by him and in many cases, repelled. The majority disliked him and were a little afraid of him. A minority found things to admire in him; and surprisingly, within the ranks of this minority, he was capable of inspiring an almost fanatic attachment to himself. But far and away the greatest asset of his nature was the strength he very obviously possessed.

Sellars was strength personified. For this reason even people who disliked him would follow him. This single virtue was obvious in him. In fact it shone through him, not like an inner light, but like the hidden molten glow of a quiescent volcano, sullen, dogged and unquenchable. The physical coercions of an earlier age would have wasted themselves on such a man. They could only have broken his body and left his will untouched. A few such men are born from time to time and Anthony Sellars was one of them.

And he was not insane; and he did not desire power for its own sake. Like Eli, he was a child of his time—but while Eli had opened himself to the uncertainty and self-doubt of his period, seeking, asking, letting himself be tossed in any direction in his hunting for a logic to life. Tony Sellars had narrowed himself, admitting only those questions that permitted of a clear-cut positive or negative answer. And when it became necessary to go farther afield into the grayness of an unclear problem, he judged as justly as he could and then forced a decision in terms of black and white. For his own purpose, he had reduced the problems of his day to his own common denominator; and the answer had been clear-cut—absolute control for the world, and by himself, the only man he could be sure would do each and every thing that Tony Sellars believed should be done if the race was to continue.

And now he had done what he ought and won what he should—with the single exception of Eli. He regretted having to destroy Eli for the loss of talent it entailed. He did not like Eli, the natures of the two men had been too antipathetic for that. But that did not enter the problem, for the dislikes as well as the likes of his emotional being had long since been whipped to heel by his imperious will. He neither loved nor hated. He neither felt joy nor sorrow. In this hour of his triumph he tramped the floor of the anteroom without elation or apprehension, or consideration of reward. Personal reward to him was a term without meaning. As near an automaton as living flesh and blood can make itself, he merely surveyed the arena of his recent victory and paced away the moments intervening before the inexorable developments of events should move him to a further arena, a further struggle, and a further duty.

He looked once more at his chronometer. A few minutes yet remained.

He turned abruptly out of the path of his pacing and went back to his desk. Seating himself, he pressed the catch on a drawer and sprang it open. Then, reaching inside he took out the small white cube impressed with the notes of the speech he would make. He closed the drawer again; and, lifting the cube, placed it on the desk.

As it touched the dark, gleaming surface a sudden sensation flashed through him—as if he had suddenly come in contact with a live wire. And he froze abruptly, like a man paralyzed, one hand on the arm of his chair, the other outstretched and lying on the desk top, fingers holding the cube.

It seemed then, to Tony Sellars, so long the complete master of himself, as if contact with the desk had without warning burst open some long-forgotten unguarded door in his mind and that he now stood helpless and aghast at what entered through its rusty portal. Some thing he could neither describe nor understand reached through and held him. Caught by a strange compulsion, he sat for a moment staring at the cube in his fingers, then raised his eyes to look beyond the desk.

Before him, it seemed that the air was thickening and taking form. And, as he watched, the figure of Eli Johnstone, who should by rights have been trapped in the station his men were now beseiging, seemed to coalesce into shape before him. And the figure looked at him and spoke.

"I'm not really here, Tony," it said. "You and I are just in contact by courtesy of the Members."

Sellars' vocal cords broke free of their stasis.

"What is this?" he said.

The figure that was Eli smiled.

"I suppose you could call it a telepathic chat," he answered. "Or a meeting of minds or some such thing. I don't know anything beyond the fact that I seem to be a good subject for such things, and frankly I don't consider it important. On the other hand what I have to say, is important.''

The door still stood ajar in Sellar's mind. Looking through it he was forced to accept the truth of what he saw and heard; and the truth in Eli's words presented itself to his mind like a palpable thing. It was a weird sensation, but an undeniable one. And Sellars who had trained himself to face anything, forced himself to face this.

"So you're a Member," he said.

"No," said Eli. "You'd think so, wouldn't you? But I'm not."

"What do you call yourself then?"

"That's going to be a little hard to explain," answered Eli. "I suppose you'd call the Members who had psi-abilities—*freaks?*"

"I would," said Sellars.

"Yes," agreed Eli. "And now suppose you consider them for the purposes of argument to be just one small minority in a much larger class of freaks in the sense that they have unrecognized abilities beyond the ordinary human."

"Such as?"

"Perhaps an eidetic memory," said Eli. "Perhaps a peculiar color sensitivity, or an instinct for putting musical sounds together so that they have meaning.''

"Ordinary people can have talents."

"How about a homing instinct, an unfailing sense for direction? An immunity to all diseases? Perhaps a green thumb for growing things or a knack for handling wild animals?"

"Go on," said Sellars.

"How many of these would be recognized even by the people that possessed them as extraordinary human abilities? What if the race is multi-talented, much more so than has been recognized, but that only during these latter years of our civilization have ignorance and social pressures abated enough for the more dramatic talents to show themselves?"

"Suppositions," said Sellars. "But go on."

"Well then," continued Eli, "there might be more "freaks" in the world than anyone suspects; and some of them might live and die without calling any undue attention to themselves because their particular ability could find no use in the society of their time."

"I can guess that this is all leading up to your own supposed ability," said the older man, immovable. "Let's get directly to that."

"You want to know what I am?"

"Yes."

"I'm an instinctive leader," said Eli. He looked at the other, at Sellars' flat, expressionless face above the desk. "Not a ruler, Tony, a leader, a forerunner of the race. My instinct is to pick a path, like the bellwether of a flock of sheep; so that the rest can follow safely behind me."

Sellars smiled, one of his rare, wintry smiles.

"*This* is your ability?" he said.

"No," for a second Eli looked a little sad. "No, Tony, that's just my instinct, the thing that drives me. My freakish ability is something different but very handy for a bellwether. I have what you might call 'understanding'."

The hint of an impatient sigh escaped from between Tony Sellars' straight lips.

"Understanding," he echoed, with faint derision and disgust.

"Not ordinary understanding," said Eli. "Listen to me, Tony. This is something based on empathy and refined to a point of complete comprehension. It's like seeing or hearing. I *must* understand; I can't help myself. When I was a child it bothered me so much that I deliberately drove myself into partial insanity to escape it."

He looked at the unyielding face of the man before him.

"Anything that lives," he went on softly, "but most of all my own people. To come into contact with anyone is to know them completely. Don't ask me how I do it. Some of my understanding comes from what I see and hear them do. I meet them and I feel immediately what it is like to *be* each one, individually. And then I know them, mind, and body and soul." He looked at the other man and spoke gently, "As I know you, Tony."

"Of course," said Sellars, with quiet sarcasm. "You know me. You understand everybody. And you're a natural leader. So now you've shown up with the help of the Members to kill me and take over the government."

"No," answered Eli. "I can't kill anything—as you can." And his eyes accused Sellars.

"You're thinking of the Member leaders I had executed, no doubt," said Sellars, unmoved.

"Yes."

"I doubt if your understanding reaches to a comprehension of that," Sellars told him, "of the very necessary reasons for getting those troublemakers out of the way before the general population could have its inevitable change of heart."

"You're wrong," said Eli. "I do understand why you thought it was necessary. I tell you no one has secrets from me now, Tony."

Sellars made a sudden impatient effort to break loose from the compulsion that still held his body bound to the chair he sat in. A glance at the chronometer on his wrist told him it was now time for him to make his entrance into the Council Room beyond the door. But he could not move.

"Let's get this over with," he said harshly. "You're here for a reason. Get to the point."

"All right," answered Eli. "Your coup is all but completed. The world is practically yours."

"It *is* mine," said Sellars grimly.

"Not quite yet," said Eli. "It can still go in a different direction from what you planned."

"No, it can't," retorted Sellars. "My organization is in control. There is no possibility of going back. The Groups have been discredited forever as a form of government; and no one will ever trust them again."

"You're right," said Eli. "There *is* no going back. But there is another way of going forward."

"No," repeated Sellars. "No one can change the path of development now. Even if I'm killed or removed the world will go on in the direction I've pointed it. No one can change that now."

"Yes," Eli looked at him. "There is a person who can. A single person."

"You?" The wintry smile was back on Sellars' lips.

"No," said Eli. "You."

"Me?" The older man stared at him.

"If you changed your mind," Eli said. "If you saw a different path and took it, even though it meant giving up your personal gains, the world would go that way."

For a moment Sellars said nothing. Then he spoke.

"You *are* insane," he said, with almost a touch of awe.

"No," said Eli. "Remember, I said I know you, Tony. I can speak to you with the voice of your own conscience. That's what puts me in the bellwether position before all others. And because I understand individuals I understand the race that is the sum of the individuals; and I know which way the race should go."

"You do?"

Eli nodded.

"It should govern itself and follow me."

For a long moment Sellars just looked at him.

"Sweet Heaven!" he said at last, breaking his self-control for the first time since he had been a very young boy. "You'd *talk* me into letting go of the world?"

"I have no weapons but words," answered Eli. "Listen," he spoke swiftly, "let me tell you first why you want to bind the Earth together under your own single rule. You thought that people had outgrown the Groups, and you were right. They outgrew the Groups as they had outgrown all other forms of government in the past. Down through history, you said to yourself, the pendulum has swung, first toward the extreme of a strict rule, then toward loose rule; first toward a centralization of power, then toward a dispersal of power. The cities of Greece to Alexander, Republican Rome to the Caesars. Feudalism to the strong monarchies. And so on down to our own time with the Groups foundering in their own dissentions, tangled in their conflicting authorities, and the world at a standstill."

"This is fact," said Sellars.

"As *you* see it."

"As it is," insisted the older man. "The world is sick. I've operated to cut out the cancer of a sick government. My way was the only way."

"No," objected Eli softly. "There is a better way and I will show it to you. And you will take it, because you must obey your conscience. Now listen! Down through history, the same history that you surveyed, two points of view have marched side by side. One has always said, 'This is the way it has gone in the past. Therefore accordingly, this way it must continue.' And the other has said, 'All things develop or die. What is past is gone forever. The road ahead is always new'."

"In the end everything follows the cyclic theory," insisted Sellars, "always repeating and repeating."

"So the amoeba said, floating on the surface of the ocean, with his highest point the crest of the wave and his lowest the trough between two waves," replied Eli. "And if he was right, what are we doing here, a hundred feet above the water level of mid-Atlantic? But suppose it was true? Is there any reason it must continue to be true? And if it was true, what useful purpose do you perform by assisting what needs no assistance to continue?" He paused and looked at Sellars. "That reason wasn't your real one. I know what is."

"Oh?" said Sellars.

"Yes," answered Eli. "And I'll tell you what it is without your asking. Because I know you won't ask."

Sellars' eyes had dropped toward the desk top. He did not look up as Eli went on.

"You're a strong man, Tony," Eli said. "Almost too strong for your own good. You can't face a problem without doing something about it. If it can't be resolved you find a solution that, if nothing else, will make it appear to be settled for the time being. And that is exactly what you've done with the world at the present time.''

Still Sellars said nothing and did not raise his head.

"Regimentation," went on Eli. "Forced order and activity commanded by a single central head. All the appearance of progress and development. That was your idea. Keep the pump going, even if the well is dry. Pretend that we have not yet reached the decisive end-point.''

Sellars raised his eyes finally. His face was hardened with pain.

"What else is there?" he said.

Eli smiled.

"Thank you, Tony," he said. "You asked. And I'll tell you.'' He smiled again at the bitter incredulity in Sellars' eyes.

"The Members had the right instinct, you know,'' he said. "They've been dreaming of a superman without the faults of man. It was a young immature dream, because it assumed that we would suddenly hop to the top of the mountain without the labor of climbing it. But they were looking in the right direction. Man has battled his external world and won. Now he begins a new campaign to conquer his inner self. The old time of physical struggle is behind us. From now on we march into new land, so different and unknown and vast that no one can even guess at what lies waiting for us there.''

He stopped and looked at the other man.

"Well, Tony?" he said.

Sellars was free of the compulsion that had been holding him. But he did not notice. He put his elbow on the desk and leaned his head against his hand, wearily rubbing his forehead with slow movements of his fingertips.

"If I believed this . . .'' he said. "If I could believe this . . .''

"Why do you think I've come here, except to prove it to you?" replied Eli. "The proof is here for you to discover for yourself. The first and biggest block we face—''

"No!" said Sellars suddenly and sharply, interrupting

him. He straightened up behind the desk and shook his head
briefly, like a man coming out of a daze. "This is fantastic.
No, Eli!" He put both hands palm down on the desk and
shoved himself up onto his feet. Solid and unyielding he
looked across the desk at Eli.

"It was a good try; and you almost made it," he said. "But
I'm a little beyond the years of believing in fairy tales just
because they're what I want to hear. Sorry." And he stepped
out from behind his desk and turned for the door, picking up
the mnemonic cube with his speech notes.

"Fairy tales?" said Eli. "Are you sure that what I told you
was just a fairy tale?"

Sellars paused and faced him once more.

"I'll become sure," he answered. "One day I'll be positive. And what will you do now?"

"Nothing," said Eli quietly. "I told you I had no weapons
but words. There is your door. Beyond it, your representatives are waiting for you. If you choose to walk to and
through that door without facing what I have to offer you, all
I can do is stand and watch you go."

Sellars lowered his head and started toward the door.
There was something ponderous and awesome about this last
gesture. It was as if his great will had such mass that sheer
momentum must carry it slowly but inevitably to disaster, as
the thousand-ton ocean liner turns slowly from a broken
towing cable and with deceptive and terrible gentleness
swings in toward the silent, waiting crowd on the fragile pier.
He almost made it to the door, but before he reached it, his
feet had slowed to a halt and he turned painfully and with
hesitation to face Eli; this man who had never hesitated over a
decision in his life now stood torn and helpless with the
agony of his indecision.

"Damn you!" he said. "What's your proof?"

Eli moved toward him until they looked into each other's
face across a distance of only inches.

"First," he said, "comes trust. It is the first step for all of
us on this new road we walk. The walls of secrecy and shame
and hidden fears must go down. If you want to, Tony, you

can look into my mind with the help of the Members and see that what I told you of the future is true and possible. But the only way this is possible, is for you to let me, at the same time look into your mind. If we do this, we will have no secrets from each other; and no one can force you to it. You must agree and be willing to trust.''

"Trust . . ." echoed Sellars, his voice struggling.

"The time will come when everyone will trust and be open with each other,'' said Eli sympathetically. ''For people brought up as we are in our time it is very hard. I can do it because I know in advance now, what I will see and meet. It's my particular strength. But everybody has his own—and yours, I think, lies in your urge to be right, no matter what the cost. Can you do it?''

"Yes," said Sellars. He seemed to gather himself. "I can do anything," he said.

"I know you can," answered Eli softly.

Sellars lifted his eyes to Eli's and there found reassurance.

"I think I could trust you anyway," he said.

And with those words the barriers between them fell forever.

"You see?" said Eli, after a long while.

"I see," said Tony Sellars.

There was a deep emptiness in his voice. He walked over and sat down heavily at the desk.

"What will I do now?" he asked hopelessly, suddenly very human and defenseless.

"Believe in a different future, that's all," said Eli. "And work for it. Work is something we'll never lack. Not this generation, nor the next, nor even the next after that, will everyone in the world be willing to do what you've just done." He moved forward toward the desk. "You think I've taken something from you, Tony; but you're going to find that in losing that you've gained something much bigger and better to replace it. Hope, Tony."

"Yes, hope . . ." As if roused slowly from his preoccupation with himself, Tony's eyes went to the screen on his desk which showed his ships still clustered about the station. He reached out with one hand and depressed a stud. Invisibly a direct connection flared between his desk and the pilot room of the lead ship. The scene vanished to be replaced by the features of a slim young man wearing a pilot's uniform on which the green Transportation facings were still to be seen.

"Your orders are canceled," said Sellars wearily. "Return to Cable Island." And he cut the connection in the face of the young man's startled expression.

"Thanks," said Eli. "And now?"

Sellars took a deep breath and rose to his feet.

"Now," he said, his voice gaining firmness as he spoke. "I'm due to talk to the Group heads in the Council Room."

Across the open channel of his understanding, the cost and meaning of this statement reached through to Eli.

"I could tell them for you, Tony," he said.

"No," Sellars shook his head. His old certainty was flooding back. "The mistake was mine. The explanation will have to be mine."

He turned from the desk and made his way toward the door as Eli watched him go. With his hand on the button of it, he turned and looked back."

"Those Members," he said, "the ones I had executed. I suppose the Members I hadn't caught told you about them."

"No," answered Eli. "I'm not ordinarily telepathic, but that one time I was in actual contact. One of the men executed was Seth Maguin, a half-brother of mine."

Sellars' face went bleak. "I see," he said. He paused for a moment. "I'm sorry."

"I know," said Eli softly.

For a second more, Sellars hesitated. Then he turned and pushing the door open, went through it. It started to swing closed again, but some invisible force caught it and held it open.

"Thank you, whoever that was," said Eli. "I did want to watch."

He drifted forward to where the angle of the room hid him from the eyes of those in the amphitheater. Beyond the square, flat back of Sellars he saw the faces of the Group leaders in their sections about the room, silent and waiting.

"Spokesmen and representatives," began Sellars and hesitated, as if gathering strength.

Eli turned and saw a movement in the air beside him; and as he watched he saw Jenny coalesce out of nothingness.

"I wanted to come, too," she said, looking up at him. "Eli, do you know you don't limp any more?"

He put his shadow arm around her shadow shoulders, feeling, distant miles away across the ocean, in the station, the warmth and softness of her as his physical body duplicated the action. He smiled back at her.

"That's because I've given up being a cripple otherwise," he said. "Now hush. And listen. This is something that in our present civilization it takes a great man to do."

They fell silent. Out before them Sellars lifted the cube he held in his hand and looked at it for a second. Then quietly, he dropped it into the disposal slot of the desk before him and watched it being incinerated. He looked out once more at his audience and put both his big, square hands palm down on the desk in front of him. He leaned forward and began to speak.

"Gentlemen," he commenced simply, "I have made a mistake . . . ."

DELUSION WORLD

CHAPTER I

"THE POINT IS," Humboldt was saying, "you can pass as a technique trader."

"Beg your pardon," said Feliz. "I *am* a technique trader. The point is whether I can pass as a spy. And the answer to that is no—not even if I wanted to."

They had come around to this point in the argument now for the third time. Feliz Gebrod looked out through the un-opaqued north wall of the comfortable office lounge, down at the carefully laid grounds of the Defense Center, where a chilly spring wind was nipping the new buds on the maple trees. Feliz had not been back here to Earth in a long time; and when he had planned this little vacation he had been prepared to be properly sentimental. But his plans had not included the problems of the director of defense and Psi-Man Philip Verde. *I'm not a stubborn man,* thought Feliz mutinously, *but damn it to hell . . .*

The thought was so satisfying, he looked back at the two other occupants of the lounge and said it out loud. Psi-Man Verde showed nothing. Why should he? He had known Feliz was going to say it. But Donster Humboldt's florid face went even darker.

"You don't owe us anything, Gebrod, is that it?" said Humboldt.

Feliz looked at him with new interest. He had been almost sure it would be impossible to get under Humboldt's skin.

But evidently, he finally had. Feliz hunched his massive shoulders a little deeper in his chair and gave the other two the eye.

They were not at all alike—Humboldt, the director of defense, and Psi-Man Verde, director of the Talents Department—but Feliz was so different from both of them that he put them both together in a different class. For Feliz was half Micturian, on his mother's side of the family.

Since the Micturians were original human stock which—back in the bad old days a hundred and fifty years before laws were standardized on all the human-occupied worlds—had been deliberately mutated to allow them to settle a planet where the best chance of survival depended on resembling something double the size of an ordinary human and possessing harder bone and tougher flesh, Feliz humself was something of an oddity. He was *not* ten feet tall, and his skin was closer to the texture of ordinary human skin than that of well-tanned oxhide. Among Micturians he would have been considered a dwarf, a mere six foot half-breed.

Among unmutated humans, though, he was something else again. He did not get the low-gravity sickness that his mother's people were prone to suffer when they visited the regular human worlds. His head was normal human size, and so were his hands and feet. His shoulders, however, were abnormally broad for a human; and anyone looking closely at the extremely loose cut of his tunic would begin to notice his differences. There was a reason for the baggy tailoring of his clothes—to wit, biceps eight inches in diameter when relaxed, and thighs twelve inches ditto, under similar conditions. For all practical purposes his waist was indistinguishable from his chest, but the width of his shoulders and the loose tunic hid this.

His face was quaintly humorous, its underlying features being made up of very large bones crowded together in a relatively small area. He was so ugly, as the saying goes, that he was almost handsome. His nose was short and wide, his broad mouth concealed some magnificently massive teeth. His eyebrows were miniature forests under a broad forehead, and a touch of premature gray streaked his unruly brown hair. His eyes were the same guileless blue as the near-boiling-temperature volcanic pools in Yellowstone National Park—some twelve hundred miles due west of where he happened to be seated at the moment. Someday, he supposed, he would marry and settle down. But there were a good many comfortable years yet before he need seriously consider it.

Humboldt, on the other hand, was a normal, slightly over-weight human in his mid-fifties who had been a hammer-thrower in his college days and had a mind like a cocked and loaded rifle. He was director of defense, because there was an intelligent and technological race called the Malvar abroad in this part of the galaxy and they threatened to run ordinary humanity back into its holes and then stop the holes up for good. The fact that this would not be accomplished for somewhat more than eight hundred Earth years, according to the best forecasts, made no difference. Nor did it matter that, at the moment, the Malvar and humanity were officially the best of spatial neighbors.

The crucial moment in history was not to be eight hundred years from now—when it would be too late—but now, and for the next twenty years. It was a time to damn the consequences and put the most effective man in charge. And so Donster Humboldt was in charge. He would have been in charge even if he had been a worse devil in other aspects than Genghis Khan. Actually, he was not a devil. He simply believed in getting results, no matter who wept. Secretly he thought of all other people as amiable but rather half-witted, soft-natured animals.

Psi-Man Verde (people called him Philip to his face) knew that Humboldt thought of other people this way. He also knew that Humboldt did not even have *that* high an opinion of Psi-Man Verde. Psi-Man Verde knew that Humboldt's opinion of the psi-man and his corps of psionically talented people was literally unmentionable; and that tucked away in the back of Humboldt's mind was the thought that once the current trouble was over and the Malvar taken care of, it would be a pleasant thing to make sure that all those with

Talents were neatly removed from the scene—liquidated, and poured down some conveniently handy drain.

Psi-Man Verde knew all this; and yet he drove his frail, six foot nine, hundred and twenty pound body and sensitive mind to execute all the miracles that Humboldt daily required of the psi-man and his staff. Not only this, but he put up with Humboldt's arrogance and intolerance and unthinking brutality; and without Humboldt's knowing it, took extra burdens on himself and his people to spare Humboldt's energies as much as possible and make life an attractive thing for Humboldt.

Psi-Man Verde did all this because he, too, wanted to win the silent war they were engaged in. And also because, since he could see so much more of Humboldt than Humboldt could see himself, he pitied the other man.

So there they were, the three of them. Most of what the other two were was unknown to Feliz. If he had known it, he would have hated Humboldt and been embarrassed by the psi-man. But he did not know it, would never know it, and it did not matter anyway. Each in his own way, all three of them were concerned only with results. And *that* was what was important.

Accordingly, right at the moment Feliz was grinning internally. Humboldt, he recognized, had been trying to get under his skin with that crack about not owing them (the normal humans, that is) anything. He thought Feliz might be sensitive about being a half-breed. While actually—aside from the fact that Feliz had about as much sensitivity as a rhinocerous hide—Feliz was, in fact, proud of his freakishness. After all, it allowed him to take advantage of the advantages of both strains of humans.

So what Humboldt had really done was allow himself to get impatient and lose a point.

"Well!" said Feliz, loudly hiding his delight from all but Psi-Man Verde. "I'm a taxpayer, and you've got no authority over me. I don't have to sit here and be insulted!"

He rose to his feet with an injured air. Humboldt went pale and then red again.

"Just a minute," said Psi-Man Verde, speaking for almost the first time since Feliz had been ushered in by the Defense Department secretary who had dug him out of his hotel room in town.

Feliz checked and turned cautiously. The psi-man was another kettle of fish.

"I'm afraid all this is my fault," said Verde.

Danger flags popped up and alarm bells began ringing all over the trouble-sensitive section of Feliz's alert mind. People who started out by apologizing were liable to drive the hardest bargain in the long run.

"I'm afraid I've been less than honest with you," said Verde.

"Quite all right," said Feliz. "Don't bother. I was just leaving." He picked up his hat from an end table to prove it.

"For Dunroamin," said Verde.

Feliz paused. A puzzled look crept onto his massive face, giving it an almost comical expression.

"Beg pardon?" he said.

"I said," Verde repeated, "you're leaving for Dunroamin."

"No, no," said Feliz. "Back to my hotel in town. You see—" He broke off suddenly as he felt his hand replace the hat on the table and his body walk back to the chair it had just left, and reseat itself. There was a moment's pregnant silence in the office. "Good trick," said Feliz in a strangely colorless and unemotional voice. "I didn't know you boys could do that sort of thing."

"I wish we had someone besides myself who could," sighed Verde.

"You can't do this to me, you know," continued Feliz in the same dispassionate voice. Under the loose fabric of his clothes certain of his great muscles were swelling and writhing like pythons—but to no avail. "It's illegal."

"I know," said Verde. "I'm very sorry. But I'm afraid we've got some more talking to do."

"You can make me sit here," said Feliz. "But I've got a hunch you can't make me take a ship two hundred light-years into Malvar territory and play spy effectively. Want to bet?''

"No. Because I'd lose." Verde came around to stand in front of Feliz. "My only hope is to convince you to co-operate willingly. Perhaps, as I say, if I'm more truthful with you—"

"Now now," said Feliz grimly.

"We'll see," said Verde. "Tell me, what do you think about the Malvar?"

"I don't," said Feliz.

"Waste of time," commented Humboldt from where he stood.

"It won't hurt to try the truth on a man like this," said Verde.

"I don't butter up!" growled Feliz.

"I wasn't going to try," said Verde. "We've been asking you to go into the Malvar area of space to do a job for us. We didn't tell you what the job was, because we wanted to know you were willing to do it, before we started letting any secrets out of the bag. But your answer was no."

"Spelled N-O," said Feliz. He made another effort to get up and found he still could not.

"I think if you knew the job we had in mind, you wouldn't refuse," said Verde. "It's not spying."

"Come on now," said Feliz. "The Malvar are double-hearted, cold-blooded, communal-living lizards. What would any human be doing in their area of space, except spying on them?"

"I take it you don't, at least, prefer them to your fellow humans?"

Feliz found his shoulders were free enough of Verde's control to allow him to shrug. He did so.

"Live and let live," he said.

"You've read and heard that the way things are going they should completely overwhelm and occupy the human worlds within the next thousand years?"

"Statistics," said Feliz. "A lot of fancy figure-juggling and guesswork. A lot can happen in the next thousand years. They're no better than we are."

"Yes, I'm afraid they are," said Psi-Man Verde.

"Oh?" Feliz stared at him. "Since when?"

"Since the early days of their technology—in one small area. They have devices capable of broadcasting telepathic orders. Orders they have the natural ability to receive."

"So they hup, two, three, four without the need of words," began Feliz. "They can't broadcast to us, so we just pay no attention when they order us to move out and let them take over—"

"It's not that simple," interrupted Verde. "You see, the human race happens to be telepathic too."

"I—" Feliz blinked and stiffened. "Say that again!"

"The human race is also telepathic. You, for example, are telepathic."

"You're crazy."

Verde shook his head.

"The Malvar have a native, inborn ability to receive telepathic commands. They have developed devices to broadcast in that area, so this adds up to a plus talent for them."

"I never heard even a telepathic murmur in my life!"

"Of course not," said Verde a little wearily. "Except for a tiny percentage of unusual people such as we have in the Talents Department, the human race is telepathically as deaf as a race of doorposts. Which is a life-saving thing for them."

Feliz frowned. "I don't follow you."

"You would," said Verde, almost grimly, "if you were one of the receptives on my staff. Except when you were under drugs or sleeping, you'd be driven half-crazy. The human race normally can't hear a thing telepathically. But, barring a few freakishly crippled individuals where that department is concerned, every mother's son and daughter of them broadcast on the telepathic band like champion hog-callers in a contest."

Feliz stared sharply at the psi-man.

"That's the truth?"

"Yes," said Verde. "And the Malvar can not only receive

telepathically—they can control the power and use it. But while it's possible to construct a physical device that will emit a telepathic signal, it is completely impossible—according to all presently known laws of physics—to build a device that will allow the telepathically deaf to hear. You can boil down the situation between us and the Malvar accordingly, for yourself.''

"For all practical purposes," said Feliz. "They're telepathic, and we're not.''

"Within their own group only, of course," said Verde. "But this is the sort of small but constant advantage that can give them victory in the end. And since we both like to settle the same sort of worlds . . .''

"I see," said Feliz thoughtfully. Absently he rubbed his nose, without noticing that the compulsion of Verde was no longer holding him. He thought the matter over for a moment. "I'm still no spy," he said.

"We don't want you to be a spy—at least upon the Malvar," said Verde. "It just happens that some of our sharpest perceptives have been monitoring pretty deep into Malvar territory to keep tabs on their telepathic broadcasts. And they've been receiving some signals that aren't Malvar.''

"Aren't . . .?" said Feliz.

"They're human," said Verde.

"Human!" exploded Feliz. The two stared eye to eye for a second.

"Exactly," said Verde. "We can't make out much of anything. But they're human. A check of our records has brought up the fact that about six hundred years back, in the Lawless Era, there was a planet settled by an independent human group about where these signals are coming from. It's registered under the title of Dunroamin. That's all we know about it.''

"But how've they survived in the middle of the Malvar all this time?" said Feliz. "How come the Malvar haven't—''

"That's just what we'd like to know. And the Malvar aren't likely to agree to our sending a commission in to find out.''

"I see," said Feliz. He thought a minute. "But why me?" he said.

"Human telepathic emissions have individual and family characteristics," said Verde. "Some of the original settlers were connected to your father's side of the family. You've got relatives there now, undoubtedly. If you can get in there fast enough, and out again fast enough, it just may be that the Malvar may not notice someone from outside has made a visit at all. They'll think you're one of the natives for the duration of your visit."

"Relatives," said Feliz glumly, breathing a little heavily through his nose.

"That's right," put in Humboldt.

"This is all assuming, of course," said Feliz, "that these settlers have found some way to keep the Malvar at a distance, and that they'll be free to talk to me when I get there."

"Yes," said Verde. "If they've found a way of keeping off the Malvar, we want very much to know what it is."

"Hundred to one they haven't," said Feliz.

"No," agreed Verde gently. "You may well find the Malvar have them all in bottles, or some such thing."

"Bottles . . ." said Feliz.

There was a second or two of no talk at all in the office. Feliz stood up heavily. This time, nothing restrained him as he walked over and picked up his hat.

"All right," he said. "You've got me." He clumped toward the door of the office. With his hand on the button that opened it, he checked suddenly and whirled about.

"*What* did you say they named that planet?" he demanded.

"Dunroamin," said Verde.

"Done roaming?" echoed Feliz incredulously.

Verde spelled it out for him.

Feliz shook his head slowly and wonderingly. Still shaking it, he opened the door and went out.

CHAPTER II

FELIZ made it almost to Dunroamin in his own little trader's ship, before he ran into trouble. First came little trouble, then large trouble piling on top.

The little trouble had to do with Feliz's hat. Feliz was partial to wearing a hat, like most technique traders—a jaunty flat beret rakishly tipped over one ear. There was no logical reason for it. It was just a custom, a sort of badge of occupation among the men who went hopping from world to world, picking up new techniques and knowledge developed on one planet for later sale to people on other planets who had not yet developed or imported the necessary skills or information themselves.

The trouble began just a few hours ship-time out of Dunroamin, shortly after Feliz had come out of no-drive and set the course on conventional for that nearby planet. It suddenly occurred to Feliz then that he had not, after all, destroyed all personal identification aboard his craft. His hat, he remembered, had his name and Interstellar Trader's Registry number on the sweatband in gold letters and numbers.

He got out the hat with the intention of removing this betraying item from the sweatband, and switched on the small Mark III plastic converter on the ship's worktable. The converter was necessary for the reason that the hat was made of cast plastic and practically indestructible, being in essence nothing but a single giant molecule stretched out into a single thread, and then cut and woven in shape by a Mark III. A Mark III—when it is properly constructed with a correct governor—can mold, join, or separate cast-plastic like a fairy godmother twinkling a pumpkin into a coach.

Unfortunately, when the Mark III is properly constructed but with an incorrectly set governor, it is liable to vaporize all cast plastic within range of its beam. For example—a hat, and everything in the closet just beyond it, except one outfit that happened to be lying on the bed in the inner of the ship's three rooms.

When this happens, a man—when he is half Micturian and can straighten out horseshoes without hardly trying—is liable to lose his temper and start mashing up the defective Mark III into a neat little lump, to be returned to the retailer who sold it at the first opportunity. Feliz was doing just this when his ship's collision alarm blasted in his ear. Enter large trouble.

Ten seconds later, he was at the controls of his craft and doing his best to get away from a cruiser-sized ship of the Malvar. He was too close to the sun of Dunroamin to go back into no-drive safely; and the Malvar could take more acceleration than even he—with his Micturian blood—could stand. There was no place to go but Dunroamin itself, and hope against hope that it was indeed a human sanctuary standing firm against hostile aliens.

Feliz streaked for the planet.

He was only a few thousand miles out and thinking to himself that Psi-Man Verde might have emphasized a little more the parting advice he had given Feliz—concerning the wisdom of keeping one's emotions (and consequently one's telepathic emissions) down to a whisper is Malvar territory. Because, unfortunately, while the Malvar could not cross the barrier of species and read what was in his mind—no more than Psi-Man Verde could read theirs'—they could sense his human-type emissions, and even the tone of them, like a voice shouting in a foreign language.

The looming disk of Dunroamin was swelling in his viewscreen and he was trying to cheer himself up with the fact that at least he was close enough to dive in and burn up in the planet's atmosphere so that the Malvar in the ship behind him could not take him alive. He had done business with Malvar hither and yon about the stars, and they were fine fellows to deal with. But one would not want to be taken alive by them after being discovered spying in their territory.

His communicator sounded a dulcet note and the lean face of a Malvar replaced the image of Dunroamin on the screen. Feliz tensed instinctively, although he knew the Malvar was merely putting out a call signal and could actually have no idea whom he was talking to. Still, Feliz could not help his reaction. It was instinctive. The Malvar were really not lizards, as he had remarked to Psi-Man Verde, nor were they really double-hearted and cold-blooded. They were simply the evolutionary end-product of a different sort of ancestry than the human. They had a joined, twin-chambered organ for pumping blood, instead of the four-chambered human heart, and operated their bodies at a temperature about twelve degrees under the human.

The Malvar were really not lizards, and Feliz knew it. But they *looked* like lizards, and that did it.

"Halt!" ordered the Malvar on Feliz's screen, in the common lingua franca of space around the human-Malvar area. "You are in Malvar territory. Please identify yourself!"

"No, no, a thousand times no," hummed Feliz thinly between his teeth, stepping the acceleration up another fraction of a G. *"I'd rather die than say yes."*

The Malvar gained. Feliz fled.

"You must halt or be taken prisoner," said the Malvar.

Ah, well, thought Feliz sadly, and disconnected the automatic safety that would have prevented any accidental destructive plunge into a planet's atmosphere.

"You've had your last war—" The Malvar in the screen broke off suddenly. The Malvar's picture disappeared and the green face of Dunroamin reappeared. Feliz stared. He glanced at his instruments.

The Malvar ship was curving away sunward. In the tracking scope it looked as if it was still hot on Feliz's trail, but the telltales reported it had altered its course half a second of arc to sunward.

"Now what—" began Feliz, and was cut off short as the collision alarm blared again.

He looked at his instruments. Another object was approaching him, emerging now around the curve of the planet which had hidden it before. He punched at the screen.

The screen clouded, wavered, and finally cleared (it had needed overhauling six months now, that screen) to reveal something that could only be said to resemble a six- or seven-room house put together in a vacuum by either a child or a madman. For a long moment Feliz stared at it without comprehension, then memory of an ancient-history course he had taken years ago came back to mind.

"Twist my head off!" said Feliz. "A space station!"

He punched assorted buttons on the communicator. There was an answering beep in a broadcast range that had not been used at any time that Feliz could remember; and the screen lit up with a picture of a ramshackle room and several lank individuals in tattered black uniforms. One, who badly needed a shave, leaned into the screen and waved a handgun at Feliz.

"Surrender!" howled this unwashed character. "Surrender at once, or be destroyed. Man the guns, you men. Send a shot across his bows. Fire one! Fire two! Fire—"

And Feliz's instruments suddenly began to report hurtling objects emanating from the space station which, it abruptly occurred to the half-Micturian, were probably loaded with high explosive—an ancient and barbarous instrument of war. He snatched at his ship's controls.

"He runs!" yelped the speaker in the screen. "After him!"

This, since the speaker was broadcasting from a station in free fall, should have been an impossible order to obey. However, Feliz was in no mood to sit around and check on its impossibility. If the man could say it, they might be able to do it—and that was enough of that. Feliz's ship and the station were headed directly for each other at the moment. He kicked his own vessel hastily toward the night side of the planet.

The penumbra was looming, its dark shelter just before him, and most of the shells lobbed by the station were missing him wildly, when there was a heavy shock at the rear of his ship. The lights flickered, dimmed and came on again.

And he tumbled out of control, into the night side of Dunroamin, falling planetward.

CHAPTER III

WOBBLING down on its emergency nose jets, Feliz's ship tottered within a few dozen feet of the ground, did a back flip under the influence of its gyros, and landed heavily. For a moment there was silence under the peaceful-appearing Malvar stars in the Dunroamin sky. Then slowly the hatch opened, a boarding ladder stuck itself out to the ground below like a reluctant tongue under doctor's orders, and a battered Feliz climbed out and down onto the turf with an ungracious grunt.

"Malvar!" he growled. "Boneheaded idiots in bone-headed space stations! Pin-headed psi-men—"

He stopped talking suddenly to listen, his massive head cocked on one side. He could have sworn he had heard the sound of a woman, weeping. After a second he decided it must have been his imagination. After all, he was out here—wherever it was—in the middle of nowhere.

He looked at the sky. It was a pleasant, warm summer night under conditions of near Earth-normal gravity. A gentle wind was bringing him the scent of pines—earth-ancestered pines, no doubt, adapted long since to Dunroamin conditions. *To work, to work,* thought Feliz. He hitched up his baggy pants and went around the ship, inspecting for damage.

There was no moon in Dunroamin's sky; but Feliz's Micturian relatives had been adapted to a moonless situation themselves, and consequently Feliz did not miss one at the moment. His pupils dilated like a cat's, he poked about his ship and discovered the explosion which had crippled him had done only minor damage. It had taken off about half of one of his stabilizer fins and jammed shut three of his landing tubes. He could weld a new piece on the fin but the tubes were beyond his repairing in these primitive surroundings. No matter; now that he knew which ones were choked off, he could alter his firing pattern to balance the thrust. The rocket tubes, like the fin, of course, were only necessary in an atmosphere. Once well away from the planet he would be as good as ever.

He went back in through the hatch, regretfully tore out one of the interior partitions of the ship—reducing it to a two-room vehicle, instead of a three—and emerged once more onto the grass below with this in one hand and a welding torch in the other. He had to fold up the partition to get it through the hatch. He unfolded it now, and set about using it to repair the fin.

Something like a mutated variform of an Earth rabbit hopped up to the ship out of the darkness and barked at him.

"Go away!" snarled Feliz. Rather to his surprise, the rabbit did. Feliz paused in his welding to worry slightly. Had he perhaps offended some intelligent native life form? No, the rabbit was too small a creature to meet the physiological requirements of an intelligent life form.

But it had obeyed with suspicious swiftness.

He went back to his repairs, and was still occupied at them about an hour and a half later when the night sky began to pale. Casting a glance upward, Feliz became aware that he had not fallen as far inside the night area of the planet as he had thought, and that daylight was close upon him. Congratulating himself on the fact that he had got to work on the fin promptly, he put a few final touches on the repair job; then, torch in hand, he headed back toward the hatch and the familiar surroundings of the ship's interior. He would, he told himself, have a bite to eat, and figure out his next move on a full stomach. A peculiar result of Feliz's half-Micturian ancestry was a metabolism that left him hungry on at least six large meals a day. And at the moment he had not eaten for nearly ten hours.

He thought of eggs, sausage, and steak. He put his foot on the first rung of the landing ladder—and stopped, hearing something.

It was very definitely the sound of a woman crying. He realized now that he had been hearing it for some time. It was a thin little sound that—having once dismissed it as *not* the sound of crying—he had been vaguely identifying as the ululating of some night creature; possibly some relative of the barking rabbit. Now, however, there was no doubt of what the sound actually was. And, as he listened more attentively now, it was borne in on him that the person making the sound was either young, or pretty close to it. He was made aware of this fact by short and not uninteresting statements mixed in with the sobs.

"Oh, dear . . . what's going to happen to me now? Why couldn't I stay adjusted? Oh, I'm so *hungry!*"

The bit about being hungry struck off a spark of fellow-feeling in Feliz. He knew just how she felt. He laid the welding torch down against the ladder and went off in search of the unseen mourner.

He found her within about fifty feet, sitting on a rock and crying into her hands. She was, as he had suspected, young. He stood over her for several seconds without attracting her attention.

"Hey!" he said at last.

She paid no attention.

"Hey, *you!*" barked Feliz.

The girl glanced at him briefly and went back to her sobbing.

"I'm so hungry," she sniffed. "And there just aren't any nuts out here at all."

Feliz found himself disagreeing with her. There was, he felt strongly inclined to say, at least one nut growing on a rock not fifteen feet from him. However . . . perhaps she had just been brought up not to talk to strangers, or something.

Feliz went back to the ship, climbed inside, and made a thick sandwich of canned roast beef. Eying it hungrily himself, he fought a brief battle with his baser appetites, then nobly shoved these aside and returned to the girl. The sun was well up by the time he got back to her. She had stopped crying—out of moisture, was Feliz's private opinion—and was merely seated on the rock gazing dolorously at her hands, which were none too clean.

"Will I ever paint again?" she was asking herself out loud. Feliz made no attempt to answer her. He merely shoved the sandwich into her hands.

The girl stared at it in surprise, looked up at him, back at the sandwich, and burst into a fresh wail.

"Now I'm getting tactile hallucinations!" she choked.

"Hallucinations!" exploded Feliz. "That's real, you nitwit! Taste it!"

For the first time she really looked at him. And, in the first young light of the new day, Feliz could see in return that she was indeed young. And, in fact, pretty. Blue eyes, rather reddened at the moment, looked up at him out of a small, pointed face beneath a crown of fluffy, light-blond hair. She was dressed in sandals with a thong between the first two toes of each foot, and a sort of dress of many colors. Feliz braced himself for the embarrassment of tearful thanks.

He was afflicted by no such discomfort.

"Oh, shut up!" she said. "If I hadn't paid any attention to you hallucinations in the first place, I'd be home in my own bed right now. I wouldn't have to be out where nobody is and there aren't any nuts or fruit or anything to eat."

Feliz checked the temptation to argue the question of his own reality. The girl was obviously unbalanced.

"What are you doing out here anyway?" he demanded.

"Where else can I go?" she sniffed. "Now that I don't exist any more?"

"You," said Feliz, thinking perhaps shock treatment

would prove effective, "are out of your head."

"No, I'm not," said the girl. "I'm out of my body and that's worse." And she began to cry again.

"Quit that!" roared Feliz. And so effective was the half-Micturian volume of his voice that she did. And sat staring at him, apparently half-stunned, with her mouth open.

"Look," said Feliz, trying to hold his voice down to tones of gentleness and reason. "Forget about hallucinations for a moment. Where'd you come from? How'd you happen to be here?"

The girl swallowed and closed her mouth.

"They disintegrated me because I kept seeing hallucinations," she said in a small voice. "Now nobody can see or hear me." She looked at him. "Nobody real, that is."

Staring down at her, Feliz had an idea. It was a far-fetched notion, but what had driven this young girl into a state of imbalance might just possibly have some connection with what he had been sent here to investigate. If there was a breeding source of insanity on Dunroamin, that might explain why the Malvar left it alone.

"Here," said Feliz, attempting a soothing tone, "you come along with me and—" He reached for her.

The girl gave a sudden scream, tumbled backwards off the stone and rolled away from him in a frightened swirl of colors and flashing limbs Before he could move, she had bounced to her feet and run off, still carrying the sandwich.

"Stop, dammit! Stop!" roared Feliz, and took off through the trees after her at a lumbering gallop.

The trees stretched in all directions, and the girl had vanished among them. Feliz charged in after her, tripped over a root, fell sprawling, caught a flickering glimpse of color somewhere farther on, got up and galloped on again, expecting every minute to come upon her but not doing so. Finally he collapsed against the trunk of a sturdy poplar-like tree, snorting for breath.

His body, as no one knew better than he, was built for

power rather than fleetness. For short distances he could hit up to thirty or thirty-five miles an hour, and then he bore a rather awesome resemblance to a charging rhinocerous. But he was no cross-country artist. Panting, with heaving lungs, he told himself that he was a tin-skulled idiot; that the girl, insane or not, obviously knew how to take care of herself. That it was her world, after all, and it was not any of his business anyway. That he had other things to do, and one of the best of them was to go back to the ship, eat a decent breakfast and get himself armed before sticking his neck out any further on this nut-filled planet.

With this, having recovered his breath, he stood up away from the tree and prepared to turn back to his ship.

Only—the thought suddenly occurred to him—in what direction was the ship?

Jerked suddenly into an awareness of his situation, Feliz turned about on one heel, peering through the trees. On all sides the green corridors stretched away into solidity. Every way looked alike. Each looked like the path back to the ship.

This, thought Feliz furiously, was ridiculous.

The ship, he told himself, must be just out of sight, one way or another. He had hardly done any more than turn his back on it. It was simply a matter of getting his bearings, of thinking the thing out.

Feliz calculated. He tried to remember over which shoulder he had first seen the sun, and how many times he had altered course while chasing the girl. After a while he decided to ignore everything but the position of the sun, which he seemed to remember had been rising ahead of him as he chased the girl. Accordingly, he turned his back on it now and strode off.

He made good progress, but twenty minutes later found him still walking among the trees and with no open spaces in sight. He stopped again—and inspiration came to him, from a book on woodsmanship he had read in his boyhood days. Find a high spot, that book had advised. If nothing else provides, climb a tree and look about you.

Feliz, skinning his knuckles and breaking a good many

branches in the process, climbed a tree.

From as high up the tree as he dared go—his weight was making it sway and creak alarmingly as it was—he did spot an end to the forest about a couple of hundred yards off. Beyond this ending was an open slope down what looked like a valley containing a good-sized town or even a small city. Feliz slid recklessly down the tree and headed in that direction.

A few minutes later he saw the trees become sparser about him and he broke out at last into a gently sloping meadow. Ahead, about a mile or so away below him, he could see the city, a composite of buildings no more than four or five stories high at the best and with a fairly thick belt of smaller homes surrounding these taller constructions. The building material was evidently native wood, stone or cement—and the architectural style was a hundred years or so out of date. No matter. It was, in Feliz's estimation, civilization.

He started forward, and only then did he notice a low, unmortared, rustic-looking stone wall just a few feet from him. The wall also ran down the slope toward the city; and seated on the wall only a few feet off was a venerable old gentleman who beamed at Feliz.

"A morning to remember, is it not?" said the old man.

Feliz looked and blinked.

The oldster had arranged his many-colored kilt warmly around his knees as he sat on the wall. It was perhaps a blessing that he had, for his thin, hairy, ancient legs from the knees down seemed to be things of knotted muscle and angular bone. The long arms protruding from his short-sleeved and also many-colored tunic were likewise thin and bony and rather unadmirable. His white beard was so long it had been tucked into a belt at his waist. His hair was similarly white and stood up like a fuzzy wig. Below it, the old man turned on Feliz eyes of a gentle and guileless blue; and, under a long and stick-thin nose, smiled at Feliz with a mouthful of brilliant white teeth marred only by the fact that one incisor was broken off near the root.

Feliz stared distrustfully, searching the old man's face like a suspicious customs agent who had never heard of technique traders before. The old man smiled more widely and more gently.

"Something about me," he asked, "suprises you, young man?"

"I just ran into a woman who was mad as a hoot owl," answered Feliz bluntly. "I thought perhaps you might be another of the same."

The old man chuckled happily, in fact so hard that he had to wipe his suddenly damp eyes with the end of his beard.

"Dear me! Dear, dear me!" he gasped at last, recovering himself. "You must forgive me for going off in such a fit of humor. It was the irony of your question that set me off. That you should suspect me of insanity! Well, well." He managed to sober up finally. "It's not a subject to joke about, I'm sure. But just to reassure you, my young friend—among my other other modest virtues, I think I can truthfully say that I am without a doubt the sanest man in the world."

CHAPTER IV

"OH YOU ARE?" said Feliz. "The sanest man in the world, eh?"

"Indeed. Without a doubt," said the other. "Hoska's the name. El Hoska. You've heard of me, no doubt."

"No," said Feliz.

"You haven't!" El Hoska stood up in surprise. "Imagine that! It's almost inconceivable—but then we must all keep open minds. Anything is possible, including the fact that you might, indeed, never have heard of me." He indicated the city below. "I'm the mayor down there."

"You are?"

"Indeed, yes." El Hoska slipped a friendly arm through Feliz's. "And one of the most pleasant, perfectly adjusted little communities you ever saw, it is indeed. Come along with me and meet my people. We see visitors only at such rare intervals."

"It comes from shooting at them from space stations," said Feliz dryly.

"Beg pardon?"

"If the shoe fits," said Feliz restraining the mayor's attempt to lead him down the slope by the simple expedient of keeping his three hundred odd pounds, Earth-weight of bone and muscle solidly planted on motionless feet. "Sorry, I can't meet your people now. I've got to get back to my ship."

"That's too bad," said the mayor, reluctantly releasing

him. "However, if you must, you must. I'll be happy to tell people you passed by, in any case. Would you care to give me your name and profession?"

"I'm a technique trader."

"But this is magnificent!" cried El Hoska. "That changes matters. You absolutely must stay. You must come down and get acquainted. This is just what we've been waiting for. We have a warehouse full of techniques to be traded and at least one other full of old ones needing mending. I'm sure we can give you a lot of business."

"Just a minute," said Feliz. He explained what a technique trader actually was.

"Dear me!" said El Hoska, when he was finished.

"Yes," said Feliz.

"What an embarrassing blunder! I'm afraid I just assumed you were something like a tinker or a dealer in hides. Can you possibly forgive me? Of course, you are a thousand times more valuable. Pardon me—but the best teachings advise us not to bottle up our happy emotions, any more than our unhappy ones; but give immediate expression to them."

He stood on his head, to Feliz's astonishment. His skinny old legs waved happily in the air. It was an unlovely sight.

"Well, so long," said Feliz. He turned and started back into the woods.

His legs, operating independently, immediately turned him around and headed him once more down the slope, toward the city.

"Hey!" yelled Feliz. "What is this?" But even as the words emerged from his lips, he was answering that question himself. The memory of Psi-Man Verde forcing him to sit still in a chair was still painfully green.

"The will of one," replied the mayor solicitously, stepping up to walk beside Feliz, "is the will of all. As the mayor of my people I express their united desires. That is all. We are a simple people," he continued, as Feliz's captive legs carried him on down the slope. "Though we live in the city, you could say we are not of it."

"Could you?" gritted Feliz through closed teeth, straining without success to regain control of his own lower limbs.

"I think you could, yes," replied the mayor thoughtfully. "A somewhat romantic phrase, of course, but true in essence. Yes, we are really children of nature and the spirit. A sound body and a clean mind are almost our only necessities—which is why you had the luck to bump into me on the hillside this dawning, as I was doing my deep-breathing exercises. Yes," sighed the old man happily, "with a spiritual return to nature has come a harmony between the flesh and spirit. . . ."

And he rambled on as they continued down the hill, his bright old eyes gleaming, his creaky voice expounding. Feliz reached out one of his uncaptive arms, and fingers that could crumple half-inch steel plate grasped at the back of El Hoska's neck.

But the mayor, innocently galumphing along with his kilt flapping about his bony knees, was about six inches out of reach.

They went down into the city together. It was, Feliz discovered, in an advanced state of decay. Best kept up were the small family houses toward its outer edge in which people obviously lived; but even these showed startling differences. There seemed to be a group of homeowners who believed in keeping their buildings up; but at least an equal number had let theirs go to not-so-picturesque ruin, though these latter had kept up their lawns and flower beds. The larger business and office buildings of the area near the center of the town were slovenly and broken-windowed almost without exception. No wheeled traffic was about the streets and there seemed to be a startling lack of industry.

"Here," said El Hoska, as they at last reached the center of town, "you see our public square."

He waved at a plastic-floored area of about two acres. Scowling helplessly, Feliz looked it over. Its black-and-white checked surface was nearly deserted except for a few individuals as brightly and colorfully dressed as El Hoska. Occasionally, a man in the black tunic and breeches of the men Feliz had seen in his screen at the time he was dodging the space station, marched from one building to another. The more gaily clad people ignored these uniformed men. And, as far as the uniformed men were concerned, from what Feliz could see, the feeling was mutual.

"Wait here," said the mayor, beaming at Feliz. "Wander about and steep yourself, if you will, in the storied grandeur of these buildings surrounding us. Meanwhile, I will gather a few of my people who will wish to meet you, and whom I am sure you will in turn enjoy meeting."

And he skipped away. Feliz stared. For the mayor was actually *skipping*, the way a four year old child might. He skipped across the square, waving gaily to the other brightly dressed strollers and loungers as he passed them; and disappeared from sight down one of the streets.

Still skipping.

Feliz took an experimental step and found that the compulsion the mayor had been holding upon him was no longer operating. He was free to move about as he liked. He took one long stride back the way he had come, and then caution stopped him.

It would be best to find some other way out of this town. The road back was in the same general direction in which the mayor had disappeared. Feliz had no wish to be recaptured.

Feliz scowled about the square. He still had no idea what it was that kept the Malvar at a distance from this planet; but if most of the world's inhabitants had the mental punch and grip of the mayor, then there was at least enough here to give the aliens pause.

Incongruously, as Feliz looked about for other exits from the square, there came back to his mind the matter of the barking rabbit. Being a technique trader had taught him that all mysteries on a strange world are usually connected to the general fabric of that world at many points. All things are eventually related; and when in search of a solution to one puzzle, you bump into another, the chances are better than even that both are different aspects of the same problem. Why should a rabbit—a very Earth-like rabbit—bark? The incongruity of it stuck firmly in his mind and would not be shoved aside.

Meanwhile, he had spotted what looked like a little alley leading off from the square. An alley between blank and dusty commercial buildings whose appearance suggested that nobody had gone that way for weeks. Feliz took off.

"Halt!" shouted a voice behind him. Feliz stopped, and the back of his neck crawled. Had someone been keeping a watch on him all this time? He turned.

Two of the black-clad men, brandishing night sticks, were approaching him across the square at a run. As he finished turning, they slid to a stop on the slippery plastic about him.

"How did you sneak in here?" shouted one.

"Answer immediately!" shouted the other, who was somewhat skinnier and shorter than his companion. The second-speaking one also had a bad case of halitosis. Feliz caught a full blast of his breath and backed off slightly.

"Halt!" shouted the taller one. "We order you to halt."

"I am halted!" growled Feliz, taking another backstep to get away from the smaller man's exhalations.

"Then stop trying to sneak away!" The taller one waved his night stick ominously. "Answer immediately!"

"Answer what?" snarled Feliz. His own temper, never one to win any records for length and sweetness, was beginning to warm to the occasion.

"Who are you?" shouted the taller of the two. Then, before Feliz could answer, he shouted, "That is a lie!"

"What's a lie?" roared Feliz.

"Silence! You are here to answer questions, not ask them. Speak when you're spoken to."

Feliz, getting a grip on his temper, closed his mouth and said nothing.

"Well?" shouted the taller. "Why are you stubbornly silent?"

"*Stubbornly silent!*" exploded Feliz. He gasped air, closed his mouth, felt his face heat up like a furnace, clenched his fists and said between his teeth, in an artifically calm voice, "Because I am here to answer questions, and to speak when I'm spoken to.

"Slippery answers," shouted the smaller one with the halitosis, "will not help!"

"You would do well to co-operate," said the tall one threateningly. "We're trying to treat you with kindness."

"And patience," said the smaller one.

"But you continue to avoid answering."

"Answer at once. Who are you?"

"I," said Feliz. "am a technique trader."

"That is a lie!" both shouted at once.

"Shut up!" thundered Feliz, finally and completely losing his grip on his temper. "I'm trying to tell you what I am, and you—"

Too late, he saw the night sticks descending toward his skull.

"Resisting arrest!" he heard the small one shouting, dimly and from a great distance, as the black and white of the pavement rushed up to meet him. "Hit him a good one, Harry! Hit him again!"

CHAPTER V

Splash!

Feliz snorted water out of his nose and tried to come up swimming. It was an ocean. No, it was merely a bad flood. No again. It was a local cloudburst of some sort . . . . Feliz came fully to his senses and recognized the fact that someone had just emptied a pail of water over him.

The someone in question wore a black outfit like a uniform. There were two more black outfits behind a desk. The one who had just dumped the water went back and sat down alongside the others. Feliz blinked water out of his eyes and straightened up slightly in the stiff-backed chair in which he seemed to be sitting. He stared at the three. Like a trio of suspicious rather than wise monkeys, they stared back.

"I want a lawyer," Feliz said.

"Silence!" snapped the one in the middle. "Alcoholic beverages are forbidden, except by express permission of the controller."

Feliz's vision cleared completely. He looked about him and saw that he was seated in a Spartan sort of office with walls of dirty white. A spider was setting up house in one high corner of the room within Feliz's range of vision. Directly before him, in that order, were the desk, the three behind it, and a large window through which sunlight came to smite Feliz in the eyes. The men behind the desk were haloed against it. Feliz squinted and became aware suddenly of a piercing headache which exploded upward for a second as he noticed it, then subsided to a dull, persistent ache.

"All right, spy!" grated the one in the middle. "Talk!"

Feliz pulled himself all the way up in the chair. With a movement so swift that Feliz had trouble convincing himself that he had seen it, the man behind the desk whipped out what appeared to be a needle-snouted handgun and pointed it across the desk at Feliz.

"Be very careful!" he said.

"Oh, yes. Yes," said Feliz. "I will!"

Slowly, the middle man put the handgun away. Feliz stared at the three. All bore ingrained frowns of suspicion upon their tight faces. They looked like wrinkled crabapples, knotted and gnarled before their time. The middle one seemed to have the authority. He was a tall, thin man with a long, oval face. His nose was fleshy; his lips were thick and they parted a little with each breath. Dark eyes glared at Feliz from under untidy brows.

"Well, spy?" this man said now.

"I'm not a spy."

"Don't lie to me! I'll have you shot!" shouted the middle man.

"You tin-whistle idiot!" roared Feliz, losing his temper in spite of the recent caution imposed by the sight of the handgun. "I'm a perfectly legitimate technique trader!"

Oddly enough, his violence and abusiveness seemed to relax the others at once. It was as if he had just proved himself to be a member of the club, so to speak, and the first natural stiffness between them could now be abandoned. One of the black-clad sidemen put his elbows on the desk, and the middle one leaned forward.

"Don't try to lie to me!" he said—but he said it almost genially. "What's that?"

Feliz explained, for the second time that day. Memory of his first explanation reminded him of something that might be useful. "Listen," he wound up, "you people probably came too late to see it when you picked me up; but I'd just finished talking to your mayor—"

The clubbish attitude suddenly vanished.

"Mayor!" cried the central one. "What is this nonsense! There is no mayor in this city. There is only the controller—me, Taki Manoai! Talk to me of mayors and I'll have you shot!"

"Well, he called himself the mayor," growled Feliz. "He had this kilt and tunic on, colored red and purple and blue and yellow and—"

"Enough of such deviationist talk!" shouted the controller. "Kilts are decadent. Tunics are forbidden. The aberrant strain of impure breeds among us that pretended to see different shades in the one color black has been eradicated from this world many years ago."

"Look around you, man—" began Feliz; but the controller began to foam at the mouth and the ceiling fell in. There had, it seemed, been night sticks hiding not too far behind Feliz's chair.

Feliz explored his tender head with careful fingers. While his brain was as susceptible to being jarred into unconsciousness as any other human brain, his skull—thank Micturia—was somewhat thicker than a normal human's. No permanent damage seemed to have resulted from the night-sticking; though he would scarely like to have made a practice of being on the receiving end of that department.

He stopped feeling his head and contemplated the bowl of lukewarm protein gruel set before him. It was the first prison he had been in where the jailer was not bribable in direct proportion to the badness of prison conditions. The place he was in at the moment might have been a good place once— about a hundred years before. But it had suffered from a sad lack of care for at least the last fifty years or so.

"Steak?" Feliz had suggested hopefully when the jailer brought him his gruel.

"Steak?" said the other, interested. "What kind of a machine does that come out of?"

"It comes off an animal," said Feliz sourly. Then he brightened. "But you can get a sort of poor substitute out of the same machine that produced this slop. You just change the settings—''

"Sabotage!" said the jailer. His eyes lit up, then faded again. He shook his head. "No, no," he said sadly. "I'm too old. You don't get me to commit no sabotage."

"Oh, get out of here!" Feliz snarled, picking up the gruel. After all, there were calories in the junk and by now his stomach was shrunk—if he could judge by the way it felt— almost to pea-size.

"I committed some sabotage once," said the jailer, lingering.

"I'll bet," said Feliz, swallowing a spoonful of the gruel and grimacing at the taste.

"Watered the coffee in the bachelor's mess to make it go farther."

"Uh."

"Yep," said the jailer. "Just poured myself a full pint of plain water and dumped it in. Nobody ever suspected."

"Yeah."

"But I was young then," said the jailer with a sigh. "A man gets older, he gets to thinking before he goes about taking harebrained chances and defying authority like that. Nowdays I just stand in line with my cup like the rest, and if there isn't enough coffee to reach down to my end of the line, I just count my blessings and take a cup of plain water."

"I'll bet you do," said Feliz, eyeing him.

"That's right. You've got to learn to live with life, that's what I say," said the jailer, and went off.

Left alone, Feliz ate his gruel and got up to have a look through the dirty translucent pane that pretended to be a window in his cell. He had evidently been asleep for some time following the second clobbering with the night sticks, for it was now late afternoon outside the building. He crossed to the bars that screened the corridor side of his cell and wrapped his two thick hands around them.

He could handle a good many things that would baffle the strength of an ordinary man. Attitude, thought Feliz, had a good deal to do with it—although of course strength was important also. But it was the determination not to be conquered . . . He took a good grip on the bars, planted his feet firmly and tried to force two of them apart. The muscles creaked and cracked in his arms and spots began to swim before his eyes. He felt the bars give slightly, and stopped, gasping, to look at them. He had spread them about an inch and a half—to a new width of about nine and a half inches.

On the other hand, thought Feliz wisely, sitting down on the cot in the cell once more, brains are better than brawn any day. The intelligent man *thinks* his way out of a bad spot.

Just then the corridor lights—evidently thousand year automatics—glowed up into brightness to compensate for the rapidly dwindling daylight. Feliz blinked in the sudden increase of illumination and heard a small voice suddenly address him out of the glare.

"Pardon me," it said timidly. "But are you really not an hallucination after all?"

Feliz blinked and got to his feet. With the adjustment of his dazzled eyes, he became suddenly aware of a face peering around the edge of the wall that separated his cell from the next, where that wall met the bars of the corridor. It was the face of the girl in the woods.

"You!" bellowed Feliz.

The face disappeared. Feliz jumped to the bars and pressed his face against them. He was just able to make her out, shrinking against the bars of the cell alongside.

"Come here," said Feliz.

She shook her head.

"Come here!" snapped Feliz impatiently. "I won't grab you. Can't you see I'm locked in here?" He shook the immovable bars, or attempted to shake them, by way of making his point.

Shyly, she approached.

"Are you sure you aren't an hallucination?" she repeated.

"Do I look like one?" roared Feliz.

"Oh, yes," said the girl. "You aren't wearing the right kind of clothes for a real person at all."

Feliz stared at her.

"What kind of clothes do real people wear?" he finally asked.

"Why, *real* clothes," said the girl. "Of course. Like mine."

"Oh."

"Of course, your clothes are brown instead of"—she blushed—"black. That's one of the reasons I came here looking for you. When I thought of that, I mean."

"Oh, you did, did you?"

She blushed again.

"Well, of course, when I bit into it—"

"Bit?" Feliz found himself hanging onto the bars like a boxer on the ropes.

"Well, after all," said the girl, bursting suddenly into rapid and obviously highly embarrassed speech, "there's nothing more natural than a person having an hallucination about something she wanted very much, and who would have thought there would be food of that shape and color and taste that you gave me. I mean, how was I to tell it was food at first? But after I ran away with it and I couldn't resist taking a bite because it sort of *smelled* like food, and it turned out to be so good, I ate it all."

"I bet," said Feliz, thinking of those two thick slices of honest bread and that one gloriously thick slice of cold roast beef. He salivated.

"It was *so* good!"

"I know," said Feliz.

"Just delicious."

"I know. I know."

"That stuff in the center. It had such a chewy, nutty, tasty—"

"Will you stop it!" roared Feliz, in agony. "I haven't eaten anything in six months!"

"Six months!" said the girl, staring at him round-eyed.

"Nearly. Nothing decent!" growled Feliz. "And I can't get out," he added despondently. "I'll starve in here."

"Oh, don't do that!" said the girl. She ran to the door of his cell and did something. There was a click and it swung open. She came in and took him by the hand. "I'll take you back to that funny house of yours and you can get some stuff to eat for yourself."

Feliz looked from her to the open door of the cell. He opened his mouth and then closed it again.

"What?" said the girl. "Is something wrong?"

"No," said Feliz with great feeling. "Nothing is wrong. Nothing. And nothing is going to be wrong until I can look at it from behind a full stomach. Let's get out of here." And he started off up the corridor in the direction in which he had first seen her retreat.

"Not that way," she called after him. "Let's go out this way. There's a hole through the wall. It's quicker."

CHAPTER VI

THEY went out through the hole in the building, up through dark streets in a gloaming only spottily relieved by the few undamaged streetlights remaining, across the square and toward the edge of the city. The few black-clad people they met paid no attention to them. Neither did the color-dressed people—which brought the girl down in a slight case of sniffles by the time they reached the edge of the city.

"Going to be a fine walk in the dark," said Feliz gloomily.

"Well, it's not far, anyway," said the girl.

"Hah," said Feliz. "Don't tell me. I've walked it."

"Yes, but you went all crooked," said the girl. "I was watching you. Actually, we should be there in about ten minutes."

She was right of course.

"Wow!" said Feliz, as he helped the girl through the hatch and closed it behind them. The interior lights in the control room and the cabin, and what had once been the galley, went on automatically. "I could eat a horse and sleep for a week."

"What's a horse? Could you?" said the girl. "Why?"

"Ever hear of an accelerated metabolism?"

"No."

"Well, that's what *I've* got—naturally," said Feliz. "I need sleep and food. Lots of both. Of course, I have a fair amount of energy—" He was opening the food locker and

148

hauling out items already processed and prepared. "Ah!" he had just found the remains of the beef. He tore off a large piece and put it in his mouth. Manna from heaven, that's what it tasted like, he thought. "Help yourself," he mumbled to the girl.

She poked interestedly among the pile of comestibles.

"What funny food."

"Funny?" said Feliz around a mouthful of cheese and bread. "What's funny about it? What do you eat?"

"Fruits," she said. "Nuts. Vegetables, raw. Natural food. Nature's bounty."

"How about that synthetic gunk I got in that prison?"

"Oh, that—that's what the hallucinations eat."

"Hallucinations!" barked Feliz. "Don't start that again."

The girl sat down suddenly in the pilot's control board chair with a thump and began to keen like a rejected puppy.

"Oh, I'm so mixed up," she wailed.

"Hold it! Hold it! Cut it out!" cried Feliz hastily. "Maybe I can help you."

The girl stuck her head up.

"Would you?" she said.

"Can try, can't I?" growled Feliz. The girl uncurled and sat up in the chair. "Suppose you fill me in on what happened to you anyway."

The girl sniffed, but kept control of herself.

"Well," she said, "I'm an artist."

"Go on. Go on."

"Well," she said, "I mean, we're all artists of course, in the sense that the human mind needs to find one means or another for creative self-expression. But I'm a painter, of the new classic school of expression."

Feliz's eyebrows went up.

"You mean you don't know? I thought everybody knew that. The new classic school of thought believes in interpretative representationalism."

Feliz's eyebrows stayed up.

"Well, you *know!* No, I suppose you don't. Well, you know what representational painting is, don't you? You see a

house and you paint a house. It's like making a print of it.
Well, interpretative representationalism is when you represent the house exactly as it is; but through the modified use of
color and the addition of imaginative detail you interpret the
scene in terms of your own personalo-creative essential and
make it manifest.''

Feliz's eyebrows came down, defeated.

"You do understand what I mean?'' she said.

"Absolutely," he told her.

"Well, there you have it. It was all so wonderful, and
then''—the girl's voice began to grow moist again— ''I
began putting in imaginative details that were just like hallucinations.''

"Hold it," said Feliz. "Please."

"I was a fool!'' said the girl, covering her eyes with the
palm of one hand and extending the other at arm's length,
palm out, as if warding off something. "Wasn't I a fool? Tell
me I was a fool.''

"Why?'' said Feliz. "How should I know if you were or
not?''

The girl took the palm away from her eyes, indignantly.

"You aren't very helpful,'' she said.

Feliz yawned hugely. He was having trouble keeping his
eyes open, now that he had no empty stomach to prod him
awake.

"Need . . . little sleep," he said.

"But I'm not finished.''

"Oh . . .'' Feliz yawned again. "Okay. Go on.''

"Well, sooner or later I was bound to be discovered. I said
to a good friend of mine, Esi Malto—I said to her, Esi, I
really shouldn't mention this to a soul . . .''

Feliz dozed off, in spite of his good intentions.

'' . . . and *bang!* I was disintegrated.''

Feliz sat up with a jerk. He had missed a lot evidently. No
matter. Tomorrow was another day. What was he thinking
of? A couple hours of nap and he would be fine.

He lurched to his feet and across the control room to the
cabin.

"Twen' winks . . ." he muttered, fell on the bunk and was lost to the world.

When he woke, the hatch to the ship was open, letting sunlight flood across half the floor on the control room. Was it . . .? Yes, it was morning. Must be. Feliz sat up, massaging the stiff cords of his neck.

"*Hark, hark,*" the girl was singing, somewhere outside the ship:

> —*the lark doth greet the new-born day.*
> *With joyous heart and bright array.*
> *'Joy! Joy!' doth say.*
> *And air-borne, flitteth on his way.*

"Snubg, smudg," grunted Feliz, scrubbing his wire-bristled, forty-eight-hour beard with a sleep-numbed fist; and, earth-borne, clumped heavily into the ship's washroom, where he undressed, climbed under the shower and turned it on, smoking hot.

About twenty minutes later, shaved, cleanly dressed and awake at last, he emerged. The girl, he found, was seated at the control desk. From somewhere she had produced a stick of charcoal and was drawing something on a clean page of his log book. Feliz took a closer look. It was a sketch of a sort of hairy monster in Feliz's clothes, stretched out on its back with its mouth open, asleep and obviously snoring.

"Thanks," said Feliz.

"Oh, do you like it?" said the girl, looking up. "I put a lot of myself into it."

"Yeah," said Feliz. "I'd like it better if it wasn't in my log book." Feliz was realizing just now that he'd forgotten to get rid of the log with his other identification; not that it seemed to matter now.

"Why?"

"Because—never mind," said Feliz. "I'm sure the port inspectors will understand." He rubbed his hands together. "Well! How about a bite of breakfast?"

"Are you hungry *again*?" said the girl. "You ate just before you fell asleep."

"What's that got to do with it?" asked Feliz, rummaging in the food locker. Abruptly, he stopped rummaging, stood upright, turned about and began to walk across the control room toward the open hatch.

"Are you going somewhere?" said the girl.

"Yes!" yelled Feliz, climbing out of the hatch. "Stop me!"

He reached the ground and, turning toward the city, began to march off.

"Help!" he shouted.

The girl scrambled out of the hatch and hurried after him.

"Don't you want to go?" she said. "If you don't want to go wherever it is you're going, why are you going?"

"Because I can't help myself! Something's making me go."

"Oh!" said the girl.

"What do you mean, *oh?*" demanded Feliz, looking sideways and down at her as she hurried to keep up.

"You're under compulsion."

"Yes," said Feliz. "I would say that. I would say that I was under some sort of compulsion. Yes, I think that describes it rather well."

"You don't have to be mean about it," said the girl.

They walked on a little farther and entered under the trees that reached to the slope overlooking the city.

"What did you do to get put under compulsion?" said the girl.

"I met that old unmentionable bag of bones that calls himself your mayor!" snarled Feliz, his face purple with effort from the unsuccessful fight he was making against the coercion being exercised upon him. "The misbegotten unclean article of refuse did this to me once before!"

"Oh, dear," said the girl. "El Hoska is awfully severe. He's the one who disintegrated me."

Feliz craned his neck to stare at her.

"Him? The same one?"

"He said"—the girl's lower lip began to quiver at the memory—"I'd become so maladjusted that there was no longer any hope of correcting me. He said I was a danger to the community. I would have to be disintegrated—I told you all this last night."

"Tell me again."

"He told me I'd have to be disintegrated. And he snapped his fingers and *bang!* Just like that I ceased to exist."

"So that's it," said Feliz, thoughtfully.

"What's what?"

"Nothing," said Feliz. "You wouldn't understand. Except you might as well get used to the idea that you weren't really disintegrated after all. You didn't cease to exist at all."

"Oh, yes, I did."

"Of course you didn't. You exist right now, don't you? For pete's sake!" said Feliz exasperatedly.

"Well, I most certainly do not! I guess I know whether I exist or not!"

"If you don't exist, how come I see you and hear you?"

"You're just an hallucination," said the girl stubbornly. But there was a quaver of uncertainty in her voice.

They had been following the nearest thing to a straight line among the trees. Now they came out near the stone wall where Feliz had first met El Hoska. And there, sure enough, was the elderly gentlemam, seated on the corner of his wall.

"Good morning, good morning, *good* morning!" he said, leaping to his sandled feet as Feliz marched up. "You had a pleasant night, I trust?"

"I don't suppose," said Feliz in measured tones, "that there would be any particular use in asking you to turn me loose?"

"But, my boy!" said El Hoska. "If you really, basically, did not wish to fall in with my desires, certainly you wouldn't do so. The human mind is a free entity. How can I possibly force you to do what you do not want to do?"

"Because," said Feliz between his teeth, "you happen to be a natural psi talent. Psi-Man Verde—you don't know him, but he's a lot like you—would probably give his right arm and half his left to get you on his staff.''

"Come, come," said El Hoska, gently. "This is wild talk. You are like most ignorant people who have had little contact with civilization—you instinctively fear the natural forces and science. You must understand such fears are mere superstition.''

"Superstition?" said Feliz.

"Of course! What you think to be compulsion upon you is merely a strong desire, a strong, *loving* desire on the part of all my happy people to have a closer acquaintance with you. Naturally, since I am my people's representative, the desire is channeled through me. Dear, dear," said El Hoska reprovingly, "you have never been taught that this is a moral universe we live in. No one can coerce anyone else against his will. If it looks like someone is being made to do something he doesn't wish, you can rest assured this is only an illusion. Basically, the coerced one *wants* the illusion of being dominated. This is very good science.''

"It is?" said Feliz.

"Dear me, yes." El Hoska linked his arm in Feliz's, and began to lead off down toward the city. Feliz's legs carried him right along with the old man. "I have thought of the very thing to occupy your time while you are getting to know us better here. For a long time—''

"Just a minute," said Feliz. "I just thought of something. Have you two been introduced?" And he nodded from El Hoska to the girl, who was walking along at his other side and looking mournful.

"I beg your pardon?" said El Hoska, peering around Feliz at that side of him where the girl was.

"Her!" shouted Feliz, jerking a thumb at the girl. "The one you disintegrated, remember?''

"But there is nobody here but the two of us," said El Hoska. The girl began to sob quietly. "Oh!" said the mayor suddenly. "You wouldn't—you haven't possibly happened to hear about Kai Miri, the little girl we were forced to disintegrate a few days ago? Is that who you mean?''

"That's right. Her," said Felïz. "The one walking right here beside me right now."

"There, there," said the mayor. "You are obviously a badly maladjusted young man. Think now. Look at the matter logically. When that poor girl was disintegrated, the atoms of her mortal body were scattered over a tremendous area, and the natural currents of the air will have dispersed them even further. Don't you see how impossible it would be to collect them all in one spot? Even if by doing so you could restore them to their orignal order and restore her to life."

Kai Miri began to sob louder—probably, thought Feliz, at the thought of the wide areas over which the natural currents of the air had dispersed the atoms of her mortal body.

"Never mind!" growled Feliz, patting her shoulder clumsily. "Forget it!"

"Tch, tch," said the mayor, observing. "You must really let me give you some special counseling, my boy, when we have the opportunity.

"I'm leaving," said Feliz. He continued, however, to march toward the city. They were at its outskirts now.

"No, no," said the mayor. "In your present precarious state of mental balance, it would be dangerous, extremely dangerous. Besides, wait until you see what I have for you to do."

"What?" demanded Feliz.

El Hoska folded his hands benignly together as he strode along.

"How beautiful is nature!" he said.

"What do you have for me to do?" said Feliz, staring at him.

"We who have passed beyond the stage of a mechanical civilization," he said, "have little use for the city's ancient appurtenances, beyond those required for basic shelter. There is, however, one exception. That is the public square. The ideal gathering place for social meeting and discussion—except for one thing."

He paused and paced along with his eyes closed. Feliz

stubbornly kept his own mouth in closed position. *If he thinks,* thought Feliz, *that I'm going to play straight man by asking him* . . .

"That is," said El Hoska, opening his eyes again, with no visible sign of irritation, "a lack of water. The sun, the air, the good earth is there—"

"Where?" asked Feliz, thinking of the unbroken expanse of black and white plastic pavement.

"But," said El Hoska, ignoring the interruption, "there is no water. What the spirit craves in this ideal gathering place is a tinkling fountain rising in its midst. It would be a refreshment to the souls of all who gather there. Besides, the nearest good well is five city blocks away, if one happens to be thirsty.

"I see," said Feliz.

"Yes. And you," Eli Hoska said, "being a more primitive man, used to fumbling with mechanical things, are the ideal one to construct such a fountain for us."

"And if I don't, you'll disintegrate me?" said Feliz, with a sudden ray of hope.

"How can you think of such a thing!" said El Hoska, shocked. "No, no, my boy. Someday you may basically wish to be disintegrated, and then, of course we may have to oblige you. But that day is not yet."

"It isn't?"

"Dear me, no. You can trust me. I'll let you know when you want to be disintegrated."

"Thanks," said Feliz.

"Not at all. Within this city," said the mayor as they left the last of the buildings behind and stepped out into the square itself, "you will come face to face with the reality your warped and primitive mind has heretofore denied. And, basically, you want this. Basically, you do not want to leave, I can tell that. Basically, your desire is so great that right now I do not believe you could find it in you to tear yourself from my side for any reason. With me, you will find inspiration."

"That's not all I'll find," said Feliz, beginning to sweat. Two of the black-uniformed men in the square had already recognized him and now they were approaching at a run. The order had evidently gone out to take no chances, for they were letting their night sticks dangle from their belt, and drawing sidearms as they came.

"Halt, spy!" shouted the nearer of the two. "Make a move and you will be shot. Surrender yourself, and come with us!"

"True," El Hoska was saying reflectively as they strolled along, "you will undoubtedly find this city making its impact upon you in many different ways. Come along, my boy, and do not stare so wildly at the empty air."

CHAPTER VII

"HALT, spy!" shouted the taller of the two black-clad men as they galloped up. They were, Feliz recognized without any great happiness, the two who had night-sticked him the day before. "Halt or you will be shot. Come with us!"

"Shoot him in the leg, Harry," said the small one with halitosis. "Just to show him we mean business."

"Wait," said Feliz hastily. He grinned reassuringly, revealing his mouthful of teeth in such a large way that the small man slowed immediately and ducked behind his larger companion. "I'll go. I'd like to go. But this old gentleman here—"

"Silence!" shouted the tall one, waving his sidearm under Feliz's nose now. "What nonsense is this? What deviationist, obstructionist tactics are you engaging in now! Come at once, and with no more excuses!"

"Excuse me," said Feliz to El Hoska. "But I'm afraid I have to go."

"Go where?" asked the mayor.

"Wherever these two characters with the guns want to take me!" cried Feliz.

"Dear, dear, dear me!" said El Hoska, sadly shaking his head.

"What do you mean, *dear me?*" exploded Feliz.

"That one so young should be so badly maladjusted. That such a healthy-appearing individual should suffer the persecution of such marked delusions. Sit down, my boy.''

Feliz tried with all his might to fight the mental pressure upon him, but his knees folded and he sank to the ground.

"What new obstructionist tactics are these?" said the tall man in black. "Get up at once."

"Shoot him, Harry."

"You shut up, Upi. Stand up, spy, or you will be shot."

"Think," said El Hoska, "of relaxing, soothing things. Beds of meadow flowers, a sunny day in spring, drowsy with the hum of useful insects—"

"Kai!" bellowed Feliz, in desperation.

"What?" quavered the girl who was standing just a few feet away.

"Can you see these boys with the guns?"

"Alas, yes," she said sadly.

"Well, they're going to shoot me if I don't go with them. I've got to get loose!" Feliz beckoned her toward him. "Can you hit this ancient demon here with something and at least distract him for a minute or two?"

Doubtfully, Kai looked at the mayor, looked around her, and then down at one of her sandals. Doubtfully, she took this off. Timidly, she tapped El Hoska on the head with its hard wooden sole, with about as much force as might break a normally-shelled egg.

"Ouch!" said El Hoska, putting his hand to his head and looking uncomfortable. "Dear me, my sinuses . . .''

Kai's face lit up. She beamed. She took a good, two-handed grip on the sandal and swung from left field. There was a painful-sounding thud, and the mayor folded up like a pole-axed grasshopper.

"That's enough. That's enough!" barked Feliz. Kai, looking happier than he had ever seen her, was just heaving up the sandal for another blow. Reluctantly, at Feliz's shout, she checked herself.

"Let's go," said Feliz to his black-clad would-be captors, and, jumping to his suddenly free feet, he hurried off.

"Stop!" said the tall one, catching up with him. "This way, spy!" He grabbed Feliz by the elbow and whisked him around the corner of a building near the square and in through its large but age-battered doorway, up an escalator that was not moving to a second floor hallway, and into a lofty and overfurnished apartment.

Within the apartment, the city controller, Taki Manoai, sat in a comfortable chair with his feet up on a beet-red hassock. The feet were encased in slippers; the rest of the controller was wrapped in a battered dressing robe, and there was a glass in his hand and an ice bag on his head.

At the sight of Feliz, his face lit up.

"Ah, you got him. Get out!" he said to the two captors. "And *don't* slam the door!"

"Yes, controller. Yes, sir," said the tall one. They went out, closing the door as gently as a pair of mothers tiptoeing off from a sleeping baby. Left alone, Taki Manoai took the ice bag off his head, poured the water—which evidently was all it contained—out into a pail at the left of his chair, and poured fresh water into it from a container at his right.

"Well, spy," he said, putting the cold water bag back on his forehead. "What have you to say for yourself? Jail-breakers are shot. Answer in non-loud tones, if you please."

"I know," said Feliz. "Uh, by the way, if I should suddenly try to get away again, I'd like you to have me restrained gently, if you have to. I may not be able to help myself."

Taki Manoai scowled.

"What farce is this?" he inquired. "If you don't want to leave, why should you? If you do I will certainly have you shot."

"Look, I tell you I may not be able to help it," said Feliz desperately. I know you people don't admit their presence, but these people in colored clothes have a mayor—"

"Stop!" shrieked Taki Manoai, and clutched at his head. "Stop," he whispered. "There is nó such thing as people in non-black clothes. There is nobody in this city but"—the door behind Feliz, by which he had entered, suddenly opened and closed on "us."

Feliz looked around. It was Kai; she came up to him, still

carrying her sandal and walking unevenly.

"Oh, there you are," she said. "I was afraid I wouldn't find you. El Hoska thinks he has a migraine headache, and he's gone to lie down and rest until it goes away. Everybody else who's real is out looking for you, but El Hoska can't help them, he says, until his head feels better—and maybe not then. He thinks maybe it was talking to you that brought on the migraine. So you're all right now."

"All right!" said Feliz. "When these people may shoot me any time in the next sixty seconds?"

Kai Miri looked curiously at the controller.

"I guess they could, couldn't they?" she said. "It's hard to believe that mere hallucinations like that could really do anybody any real harm."

Taki Manoai had been shouting at Feliz for some time now. Feliz turned to see what it was the other wanted.

". . . and stop talking to empty air. I command you!" Taki was yelling, holding his head with both hands. "As if I didn't have enough troubles! If I were a weak person, it would be very disturbing. Stop it. That is a direct order!"

"All right," said Feliz. Taki took his hands down from his head and looked at Feliz injuredly.

"You don't know what the pressures are upon a controller," he said. "All the troubles come home to me. All the responsibility. At this rate, I'll burn myself out before I'm fifty. People think it's an easy job, but it isn't. No wonder I take an occasional drink."

"You do?" said Feliz. Taki glared at him.

"Are you attemtping to joke? People do not joke with controllers."

"Oh," said Feliz.

"Not if they know what's good for them."

Kai Miri had come up behind the controller's chair. She brandished her sandal.

"Shall I clunk him?"

"Not now!" said Feliz. "Has this business of hitting people gone to your head?"

"I find I like it," she said, taking a practice swipe a few

inches above the crown of Taki's skull. "Something that gives one so much self-satisfaction surely must be good for one's personality."

"Will you stop talking to empty air?" Taki barked. "This is your last warning."

"I'm stopped," said Feliz. "Just a slip of the tongue, there."

"It better not slip again. Listen and obey. You told me you knew a number of mechanical skills and crafts we did not know. Right?"

"Correct," said Feliz.

"Then I'm going to put you to work. Only when one works for the controller is one truly fulfilling a purpose in life. Now, I—"

"Why?" said Feliz curiously.

"Why?" said Taki.

"That's right. Why does one have to work for the controller—"

"*Why?*" said Taki, and made a grab for the water bag on his head. "Everyone knows that."

"Nobody ever told me," said Feliz. "And, frankly, I'm interested. You seem to have a pretty good setup here."

"It is perfect," said Taki. "Except, of course, for the occasional rotten apple in the barrel."

"I see," said Feliz.

"Absolutely. Since universal good is the universal desire of the populace, it follows that everybody wants to work for the good of all at all times. They need only orders, and for these they look to their controller. Which brings me, incidentally, to why I want your efforts. There is a limit to the number of orders even I can give to my eager and waiting people. It follows, therefore, that you are to build for me a sort of broadcasting unit that will take over the issuing of a great many routine orders, reminding the individual of his duties from minute to minute, so that the individual can work more efficiently."

"That's what you want?" said Feliz.

"Hear and obey."

"Oh, sure," said Feliz. "Just a suggestion, though."

"No arguments!" snapped Taki Manoai. "To work, spy." He picked up a sort of cowbell beside his chair and rang it. The door opened and Feliz's two captors came back into the room. "Take the spy out and give him what he needs to build what I want."

"Of course, if you don't want something better . . ." said Feliz.

"Better?" The controller stopped the approaching captors with an upraised hand. "What is this?"

"Well, uh—" said Feliz. "I don't suppose the news may have leaked over to you people yet, but there is a little-understood power source that seems able to control the individual's body against even his own wishes. Make him come, for example, when he doesn't even want to come. And so forth."

Taki Manoai sat up straight in his chair.

"You personally know of such a power source?"

"You might put it that way, yes," said Feliz.

"Build me one!" In his enthusiasm, the controller allowed the water bag to slide off his head. The damp black hair underneath stuck out over his ears like a crow's nest. "Build me one immediately!"

"I thought you'd like the idea," said Feliz.

"Men," said Taki to the two in uniform. "Take the spy away and give him anything he desires to accomplish this great end." He got to his feet. "I will come, spy, and see it immediately you have it finished!"

"Right," said Feliz. He went off toward the door with the other two men. Kai put her sandal back on and followed.

"Wait!" shouted the controller behind him. "When you get it done, what will it look like, spy?"

"Oh," said Feliz. "Well, you might be a little bit surprised by that. As a matter of fact, it'll be in the public square; and when I get it done it may look a lot like a fountain."

"Good. Look forward to being shot if it doesn't." And Taki genially waved them out of the room.

CHAPTER VIII

"WELL, spy," said the tall man, whose name appeared to be Harry, when they were all four once more in the street. "What sort of equipment do you need to begin work? Answer immediately."

"You go," said Feliz gently, "to blazes."

Harry blinked at him.

"Be nice to me," said Feliz, "or I'll report you to the controller for not co-operating with me." He leered at the two of them. They shrank visibly. "What about it?"

"Yes, sir," said Harry.

"Yes, sir," said the small one eagerly. "Harry was the one who hit you the second time. I told him not to, but he—"

"What's your name?" said Feliz.

"Upi Havo, sir. I t-told him not to, but he—"

"Do you," said Feliz, "know what the phrase 'keep to windward' means?"

"Oh, yes, sir!"

"All right. From now on, whenever you have anything to say to me, you will at all times keep to windward of me."

"Oh." Upi Havo scuttled around to the other side of Feliz. "Like this, sir?"

"Yes. Now, I'll tell you what we're going to do, both of you. One of you—that'd better be Harry—is going to walk about ten yards ahead of me and point out the way. The other—Upi, that's you—about ten yards behind and bring up the rear. You both may hear me talking to myself from time to time, but that's just the way we technique traders are. You will pay no attention."

They dispersed, almost cheerfully. Harry got about five yards off, thought of something, and came back. Feliz had been waiting.

"Sir?" Harry said. "Where to, sir?"

"Your tool warehouse, or wherever you keep tools and equipment."

"Yes, sir."

They took positions and moved out.

"Now, you," said Feliz, reaching back to take hold of Kai Miri's costume and pull her up to walk alongside him. "It's high time you and I had a constructive chat. How long have your bunch been ignoring this bunch in black—and vice versa?"

She merely stared at him, with very large eyes.

"Now, you know what I mean," said Feliz, gently but firmly.

"Oh!" Her face suddenly lit up. "Oh, nobody's ever paid any real attention to hallucinations . . ." Her voice faltered a little and she looked away from him. "Except sometimes the little children—"

"The children?"

"Oh, well, when you're very young, of course, you see hallucinations all the time. But when you grow up, they disappear. Except in my case." She looked almost ready to melt into tears again.

"How long," asked Feliz quickly, "have the children been seeing them?"

"Why," said Kai Miri, "ever since the world began. For hundreds of thousands of years, I suppose."

"Hundreds—" Feliz did a little staring himself. "Don't you even know your own history?"

"Of course I know my own history. The world is millions of years old. If you knew any geology you'd realize that yourself. Really," said Kai Miri, "you're quite ignorant, you know. When I first met you, I thought you knew a great deal. But I find I know more about almost anything than you do.''

"Ignorant," said Feliz. He drew a calming breath. ''It is true enough," he said, "that the world we are now standing on is about three billions years old. But the human race, to which we belong, did not set foot upon its surface until something over three hundred years ago!

"Oh, don't be silly. How could we reach such a high level of civilization in a mere three hundred years?''

"Who, in the name of all that's natural," roared Feliz, losing his temper after all, "said you'd reached a high level of civilization?''

"Oh, don't be ridiculous!''

"Who's ridiculous?''

"Well, you could just look around you. This city. And actually, we've gone far beyond it and the mechanical civilization it represents. We have returned to nature on a higher plane. So there! We don't need clumsy, material things any longer.''

"Oh, no?'' said Feliz. He reached out and grabbed a handful of her tunic. ''Look at this. Cast plastic. The same material *my* clothes are made of. The same material that's gone into the uniforms of these monkeys in black.''

She went white at his last sentence. She stopped abruptly, swayed, and would actually have collapsed if he had not caught her.

"Here," said Feliz. ''What's the matter?'' He added gruffly, "Stand up!" With an effort she got herself upright, but she clung to his arm and he could feel her trembling.

"I wish you wouldn't say things like that,'' she whispered.

"Why not?''

"It—it just makes me go sick all over when I hear it, that's all. It isn't true. You know it isn't true. Their clothes aren't like ours. They aren't anything like us. They're just hallucinations.''

"You know better than that—hey!'' said Feliz, as she all but collapsed again. ''What gets into you whenever you face that fact?''

"I don't know," she whimpered.

They walked along in silence for a while. After about half a block she let go of his arm, patted her hair into position, and walked ahead with her eyebrows raised indifferently. She hummed a little, and glanced about the buildings as she went.

Meanwhile, Feliz's thoughts had gone off in another direction.

"Hey!" he shouted, turning and beckoning to Upi Havo, who approached at a run and circled Feliz like a bird dog to end up at Feliz's right.

"Windward as ordered, sir!" he said, saluting.

"Good," said Feliz. "Uh-your name is Upi Havo?"

"Yes, sir."

"Well, well," Feliz said. "That's a fine old name."

"Do you think so, sir?" said Upi thoughtfully. "I invented it myself when name-choosing time came around."

"Oh?" said Feliz. "Oh. Well, well—a good choice, I'd say. What time do they choose names around here?"

"The usual time, sir. Twelve years old."

"And before that, you're in school, I suppose. Learning things."

"Yes, indeed, sir." replied Upi, and began to sing, to the tune of *Little Brown Jug:*

> All hail to the con-troll-er,
> Whoever he may be-e-ee;
> And hail, too, to the beautiful black,
> > Only color I can see-e-ee!

"Little nonsense rhymes like that, sir," said Upi, dropping back into prose. "They don't make sense. I mean, everybody knows there's no color but black anyway; so how could you see any other: But we play games and dance to them. It improves our co-ordination."

"I'll bet you had the best co-ordination in your class," said Feliz.

"Oh, thank you, sir," said Upi, snuffling with pride.

"But I must be honest. There were one or two others ahead of me, sir."

"How about history courses?"

"Oh, yes, sir." Upi began to recite: "The first controller was named Og Lokmann, and he was kind and generous. The second controller was named Jak Lossu, and he was good, as well as kind and generous. The third controller—' "

"That wasn't exactly what I had in mind."

"You don't mean civics, do you sir?" asked Upi. " 'Citizens out after curfew will be shot. This is because sixty years ago an evil citizen by the name of Sey Sessi used to sneak out at night to get drunk on the squeezings from the mash in the controller's still; and under our thoughtful twelfth controller drunkenness was expressly forbidden except on special order from the controller himself.' "

"Not exactly," said Feliz. "I—"

"The thoughtful twelfth controller so hated drunkenness that he used to order himself to get drunk periodically just to show the citizens what a terrible thing it was."

"Yes—"

"Personally," said Upi, "I never drink. I don't believe you could force a drink down me, sir."

"I'm not going to. What was your history like before the first controller?" said Feliz, quickly.

"Oh, a terrible time, sir. Chaos." Upi shuddered.

"Chaos?"

"Yes, sir. The world was then full of aberrant people. Oh, it was a terrible time."

"Why?"

Upi looked puzzled.

"Why?" he repeated. "Well—er—it must have been terrible, sir. In fact," he said more strongly, "there can be no doubt about it. History tells us so."

"Tell me," said Feliz, drawing closer to the little man in a confidential manner. Upi drew back in some apprehension, but Feliz clamped a powerful hand on the small wrist and dragged him close. "Tell me, do you ever see things?"

Beads of sweat burst out on Upi's forehead and his knees buckled.

"No! No!" he cried, in a high-pitched and terrified voice. "I never see anything. Never! Never!"

"Come now," growled Feliz, shaking him with the exasperated arm motion of someone determinedly trying to get salt out of a clogged salt shaker. "Tell the truth. I'm not like the rest of you, you know. I know you see things. I see things myself. That's why I know."

"No!" screamed Upi. "I don't see anything. Absolutely nothing. Even when I was a child I never saw people in impossible-colored clothes. The other kids did, but I didn't. I never have glimpses of anything. I never feel anyone near me. I'm perfectly adjusted! Perfect, I tell you. Perfect!"

"All right," said Feliz disgustedly. He let go of the man, who staggered, gained his feet and scuttled away toward his rear position in the party. "Well," said Feliz, turning to Kai. "What do you think of that now?"

She was milk pale.

"I don't know," she cried suddenly. "Oh, leave me alone!"

Abruptly, she twisted away from him and ran off down one of the side streets. Feliz growled after her. But after a couple of automatic steps in pursuit, he gave up and let her go. He had been giving her a hard time, there was no doubt of that. But his own safe escape from this planetary lunatic asylum might well depend eventually on her facing the fact of her co-dwellers' reality.

Although, thought Feliz with sudden sourness, things were just wacky enough so that he might end up discovering that he was the one who was not seeing straight after all. The whole world he was on might turn out to be an hallucination of his own. A feverish nightmare brought on by the fact that he had cracked up on landing and was now pinned in the wreckage of his ship, delirious and dying . . .

"Ridiculous!" snorted Feliz, shrugging off the uncomfortable notion. He began to feel a little guilty about having

shaken Upi Havo, however. Perhaps a more gentle approach
. . .

"Sir!"

It was Harry, his point guard, now halted in front of the
door to a large building up ahead.

"Here's the equipment warehouse, sir!"

Feliz put on speed, and with Upi Havo at his heels—but
not too closely at his heels; out of arm's reach, in fact—
entered the building.

The warehouse was just that—a lofty building well filled
with military rank on rank of machines and construction
equipment. Feliz strolled down one of the corridors between
ranks, inspecting and trying to make up his mind what he
could use—that is, provided he could make some of this stuff
run. It had been well stored away at one time, but that time
must have been at least half a century previously. It occurred
to him there might be help available.

"Harry," he said, turning to the tall man, "you've got
machinists and machine operators, haven't you?"

"Sir?" said Harry.

"People who know how to run these machines?"

"Oh, no, sir."

Feliz stared at him.

"You must have somebody!"

"I'm sorry, sir. I don't know whose fault it is, sir. I don't
have anything to do with—" Harry was beginning to sweat
and shake slightly at the knees. "We've just got barely
enough people to run the food machine and the clothing unit,
sir. Nobody was ever trained on these things. Please—"

"Oh, shut up!" said Feliz.

"Yes, sir. Thank you." Harry saluted and backed away.

Feliz turned and stumped back through the battalions of
machines. No machinists. No machine operators. No skilled
workers of any kind. No wonder the city looked like something out of a horror story. And there was no use hoping that
Kai's people had done any better. If the whole world was like
this . . .

Which brought him once more to the old question of how

in the name of even elemental reason a planet and a divided people in this sort of amusement-park funhouse condition could have continued to exist in the heart of Malvar empire. Was there a master-mind somewhere, holding the aliens at bay even while he saw to it that the ordinary humans here continued to scrape along?

Unlikely, Feliz grunted to himself. Any master-mind in this situation was undoubtedly cutting out paper dollies by this time and sticking straws in his hair. Perhaps he would have to move over and let Feliz join him. What was more likely was that the whole setup was a secret weapon of the Malvar, designed to conquer humanity—and he was the first guinea pig to be tested in the device.

"How about the other cities?" said Feliz to the two who were timidly following him. "Could we borrow some machine operators?"

"Sir?" said Harry. "Oh, no, I don't think so, sir. We never have anything to do with any place else, except to send our taxes once a year to support the planetary defenses."

"Planetary defenses!" said Feliz, stopping dead.

"Oh, yes, sir," said Harry. "We always pay our planetary defense tax, to the defense controller in New Paris."

"Do you now," said Feliz. He drew close to the man, smiling ingratiatingly. "That's very interesting. Tell me all about these planetary defenses."

"All, sir? It's a highly complicated subject."

"Take your time," said Feliz. He pushed the other into a sitting position on a post-hole digger. "Take all the time you want. Who did you say handles these planetary defenses?"

"The controller of New Paris, sir," said Harry, expanding under the effects of kind treatment. "You see, that's where the field is."

"Oh? The defenses take off from a field?"

"Well, not exactly." Harry frowned. "I mean, they're always up there. You just have to have a field—I mean, fields go with planetary defenses. Of course," he added suddenly, "the men who man the defenses—they take off from the field."

"Oh?"

"Yes, sir. They get in a shuttle ground-to-space boat, and go up every two weeks to relieve the six men already on duty. The transfer is effected by space suit through the lock in the defenses; and as soon as the new men have taken over, they run a complete six-hour check drill. Since the defenses are in a free-fall orbit about the world, this enables them to make a complete scan of local space." He stopped and looked at Feliz with a touch of superiority.

"Go on," said Feliz. "And then what do they do for the rest of their tour of duty?"

"Do? Do, sir?" Harry winkled his brow.

"What do they do with their time? Now that they're up there?"

"Why, they're busy every minute," said Harry. "Shooting down goblins. Everybody knows that, sir."

Feliz blinked.

"Goblins?"

"Oh, yes, sir. Space is full of goblins. The crew shoots down between two and three thousand on every tour of duty."

"These goblins . . ." Feliz cleared his throat. "What do they look like?"

"You've never seen a goblin, sir? Oh, I have—lots of times. All of us have, haven't we, Upi?"

"Lots of times," said Upi. "I just pull the covers over my head."

"Of course there're witches up there, too, that they have to shoot down."

"And pirates. They don't run into pirates too often though, sir. Maybe once or twice in a tour of duty. And tourists. Tourists are the worst kind. And—"

"Just a minute," Feliz finally found his voice. "What do these planetary defenses look like?"

"Why, it looks sort of like a house," said Harry. "Only there's nothing underneath it, of course, because it's up in space. That's because it's in free fall. The clever first controller of New Paris invented free fall just so we could have planetary defenses.''

Feliz closed his eyes. Printed large against his lids was the remembered image of the impossible-looking space station full of howling maniacs who had damaged his ship in the first place with solid shot from an old-fashioned explosive weapon. He wondered what he had been reported as— goblin, witch, pirate, or tourist. Possibly, considering the actual underpopulated situation of space, he had rated as a tourist.

He opened his eyes again, took one look at the machines about him, and reluctantly dismissed any hope of ever putting them to use.

"You do have shovels?" he said to Harry.

"Yes, indeed, sir," said Harry proudly.

"Well then," said Feliz. "We're all set."

CHAPTER IX

"Young man," said the mayor, El Hoska, "your attitude grieves me deeply."

It was the following day. El Hoska, having taken a day and a night to recover from his migraine headache, had gone in search of Feliz the following morning and had been agreeably surprised to find him already tearing up the center of the square to make room for the fountain El Hoska had suggested be built. The mayor had observed for a while, then gone off about his duties, only to return in the afternoon for another session of observation. It was following about twenty minutes of this that he had been moved to comment about Feliz's attitude.

"Swing those shovels faster!" shouted Feliz. He climbed up out of the hole. "Keep 'em at it, Harry." He turned to the mayor. "What's that you said?" El Hoska looked at him with benign sorrow. For some reason the expression reminded Feliz of Kai Miri, whom he had not seen since she had run off the day before. Feliz frowned at the memory. It was, of course, nothing to him what she did; but it was only natural to expect her to at least put in an appearance to prove that she hadn't fallen down a well or something. That was, after all, only common courtesy to someone who had fed you, and more or less rescued you, and so forth.

He was halfway tempted to hunt around and find her, if for no other reason than to say a few pertinent words to her on the subject of common courtesy. In fact, if it were not for the fact that two separate sets of observers were keeping him pretty steadily in their sights, he would have taken a stroll around to look for her before this.

"Beg your pardon," he said now to El Hoska. "I didn't catch what you said the second time, either."

"I am," said El Hoska, repeating himself gently and without impatience, "concerned over this." He waved a hand to indicate the fountain pit where Feliz had his black-clad shovelers at work.

"Why? What about it?" Feliz braced himself suspiciously for some new and unexpected demand.

"Come, my boy. Come," said El Hoska, linking a skinny arm through a gorilla-like limb of Feliz's. "This machinery you're using."

"Machinery?" Feliz blinked at the sweating (but fully-clad) laborers.

El Hoska chuckled and dug him considerately in the ribs with a sharp thumb.

"Of course, the machinery," he chuckled. "You didn't think I was getting so dim-eyed in my old age that transparent plastic would fool me into thinking there was nothing there? It's a little hard to see it with the sun on it this way; but after all, a pool for a fountain just doesn't excavate itself, does it? No, no. But that wasn't the aspect of your using machinery that I wanted to discuss with you. It's the moral element that concerns me."

"The moral element?"

"What else?" inquired El Hoska, drawing him cozily aside. "Oh, I'll admit that the machinery does the work faster, and possibly more efficiently. But do you realize what you're missing? Do you know how thoroughly you're blunting your sensitivity, your innate self-identification with the good earth, by avoiding contact with it? How much better, now, would it be for you to get down there and labor directly with your own two hands. You could then feel the good rich soil crumble under your eager fingers; and the living hunger for action of your straining muscles finally being satisfied."

"Oh?" said Feliz. "Have you done much satisfying of action-hungry muscles yourself lately?"

"Dear me, no!" said El Hoska.

"If you'd care to try it . . ."

"But, my boy! That would be carrying coals to New Newcastle." El Hoska chuckled again gently. "I have already spent a long lifetime attuned to nature. I have long since made my identification. It is you who have yet to do so. More and more I find myself worrying about you. I fear for your ego." He shook his head. "Yes, I fear you stand in need of a great deal of reorientation." And he beamed into Feliz's face with a gently satanic expression that sent a chill down Feliz's back. It was a chill that threw his mind into high gear. He had a sudden inspiration—was it possible that sense could be talked to the mayor after all? El Hoska seemed to be just a little bit too independent and intelligent to be the dupe of the situation he appeared at first glance.

Feliz made up his mind.

"You might be right," he said. He looked down into the hold where the work crew, under Harry, was doing as good a job as could be expected. "As it happens, there's something I could use from my ship right now to make the fountain really sing. If you don't mind walking with me through the woods to my ship . . ."

"My boy, how could you doubt it for a second?" beamed El Hoska. "The forest. The trees. Good conversation. Nature. The very thing for you."

"Yes," said Feliz. "I was thinking so. Shall we go?"

"Indeed."

Feliz took a quick glance about the square. But nobody was in sight who seemed to have the sort of authority that might try to stop him.

"Let's go," he said.

There was no trouble going out of town. In fact, Feliz could hardly believe it. They reached the edge of the woods without a single black-clad individual showing up in pursuit. A few strides further and the leafy branches hid them from the city below and behind them. Feliz let out a long-held breath and turned to El Hoska. The mayor had been babbling steadily since they had left the square.

"The monotheistic attitude of the divertent ego," he was saying, at the moment, "embranchiates and impalpates the retro-consciousness—"

Feliz looked at the man narrowly out of the corners of his half-Micturian eyes, and decided on shock treatment.

"All right," said Feliz. "You can turn it off now. We're both men of the world, after all."

El Hoska did not seem to be put out. He stopped, winked at Feliz and chuckled. He jabbed Feliz in the ribs with a knife-pointed elbow.

"Very well, my boy," he said merrily. "Let us get down to plain language then. You realize you're a danger to the community?"

"I am?" said Feliz, considerably startled. He had hoped El Hoska would rise to the bait of a frank discussion—not swallow bait, line, rod, and half his arm at once. "Well, in that case," he said, recovering, "maybe I'd better just get in my ship and blast out of here—with your permission of course."

"Of course," said El Hoska. "No. Hmm. I'm afraid it isn't that easy. You come from some place; and where you came from there must be more like you. If you go back to them, a lot may start coming here. And an influx of backward people is the last thing we want."

Feliz stared.

"You don't really believe that?" he said. "About having progressed beyond mechanical civilizations?"

A thin film, like a nictating membrane, seemed to flicker down over the old man's sunny blue eyes, turning their appearance of mild insanity to cold determination. But he still spoke gently.

"Now, now," he said. "I believe you, personally, have had some experience of what the group mind can perform."

"Group mind—guttergunk!" said Feliz impolitely. "That's you, and you know it. That's why I thought maybe we could talk sense just now, like a couple of adults. You know what the situation really is here. Admit it. Tell me honestly now. Don't you ever see people dressed in black?''

The mayor stiffened, his frail body like a dry reed leaning obstinately against the wind.

''I,'' he said, spacing his words so that they dropped into the woodsy silence individually and heavily, like single stones into a very deep well, ''see nothing but what is real.''

''All right,'' said Feliz. He threw up his slab-thick hands. ''All right, all right! I give up!''

They stalked along for some short distance in silence. Feliz swatted a small insect that came to investigate the orifice of his ear. He felt the thistle down weight of the old man's hand on his shoulder. Dark glee burst in his keg-like chest. He turned and saw the blue eyes on his own, stained deeply with sincere and heart-felt sympathy.

''You will feel better,'' said El Hoska tenderly, ''after I have reasoned with you in a more practical sense . . . .''

Meanwhile, they had crossed through the green hush of the woods, and now they came out into the meadow where the ship was. The ship rested unchanged, as it had on the morning of its landing after Feliz had repaired it. The common-sense, down-to-reality appearance of it was a shock after the last couple of days. At about a dozen feet or so from the hatch, El Hoska halted.

''I would rather not contaminate my ego with the machine, any more than is necessary,'' he said. ''In fact, I should probably have waited for you at the edge of the woods, as I have done previously. However, here we are now. I will wait at this spot.''

''All right,'' said Feliz.

''I expect that you will be coming out again shortly to return to the city with me. I expect that if you find yourself with any thoughts at variance to that, that you will set any action aside and emerge at once.''

''I expect so,'' said Feliz gloomily. He climbed up the ladder and in through the open hatch.

After the bright sunlight of the meadow, the interior of the ship, illuminated only by what reflected light came through the hatch opening, seemed plunged in dimness. Then, as his pupils dilated, the control room brightened about him.

He immediately noticed differences about it. Here things had been somewhat disarranged. There they had been put back in an order different from the one Feliz generally used. Feliz's eyes narrowed. He rose from the chair and stepped across to the cabin. The bed had been slept in and made up again in strange fashion, with the pillow under the covers in the exact middle of the bed. He stepped back into the control room and yanked open the door of the food locker.

A majority of the food inside had not been touched. But he noticed a shortage in the fruit, nuts, roast beef and bread departments. He closed the locker and had a look at his log book. The sketch of him sleeping was still there as it had been. But a small devil with tail and horns had been added. The devil was tickling Feliz's unconscious feet with a large feather.

Feliz rubbed his nose.

Well, he thought, it was a relief to know that Kai was all right. He wondered where she was at the moment. She was liable, he thought, to be anywhere. At any rate, she seemed to be making out all right. Feliz was rather surprised to find what an extremely large load it took off his mind to know this. Of course, he reminded himself, he was a natural worrier. Things like this would be bound to prey on him, where they would probably never even occur to a more extroverted, adventurous sort of individual.

That thought reminded him of his real purpose in coming here. He glanced out through the hatch, just to check; but El Hoska was seated cross-legged on the grass, half turned away; and apparently guarding his ego as carefully as possible from any contaminating contact with the machine. Feliz turned swiftly back to his communications instruments and punched a series of controls.

The screen fogged, darkened, and cleared to reveal stars. For a second it was silent and then it chimed softly, four times. At the same time, four small red points of light appeared on the screen.

A white call light began blinking insistently below the screen. Feliz whistled tunelessly between his teeth and punched the receive button. The stars blinked out and were replaced by the face of a Malvar wearing a fleet officer's collar.

"We have recorded the activity of your scanning beam," said this face. "We know you are aware we are here. You cannot possibly escape past us. You would be best advised to come out and surrender in civilized fashion." It began again. "We have recorded . . ."

"Ho, ho! And a loud ha-ha!" muttered Feliz, but without activating the transmitter at his end. "Dunroamin forever, in preference." He sneered at the screen. "If you're so tough," he said, "come in and get me." The sneer was replaced by a thoughtful frown. He cut off the receiver as the Malvar on the screen was patiently beginning his message for the third time, and turned to the other lockers about the ship.

He gathered up some impressive-looking odds and ends, some firecrackers and Roman candles he had made to demonstrate a technique in pyrotechnics he had sold on Caswell's planet three months before, the parts and pieces of the mashed-up Mark III hat-destroying plastics converter, a lucky silk scarf with good fortune wishes written on it in red Mandarin Chinese characters, and made himself an enormously thick cheese sandwich. Munching on the sandwich, he rejoined El Hoska outside.

"Let's go," he said to the mayor.

They walked away in silence until they reached the edge of the woods overlooking the city. As they stepped out from beneath the shadows of the last trees, El Hoska sighed.

"When you are old," he remarked with a note of wistfulness in his voice, "and in a position of authority, it is easy to be unfair."

Feliz looked at him suspiciously.

"It occurs to me," said El Hoska, turning his head to meet

the younger man's eyes, "that I haven't been absolutely fair with you."

"No!" said Feliz. "Not really!"

"We have," said El Hoska, as they started down the slope, "in most essentials, a good life here. Not a perfect life—who would want perfection? But a life with a good core to it." He glanced over at Feliz. "Would you like to hear our history?"

"I've been hearing some of it recently," said Feliz.

"But probably not the full story. Undoubtedly not the full story," said El Hoska. "Few of us know that. It is not a completely happy story."

"Ah," said Feliz.

"In fact, most of our people do not know it. I think they are happy not knowing how we made the final break with our culture of the machine. At one time, you see, what has now become our way of life was merely a political philosophy."

"Political philosophy?" said Feliz.

"Yes. You see, I don't try to deceive you by claiming we were pure from the start. No, originally we were merely a planet-wide political party that advocated decentralization of the government and freedom of the individual. At that time, I should add, practical politicians—so called—were in the majority in our party. And true nature worshipers such as we are today, were very much in the minority."

"That changed, did it?" said Feliz.

"It did. You see, at the same time there was another planet-wide political party known as the Authoritarian Party, which believed in extreme centralization of control. The division was so sharp between the two parties that some foolish people even feared a way would be found to resolve the dispute by war."

"You said," Feliz inquired, "*foolish* people?"

"Yes," said El Hoska. "For of course war was impossible."

"Why, naturally," said Feliz warmly.

"For the founding fathers of this world had, by unique

legislation, required that genetics and psychological conditioning be put to a wonderful use. All children for a number of generations had been conditioned from earliest infancy to a violent emotional reaction against the very idea of mass violence.''

Feliz's eyebrows went up.

''The breach,'' said El Hoska, ''with the Authoritarian Party was, however, unreconcilable. Our people, regretfully, took the only way out. We sent all members of the Authoritarian Party to Coventry.''

''Oh? Where was that?'' said Feliz.

''I was using,'' explained El Hoska, ''an old-fashioned English expression. It meant that we ignored them completely. That we went our own ways exclusively, pretending that those who disagreed with us did not even exist. It was a harsh measure, evolved necessarily to deal with a harsh situation. We did not foresee the results.''

''Well, I'll be blowed!'' exploded Feliz, stopping in his tracks and turning to the mayor. ''Then you actually do realize what happened?''

''Of course,'' said Eli Hoska. ''They all died.''

''Died,'' said Feliz.

''Yes,'' said El Hoska sadly, and wandered on again. Feliz took two long strides and caught up. El Hoska was still talking: ''Died like the dinosaurs of our original homeland. Like the flowers of the field, ignored by the sun and the rain, they perished. We noticed them grow fewer and fewer; and there came a time when none of them were to be found any more, anywhere.''

''What happened to the bodies?'' demanded Feliz bluntly.

''I imagine,'' said El Hoska, ''they were buried at first by their own kind. And then those few that were left had their remains obliterated by the forces of nature. Remember, this was many years ago. I don't imagine there were many ever to be found. Most undoubtedly left the cities and wandered in search of their own kind. And finding none, traveled on until they fell by the road.''

Feliz looked at him, and opened his mouth. Then he closed it. Then he opened it again.

"Look," he said.

"Yes?" said El Hoska sweetly. They were entering the outskirts of the city now, and their footfalls came upon plastic pavement.

"You have an open mind, wouldn't you say?" said Feliz.

El Hoska smiled again.

"The most important part of our culture is an open mind," he said.

"Are you willing to admit the possibility of something that would turn your whole system of beliefs upside down?"

"Of course, my boy."

"Then brace yourself," said Feliz. "You know those old political opponents of yours? Well, they didn't die off after all. They've gone on living side by side with you all these years, conditioning *their* children not to see you people either."

El Hoska neither laughed nor looked startled. A shadow of a sadness crossed his lean and ancient face.

"So," he sighed, "you, too. Tell me," he laid a hand on Feliz's heavy sleeve. "Tell me—you've been seeing people in odd, tight-cut black clothing, haven't you?"

"And feeling them. To say nothing of—"

"Now, now, let's not embroider the tale," said the mayor, gently. "Such hallucinations are, unfortunately, common among my people. Many come to me in each generation, seeking some means to free themselves of such. Some I can help. Others, like that poor child, Kai Miri . . ." He sighed again. "I can only tell them all what I tell you now. The hallucinations are the result of a racial guilt complex for what our ancestors did to those other, unfortunate people many years ago."

"But—" began Feliz. El Hoska held up a halting palm.

"I realize that they seem perfectly real to you."

"Oh, you do?"

"Of course. I am sure that you suffer quite as much from

them as if they were actual, real people.''

"You can," said Feliz grimly, "say that again."

"Of course. I don't want you to think that I don't understand. I quite believe you suffer as much from them as if they were perfectly real.''

"Thanks.''

"But actually, I know they aren't real at all. They are really totally imaginary. Your diseased ego and mind are inventing them. Actually—you must trust me, I have studied a good deal and understand these things—you really enjoy the suffering they cause you. That's why you invent them.''

"Guk," said Feliz.

"So, when I say I understand, you mustn't take it to mean that I have any ignorant sympathy for the discomforts you are inventing for yourself. It would be the height of ridiculousness to sympathize with a person who is actually enjoying himself—and has a weak, diseased character to boot. You, even you, would scarcely credit the lengths to which such self-delusional indulgence can take a man.''

"Oh, I don't know," said Feliz.

"Let me tell you," said El Hoska. "I once had a man come to me who believed—actually believed, mind you— that he had been accidently shot by one of these imaginary characters.''

"No!''

"Yes, indeed. So strong was the deulsuion, he actually had a wound clear through him from which he was bleeding profusely. He came staggering to me for help. I did what I could, of course—it was clearly an hysteric condition—by immediate hypnotherapy; but he kept on bleeding, eventually turned chalk-white and died.''

"Clung," said Feliz, "to his delusion to the end?''

"Yes. That man," said El Hoska, moved to a note of unusual strong emotion in his voice, "was a psychological mess!''

They walked on in silence together for a few moments, each clearly immersed in his own heavy thoughts. They were nearing the square.

"So you see," said El Hoska, almost hurriedly, "why it is of extreme importance that you remain here. This report of your hallucinations confirms the matter. It is as I suspected."

"What did you suspect?" Feliz looked suspiciously at him.

El Hoska sighed.

"You would not have noticed it yourself," he said. "But in spite of marked—er—physical differences in the body, you bear a rather striking resemblance to some of our own people. In the face, now . . . I don't pretend to know just what the connection is, but I can hardly doubt that there may be strains of relationship between yourself and us."

"Damned strained relationship," muttered Feliz.

"And if this is so, we have a duty to each other. To be truthful with you—" The mayor stopped and Feliz saw to his surprise that the old man had tears in his eyes. "Somehow things have not been working out too well for us lately. I am ashamed to say it, but there are only two others beside myself I can count on to do the necessary work properly at the plastic clothes casting complex—which is the one machine on which we still depend. And only a few will gather nuts and berries for any besides themselves or their own children, in spite of the fact that all should give to all."

"Well, the whole setup—" began Feliz embarrassedly.

"Please. Let me finish," said El Hoska, laying a hand on Feliz's arm. "I don't have a great many more years, and what will become of these people when I'm gone? There is some strange lack in us. What it is, I don't know. I have contemplated our existence many years now and have never been able to pin down what troubles us. Our life here is ideal. All are free to express themselves in the best way possible. And nature's bounty is inexhaustible. We should be thriving and growing. Instead, we wither and die. We should be happy, and instead we are confused and dissatisfied. Someone must find what I have failed to find, and save my people.

"Young man," El Hoska looked into Feliz's face with a sort of sad and wistful hope, "if such a one as you could find it in you to share my present burden and take over when I am gone, it might be the salvation of all.''

Feliz snorted in loud embarrassment.

"Well, think it over," said El Hoska.

They came out into the square. Black-clad guards, carrying guns and shouting, began to converge on Feliz from all sides.

CHAPTER X

FELIZ had time to invent a hasty excuse for El Hoska, and then he was marched at gunpoint to the controller's apartment.

"Saboteur! Traitor!" shouted Taki Manoai, bouncing to his feet as Feliz entered, his eyes popping and the cords of his neck standing out. "I'll deal with you personally! Out!"

This last word was roared at the guards, who scrambled backward and escaped through the door. Feliz braced himself, for eventualities; but no sooner had the door slammed than Taki's eyes retreated into their normal positions and the cords in his neck relaxed. He sagged limply, mopped his brow with an elaborately embroidered black handkerchief—black on black—and hastily produced a bottle and two glasses.

"Whew!" he breathed, filling the glasses, and handing one reproachfully to Feliz. "What got into you to run off like that? I thought you'd deserted me. Gone for good. Just walked off. What's the trouble?"

"Trouble?" Feliz blinked at the controller.

"Just tell me. I'll fix it. You've got me over a barrel. Name your price."

"Ah—" began Feliz.

"Nobody has any initiative!" cried the other man, pounding his free fist helplessly on the table holding the bottle, which hopped and almost spilled. "They're like cattle. Obey orders—yes, fine. But I can't issue *all* the orders! In the name of all that's black, there's a limit to what human flesh and blood can accomplish in one twenty-four-hour period. Look around you . . ." He gave a bitter laugh and gulped at his glass.

Feliz looked. He saw nothing but the same overstuffed apartment he had seen before.

"Looks like a soft life, doesn't it?" said the controller, throwing himself down in a chair. "Only it just so happens that about sixty crises a day go with it. Oh, I tell you, being controller is a man-killing job. It isn't the large decisions that get me down, it's the little, nit-picking ones—what you might call inter-departmental level decisions."

"Departments?" said Feliz, surprised.

"Hah! You didn't think a community like this one could be run without organization, did you? Certainly—a department for every soul and every soul in its proper department, as the saying goes. Oh, there's nothing wrong with the setup. The organization as a whole should tick like a Swiss watch." Taki scowled at his now nearly empty glass. "But the goof-ups, the buck-passing—I tell you, it's inconceivable until you've lived with it as long as I have. Why can't a man get responsible subordinates, I ask you? Why?"

"Don't know," said Feliz.

"I mean, is that asking too much?"

"Well—"

"Of course it isn't," said Taki, pouring himself another glassful. Feliz tasted his cautiously. It was as he suspected—rotgut, a hundred and sixty proof. "Of course it isn't. But what can you do? There's no point in shooting them. A man can't spend all his time breaking in new help. Hah!" said Taki, bitterly. "They think I can shoot people any time I get the whim. They don't know the trouble it causes me. The delays, the paperwork, the shifts in work assignments. I have to think of these things; they don't. I've got the responsibility. I've got to produce."

"Um," said Feliz, as the controller looked at him.

"I was talking to a certain individual down at the annual

Controllers' Summit Meeting, at defense tax payment time, in New Paris. I said to him—you aren't drinking!''

Feliz took a cautious sip from his glass and almost dehydrated the upper half of his gullet.

"Here, let me freshen that up a bit for you. Ooops!" Taki spilled some on the black carpet. "That's all right. Plenty more where that came from. I said to him—no. He said to me, 'I don't know how I can make it another year, the way things are going.' And I said to him, 'Herman, you think you've got it tough. I'd like you to put in one day, just one day, in my office back there in Shangri-La'''

"Shangri-La?" said Feliz, startled.

'' 'Just one day, Herman,' I said. 'Believe me, you'd take the first wagon back to your place and spend the next month counting your blessings.' Which brings me,'' said Taki, pointing a somewhat unsteady finger at Feliz, "to what I wanted to talk to you about.''

"Oh?" said Feliz.

"That's right," said the controller. "Now, you argued with me the moment you saw me. Well, I admit it took a little time to sink in—but when I had time to mull it over, I realized how wonderful that was. You don't know what I'm talking about, do you?'' He leaned forward and tapped Feliz on one baggy knee. "Think what it would be like if two men could sit down and just talk right out about a problem from two different points of view. Why, they could probably see the mistakes each other was making, and come right out and tell each other about them. There wouldn't be a chance for mistakes or errors then!''

Feliz blinked.

"Speechless, eh?" said Taki, freshening up his own drink a bit in turn and hardly spilling a drop. "Thought you'd be. But that's progress, boy, that's progress! Why this sort of two-man talk-it-over may turn out to be the greatest invention since free fall. In fact, it will. I know it will.'' He drank off half his drink as if it was soda pop. The man, thought Feliz, must have sent his esophagus out to be tanned and cured in early infancy. "So I'm about to offer you a job."

"Hey!" snarled Feliz.

"Now don't start running before the shooting order's signed," went on the controller complacently. "I'm thinking of creating an entirely new position—co-controller."

"Co-controller, you said?"

"With all rights, privileges, and duties pertaining. You see, the way it works out, I've got say, ten hours of work a day to do."

"That much?"

"Oh, it doesn't actually run like that," said Taki hurriedly. "Four, five hours a day—that's more like it. And some days nothing. Just sign a few orders, give a few verbal orders and the rest of the day's all yours."

"You're sure about that?"

"Absolutely. And look how much better, even, it would be with you as co-controller. See, if there's ten hours' work, with two of us on it, it'd only take five hours apiece."

"Well, that divides out correctly, I guess," said Feliz.

"A five hour day—two and a half hours apiece."

"Imagine that!"

"And the days there was nothing . . ." The controller snapped his fingers. "Two into nothing goes twice."

Feliz snapped his fingers too.

"You know," said Taki wistfully, nursing his glass with both hands held between his knees, and staring off into a distant corner of the room, "with two of us, we could even perhaps go fishing sometimes."

"You fish?" said Feliz.

"Well not exactly." The controller coughed. "But I've read up on it and seen pictures of it. You take something to drink and some sandwiches." He looked at Feliz uncertainly.

"That's right," said Feliz.

"And you walk up into some hills until you find some trout streaming."

"Trout stream—a creek or river."

"Oh. Until you find a creek or river in which trout are streaming. Then I'd say, 'This looks like a good spot. I think I'll try a Bonnie Prince Charlie.' That's the name of a fly.''

"I know.''

"A trout fisherman has pet names for all his flies. I imagine because it's so much trouble catching them and tying them onto those little hooks. Personally, I don't have time to tie my own. I have a man who does it for me. He's better at it now than he was at first.''

"Practice tells,'' Feliz said.

"At any rate—and then you'd answer, 'Well, I guess I'll try downstream by the falls, myself'.''

"Or upstream,'' said Feliz. Taki Manoai frowned.

"Downstream, isn't it?'' Taki said. "All the books I have specify downstream.''

"Sometimes the falls aren't downstream. They're upstream instead.''

"That's so, I suppose.''

"Sometimes there aren't even any falls.''

"No,'' said Taki decisively. "No, I won't go for that. There must be falls. If there's trout, there's falls. I mean, that's it!''

"All right,'' said Feliz. The controllers' home-mash hundred and sixty proof was beginning to get to him after all. He felt rather lightheaded and relaxed, and he made no objection as he saw Taki, filling up both glasses again, as he had several times previously. It was amazing how much better the stuff tasted as they got toward the bottom of the bottle. It was older down there, no doubt.

"All right,'' repeated Feliz. "I'll give you the falls.''

"That's better,'' said Taki, sitting back with his full glass. "I ought to insist on falls top and bottom, above and below me; but I'm not that kind of a guy.''

"Okay. Okay, it's settled,'' said Feliz. "Falls below.''

"Right. And you go off, and I start fishing—whipping the water with my line. There's a swirl in the water near it—but a trout gets there first. Suddenly a big brown strikes. My rod bends double . . . And so forth,'' said Taki. ''Li'l snapper?''

''Don't mind,'' said Feliz, ''if I do. Then what?'' He had become fascinated with the controller's fishing expedition. It was like a house of mirrors in which no one knew what kind of reflection was about to turn up around the next corner.

''Well,'' said Taki, putting the bottle back. ''After several hours you come back, and I say, 'What kind of luck did you have down by the dam?'.''

''Falls.''

''Excuse me. Falls . . . down by the falls?' You shake your head sadly. 'And you?' you ask me. I say nothing.''

''Nothing?'' repeated Feliz blinking.

''Of course not. I merely take the creel off my fishing rod, open it, and display six beautiful fish. All lunkers.''

''Lunkers?''

''Yes. Big browns are for sport fishing. But you only keep lunkers, to be fried for breakfast back at the inn.'' Taki frowned. ''Of course, swirls are only a sort of rough fish. Nobody takes those.''

''Sounds like fun,'' said Feliz a little fuzzily.

''Yes,'' replied Taki dreamily. ''I can taste those fried lunkers now.'' He reached for the bottle, found it empty; and before Feliz's astonished eyes performed the superhuman feat of becoming suddenly completely sober in appearance and actions. The controller sat up sharply. ''What is your answer?'' he snapped.

''Answer?'' Feliz sat up himself. ''Oh,'' he said. ''Answer.''

''Don't be hasty,'' said Taki. ''You might bear in mind I can't afford to have you running around loose. I don't want to influence your decision, of course, but I would almost certainly have to shoot you if you turned down my offer. Those not with me are against me. Naturally.''

''Oh, I can see that all right,'' said Feliz, valiantly struggling to roll back the fogs of alcohol that were threatening to obscure his thinking. If Taki could do it, he thought, why couldn't he? Of course, Taki seemed more used to the white lightning they had both been drinking. "Gimme little time."

"Very well," said Taki. "You might bear in mind that it's sort of a duty, too." He scowled ferociously. "I don't want you to get the wrong idea about me. But somebody has to take care of these pea-brained idiots. They need both of us."

"Think it over."

"You do that," said Taki. "Let's say you've got until that order-giving apparatus you're building is finished. By the way, when will it be finished?"

"We'll be flooding the pool with water tonight," said Feliz. "I should be able to turn it on early tomorrow."

"Excellent," said Taki. "I'll hold a full scale assembly in the square tomorrow at noon, then, for the ceremony of turning it on. That reminds me, I've been wanting to ask you," he added, standing up, "what you need all that water for?"

Feliz stood also. "Damping field. Protection," he heard himself explaining. "It's the pomrantz. Very dangerous."

"Oh? The pomrantz?" said Taki. "Well, yes. Of course. I had no idea you had something like a—one of those in it. You're sure there's an adequate safety control?"

"Certainly. Calculated carefully."

"Perhaps I'd better check your calculations."

"Very well. If you prefer. Rather hard to follow though—all in calculus of nonexistent integers."

"That should not bother me. The calclass of nonexistent tiggers was always one of my strong points."

"Very well. Have them for you right after ceremony."

"Very good. I will check them over carefully."

"Good-bye," said Feliz. heading for the door and only blundering into one small table on the way. "Back to the old rockpile."

"Carry on. You might tell them to send up another bottle on your way out. I feel a cold coming on. My head's rather stuffy."

"Right," said Feliz. He made it out the door, closed the door behind him, and almost fell over someone outside.

"Oh, Upi," said Feliz, picking the little man up and dusting him off carefully. " 'Nother bottle of prune juice for milord."

"Sir?" said Upi, staring after him. But Feliz was already tacking off down the hallway, putting one foot carefully in front of the other.

CHAPTER XI

ONE GOOD—or bad, depending on your point of view—thing about an overactive metabolism is that, if it ensures you get drunk extremely quickly, it permits you to sober up with almost equal quickness. Feliz had thrown off the effects of the controller's liquor by mid-afternoon, although he had an uncomfortable hangover until about sunset.

That night he stayed in a one-room apartment in the same building that housed Taki. The door to Feliz's apartment, however, was locked. And a guard stood on duty outside it. Nevertheless, a few hours after he had lain down, there was a clicking sound and the door swung inward. By the dim illumination of the moonlight streaming through the room's single uncurtained window, Feliz caught a glimpse of a small body which slipped through the opening of the door. The door closed and clicked again. Feliz sat up and the bed creaked alarmingly beneath him.

"It's just me," said a small, apologetic voice in the darkness.

"Kai!" said Feliz. He fumbled around for the flint and steel they had left him to light the candle by his bedside.

"Yes," said Kai, from the darkness. "Don't put on a light. I look awful. I've been crawling in all sorts of dirty, dusty places, and I haven't had a chance to get clean clothes since I first met you."

She had been feeling her way toward him in the darkness

as she talked and now her outstretched fingers suddenly came
into contact with Feliz's bare arm. She gave a sudden,
stiffled shriek and started to jerk away, but Feliz caught her
wrist.

"Let me go!" she pleaded in a terrified whisper. "You
haven't got any clothes on!"

"Certainly. Got a T-shirt!" muttered Feliz annoyedly.
"Feel." He shoved her captive hand against the cloth covering his chest and felt her go limp.

"Oh!" she said, sitting down on the bed. "I was so *scared*
there for a minute."

"Where've you been?" said Feliz. "Had enough to eat?"

"I've been back in the stacks."

"Stacks?" He waited for her to explain. She did not. He
tried again. "Steaks?"

"Stacks," she said. "At the library. You know, where the
library keeps its books and microfilms and everything. The
machinery's supposed to deliver the films of books you want,
but it doesn't work of course. I had to crawl back in the stacks
with candles and find the spools right in their racks."

"What were you—"

"Oh, Feliz!" she broke in, without letting him finish.
"You were right. They aren't hallucinations. They're just as
real as we are." Her voice shook. "They're even some of
them d-distant relatives!"

Feliz attempted to pat her unseen back consolingly, and
did fairly well. She responded by creeping into his arms like a
lost puppy.

"Hold me," she said. Feliz held her. It was a not unpleas-
ant occupation.

After a while she stopped shivering and began to talk
again.

"After I left you," she sniffed into Feliz's T-shirt front,
"I just ran and hid for a long time. I wanted to get away from
everything. From my people, from the hallucinations, but
mostly from you. I didn't care if I lived or died. I just wanted
to find a hole to crawl into, and crawl into it, and never come
out again."

"Ah well . . ." said Feliz, clearing his throat gruffly in the darkness.

"Oh, that's all right," she said, snuggling closer in his arms. "I realize now you were just trying to make me see things for my own good." She rubbed her nose in a friendly way against his chest, and Feliz found himself making a deep-chested bearlike sound in response. Her nose almost tickled. *She is,* thought Feliz, *a feather-brained young nut, but you can't help feeling protective toward her. Even me. Here I hardly know her, and I already feel like her father. Like her uncle, I mean.*

"Well, I found a hole finally," Kai said. "A building we don't use, and *they* don't either. And I lay there almost a day feeling sorry for myself. But finally I kind of reached a limit on that. Besides, I began to get awfully hungry. So I got up and went out again."

A *young uncle,* Feliz was thinking, as he beamed into the darkness above her head.

"Well, the only place where I was sure I could get food easily was your ship. So I went there."

A *cousin?* Feliz was thinking.

"And, my, that cupboard you keep food in is marvelous. You know, it never seems to get empty!"

"Yes," said Feliz, "automatic processing." *No, just an old friend of the family. A young old friend of the family; that's what Kai makes me feel like.*

"Uh," said Kai. "I'm sorry about drawing some more in that book of yours. I wasn't really understanding things yet, and—"

"Yes, yes," said Feliz, beaming into the darkness, "it was beautiful."

"Beautiful?"

He felt her head come up, and returned quickly to his senses.

"The art of it, I mean. Uh—such line. Such control."

"Oh!" Pleasure thrilled in Kai's voice. "Does my art really reach through to you?"

"It's magnificent!"

"Oh!" said Kai. "Oh! Do you really think so? What first struck you about it? How did you feel when you first saw it? Were you really impressed, right from the start?"

"Yes," said Feliz.

"You said it was magnificent. Did you mean *magnificent?* Or just magnificent? I mean, did you really mean *magnificent?*"

"I said it, didn't I?"

"Oh!" said Kai. And hugged him. Feliz hugged her back, cautiously. Suddenly, he woke up to what he was doing. *Whoops,* he thought.

"Now is not the time," he said aloud.

"Now? What?" He could feel Kai staring at him suddenly through the darkness. "Not the time for what?"

"Never mind. I'll tell you later," he said. "Go on with your story."

"But I thought we were talking about my art."

"There will be time for such a—" *What am I talking about?* wondered Feliz. He cleared his throat. "We will talk about your art. Later," he said. "Right now, the situation is urgent." *I'm not making much sense,* he thought. *Oh, well.* "Go on," he said.

"Well," said Kai reluctantly. She took a deep breath. "Well," she said, "after I'd eaten, I began to think over what you said. And I decided to get it straightened out, one way or another. So I went to the library."

"Good for you."

"Well, I did think myself that it was high time somebody did. But, Feliz! It was awful. There's all sorts of spiders and things crawling around in there, and it's dark. Nobody's been there for a hundred years! And the dust is so thick that you can't see where you're going, and you can't breathe. And I got l-lost—" She was shaking again.

Feliz held her cautiously.

"But," he prompted, "after you found out what you went after . . ."

"Yes. After all, I found it," she said. "And it's all true. First we started out not having anything to do with them. And then we began the acting and dressing differently. And then we started pretending they really weren't there at all. And all the time they were doing the same things. Feliz! You've got to let me stay with you always, from now on."

Feliz shivered slightly.

"Well, we'll see," he said.

"I don't have any people but you any more." She clung to him. "Can't we go away from here and live by ourselves, somewhere where they'll never find us? They wouldn't follow us back into the hills; I know they wouldn't."

"Well," said Feliz. "Going into the hills isn't always the solution. I mean, there's things about me you don't know."

"I don't care!" she said.

"Well, that's nice. But I'm still a prisoner here, and there's various things to think of," said Feliz. "What I really need right at the moment is to know everything you can tell me, both about your people and these others."

"Just ask me!" said Kai.

"Well—uh," said Feliz. "What would happen if you saw somebody with his clothes off? I mean—" he broke off. Kai had just given a soft little shriek.

"Oh, how terrible!" she said.

"Terrible?"

"Any decent person," said Kai primly, "wears clothes *all* the time."

"Night and day? Alone as well as in company?"

"I should think so! Why, even if you were alone, you could never be sure who might be look—*oh!*" She broke off suddenly. There was a little silence. "I see what you mean," she said.

"One of the other group might be present or watching; and even though you couldn't admit to yourself that they were there, you couldn't be sure that their conditioning was as strong as yours," said Feliz. "They might be letting themselves see you."

"Yes," said Kai unhappily.

"Also," said Feliz thoughtfully, "it might be a matter of violating the basic taboo, since someone without clothes on could not be identified as a member of a particular party."

"Taboo?" said Kai. "What's a taboo?"

"Tell you later. When did you really first start admitting to yourself that you saw these other people?"

He heard the sharp hiss of her breath, indrawn in the darkness.

"I always did!" she burst out suddenly. "I *always* knew they were there. I just pretended I didn't."

"And I'll bet," said Feliz grimly, "everybody else, or nearly everybody else, was in the same boat. A few might have been so good at autohypnosis—El Hoska, for example—that they actually couldn't see the others. But I'll bet most are just like you were."

"Yes," said Kai. "But what good does knowing that do? They won't admit it!"

"No," said Feliz. "But that's not important."

"What is important?"

"If I told you, you wouldn't believe it," said Feliz. "Both your groups here, like all social ideas carried to extremes, are starting to break down of their own weight. El Hoska has become a strong central authority out of sheer necessity, and Taki—"

"Who?"

"Taki Manoai, head of the black-dressed people. He's reached the stage of wanting to give half of his authority away."

"He has?"

"And still the Malvar don't dare land."

"The who?"

"There are many things," said Feliz, "I'm going to have to explain to you. But now now. Right now, I want you to go back to the ship and wait for me there. I'll sneak away right after the ceremony tomorrow, when that deal in the square gets dedicated. You go back to the ship and wait for me. And stay inside it."

"All right, but—"

"No buts. Stay inside."

"Oh, I will. But—" Kai yawned suddenly. "I've been

going steadily since yesterday, and I'm so tired. Can't I just close my eyes here for five minutes?''

"Well . . ." said Feliz.

"Please."

"Well," growled Feliz, "all right." He started to move out from under her so she could lie down; but Kai merely sighed comfortably and curled up a little tighter in his arms.

"Jus five minutes . . ." she murmured, and began to breathe slowly and steadily.

"Five minutes," said Feliz helplessly. He looked around the dark room, and out the dim window. In the moonlight, he could see the edge of the rooftop of the room adjoining. As he watched, the dark silhouette of a rabbit hopped into view and paused there, outlined against the night sky like a black paper kindergarten cut-out of itself. It barked.

"That reminds me," said Feliz suddenly. "Something I particularly wanted to ask you, Kai . . . Kai?"

He looked down. Kai breathed on, unconscious. For a second he debated waking her, then gave up the idea. He sighed, and looked back out the window.

The rabbit barked softly at the moon.

CHAPTER XII

FELIZ squinted at the sun of Dunroamin, a yellow, Sol-type star, which was about at its zenith above the square of Shangri-La; and above Feliz himself, where he stood on a small circle of foundation material. About him was the pool of the fountain order-broadcaster. Beside him were the visible elements of the infernal machine itself. These consisted of a long pipe, an antenna fastened to the pipe, and a Chinese silk scarf fastened to the antenna and whipping merrily in the breeze. The innards of the Mark III were wired about the base of the pipe, with their more glittery and impressive-looking parts toward the outside. Arranged around the Mark III parts were the firecrackers and Roman candles.

Out of sight, underneath the Mark III parts, Feliz had constructed a small serviceable water pump, powered from the energy pack of the Mark III.

From his small island—some ten feet or so removed from the terra firma of the square's plastic pavement—Feliz observed the proceedings. To his right, Taki Manoai was speechifying to orderly ranks of black-clad men, women and children. To his left, El Hoska was gently lecturing to a loose gathering of colorfully dressed ditto. It was perfectly remarkable to see the way the two crowds managed to ignore each other's presence. Occasionally a toddler of one faction or another made the mistake of paying attention to a toddler of equal age from the other group. But since their parents, at that moment, invariably found some transparent excuse to spank their offspring, such acquaintanceships were usually not of long duration.

Just at that moment, Taki wound up his peroration to his people, and these burst immediately into a stirring song of praise for their controller. Wiping his brow and ignoring the music, Taki turned and spoke across the three foot depth of water to Feliz.

"Well?" he inquired. "What did you think of the speech?"

"Instructive," said Feliz.

"Thank you," beamed Taki. "I flatter myself I have a knack for getting through to people from the platform. Made up your mind about that offer of mine, yet?"

"Well, yes as a matter of fact, I have," replied Feliz, showing all his large teeth in what he fondly imagined to be an engaging and disarming grin. "I've decided you stick by me and, by golly, I'll stick by you."

"What was that?" said the voice of El Hoska from across the pool. The mayor also, it appeared, had finished his address to the populace. "Did you say something to me?"

"Yes, sir," said Feliz, turning in that direction. "I've decided as long as we work side by side, you can count on me!"

"Marvelous. A wise decision," glowed El Hoska. "Is the fountain ready?"

"That broadcaster ready to go?" demanded Taki Manoai.

"It is," replied Feliz to them both and the square at large. "Here we go."

He reached down and set off the Roman candles and the firecrackers.

"Oooooh!" said the two crowds. "Aaaaah!"

He turned on the fountain. Water spurted forty feet into the air and drenched everyone with a ten yard circle. Cries of admiration arose. Taki Manoai and El Hoska glowed.

Feliz, thoroughly soaked by this time, reached down and turned on the rebuilt Mark III.

The Mark III, as the one in Feliz's possession had proved
not long since, could do a good job of vaporizing a hat.
However, there was also no reasonable reason why it could
not do a good job as well of vaporizing a lot more than that. It
was just a matter of how wide you wanted to set its beam, and
how heavy a drain you wanted to put on its power pack. Feliz
had thoughtfully set its beam on full circle aperture at ground
level, and triggered the power pack to spend all its energy in
one brief, glorious burst of annihilation.

The beam of a Mark III is not stopped by ordinary sub-
stances such as make up buildings, walls, and the stone and
earth of an everyday countryside. It followed, therefore, that
one micro-second after Feliz bent down to turn on the switch,
no scrap of cast plastic existed within the city limits of
Shangri-La, or outside them for about ten miles in every
direction. And between ten and thirty miles, any cast plastic
would be pretty badly melted out of shape.

The one exception was Feliz's spaceship. Kai would be
safe inside since Feliz's ship, like most enclosures back on
the civilized worlds, was Mark III beam-proof. Any other
arrangements would have resulted in a lot of lawsuits between neighbors.

But that was back on the civilized worlds. Where Feliz was
at the moment, in the square of Shangri-La, one second there
were two hordes of differently dressed people standing staring at Feliz. Two seconds after that there were only two
hordes of people standing like statues and staring at each
other.

And one second after that there was one horde of people.
One mass of wild, frantic, terrified people, all with only one
thought in mind—to get away from everybody within sight of
them and hole up somewhere until they could become de-
cently clothed and identified again.

People who have grown up in a more usual society,
thought Feliz, as he hastily stripped the silk scarf from the
antenna and wrapped its good fortune wishes around himself
hastily in loincloth fashion, would have found it hard to
believe it was possible to panic so on simply being deprived

of their clothes at a public gathering. Or would they? Feliz paused, struck by the idea. Possibly he should try it out sometime. Or possibly he should not. No, on second thought, it was a matter for speculation rather than for practical experimentation.

Here, of course, the nakedness taboo was much more deeply implanted than in a usual society. For generations now, they had been distinguishing between strangers on the basis of their clothing—to the point where the wrong sort of clothing rendered the stranger invisible and impalpable. Now, with no means left to distinguish, their conditioning broke down. The average horrified onlooker in the square was suddenly faced, not only with himself and his undressed neighbors, but with the sudden appearance of a multitude of naked strangers. It was too much. Everybody ran.

Almost everbody. Feliz was just putting a last knot for safety's sake into his loincloth, when there was a distant cracking noise and something whizzed past his ear. Looking around, he saw a rifle barrel protruding from an upstairs window of the closest building to the square. Some black-clad (originally) guard, no doubt, posted in a lookout's position by Taki Manoai to keep an eye on Feliz just in case.

Feliz stayed not upon the order of his going. But went.

Down in the square was a seething, howling riot of humanity, tangled in itself in its attempt to escape. The children and the mothers, luckily, had been back on the outskirts; and these were already streaming away in every direction across the square. But the men of both factions were a tangled mob, and into that mob Feliz plunged.

Fortunately it was the sort of thing he was built for. His enormously muscled legs drove his bulldozer-like body through the melee like a fullback. That is not to say that, powerful as he was, Feliz was not tossed from side to side of his line of escape, like some swimmer in heavy waters. But three hundred pounds of flesh and bone have certain advantages over other flesh-and-bone conglomerations averaging about half that weight. In a matter of seconds, scratched and bleeding from a number of small surface wounds, but with even the Chinese scarf intact, Feliz broke free into the less dense edges of the crowd and headed for the hill.

The streets were filled with other escapees, fleeing for sanity's sake toward the safe darkness of their homes, and the full closets they fondly expected to find there. These others, Feliz joined—and passed.

A half-breed Micturian can run very swiftly for a short distance. Feliz passed the people of the city at about thirty miles an hour; but by the time he reached the outskirts of the city he was huffing badly, and his heaving lungs forced him to slow to a jog trot. This pace, however, though he snorted like a rhinoceros, he grimly kept up, all the way up the slope to the stone wall's corner and the beginning of the woods.

At this point he did collapse, toppling to earth like an undercut monument, and lying almost helpless for several minutes while his breathing processes struggled to return a sufficiency of oxygen to his starving body and remove the fatigue poisons from his oversized muscles.

After a short interval he felt better. Then he felt much better. He sat up and looked back down the slope the way he had come. And saw a small group of seminaked individuals wrapped in odds and ends of black draperies, rugging and such, waving their fists at him and approaching rapidly.

They were also hauling and tugging along up the slope what looked like a medium-sized, old-fashioned, solid-shot cannon. Such a weapon as the space station had used to cripple his ship originally.

One of the figures lifted a rifle, which cracked. Something whistled by at no great distance.

With something between a growl and a groan, Feliz scrambled to his feet and went lumbering off into the woods. He had marked the direction in his memory as well as he was able from yesterday when El Hoska had walked him to the ship. Now Feliz followed what he was almost positive was the proper route. But his heart stayed inconveniently close to his throat until, finally, the trees thinned ahead of him and he saw through their partial screen the welcoming gray bulk of his spaceship, with the hatch open and waiting.

Feliz crawled up the ladder, staggered through the hatch and fell into the chair before the control board. Panting, he located the controls to close up the ship, and punched them. There was a welcome sound of metal closing against metal, behind him. He gulped air, thought of the cannon coming up behind him, and reached for the take-off controls. And suddenly his heart congealed as if his chest cavity had suddenly become filled with liquid air.

The ship, he now noted, seemed completely empty of human life.

"Kai!" he shouted, jerking to his feet. His voice thundered in the narrow confines of the control room. He turned and took one long stride toward the cabin entrance; and the door, which had been standing ajar there, slammed suddenly in his face.

"Don't you dare come in here!" cried the voice of Kai.

"Good!" bellowed Feliz. "Strap yourself into the bunk there. Lie down and buckle the straps around you." He dived back into the control chair.

"Why?" came the voice from the cabin.

"Never mind why!" roared Feliz, his hands doing complicated things with the controls. "Just do it!"

There was silence from the cabin. He could only hope she was following orders. His ship did not take off like one of the great luxury liners. Rather, like a cat with a stepped-on tail.

As he worked, he turned on the screen. In it he saw that his pursuers had just broken out of the woods into the open. Taki Manoai, wearing a black bedspread, or something that looked like a black bedspread, was directing them. They proceeded to set up their cannon and get it aimed at his ship.

Feliz sweated. He had warmed his atmosphere engines. He was now mixing fuel with a painfully steady hand on the liquid oxygen control button.

Outside, they loaded their gun.

"Now!" said Feliz to himself.

He took off. Too late, he remembered he had forgotten to strap himself in. He banged the back of his head so hard on the seat cushion, his nose began to bleed.

However, a tense half-hour afterward, they were out of atmosphere and lined out into space. Feliz leaned back, wiped dried blood from his upper lip and felt the back of his head. Then he turned once more to the cabin.

"Did you get yourself strapped in all right?"

"Yes," came the somewhat quavery answer. "What happened?"

"We took off. Strap yourself in again!" roared Feliz, diving for the controls as the interception counter began to chime as if it was trying out for a part in a grade-school rhythm band; and the now star-filled screen began to come alive with red dots representing the Malvar ships.

"Aw, come on, fellas," groaned Feliz, staring in disbelief at their number. "We aren't worth all that!"

And then he stopped groaning. There comes a time sooner or later, even to the most cheerful individual, when the hour becomes a little too late for humor. It was that hour now. Shielding the movement with his big body, just in case Kai should be watching from the cabin, Feliz pushed on a panel of the control board that was level with his belly. It slid aside in a manner never conceived by its original manufacturer, and Feliz slid his hand into the space behind it. The hand came out holding a small but powerful pellet hand gun. Feliz closed the panel with one finger, shoved off the safety on the handgun and tucked it under the top edge of his Chinese scarf loincloth. The hard part would be Kai; but if he was quick about it, she would never know what hit her. No, Malvar, thought Feliz grimly, would take her alive—if it came to that. For himself, he would rather like to get his hands on one or two of them before signing off.

If it came to that.

But, Feliz reminded himself, it had yet to come to that. In fact, there was something very important to be tried first. He looked down and the call signal was blinking under the screen. He turned the screen on, and a Malvar—they all looked alike to Feliz—wearing an officer's collar was speaking.

" . . . surrounded. You cannot escape. If you surrender,

you will be accorded all the good treatment normally accorded prisoners of different jurisdiction. If you do not surrender, we will be forced to take stern measures to halt you. I
repeat, you are surrounded and you cannot—''

Feliz switched off.

"Kai!" he called.

"What?" she said from behind the closed cabin door.

"Come out here."

"I won't. You haven't any clothes on."

"I have. I've got a fine big scarf," said Feliz impatiently.
He waited. Nothing happened. *"Kai!"*

"What?"

"I'm not joking. This is serious. Come out here."

"You *have* got a scarf on?"

"Yes."

"All right." The door opened and before Feliz's astonished eyes, his only spare outfit, from boots to tunic,
clumped into view, with Kai's face peering rebelliously at
him over the collar. Feliz stared.

"You were outside!" he yelled.

"Well, how was I to know?" she said. "I certainly never
thought—"

"I told you to stay inside!"

"Well, of course you told me. But how was I to know—"

"Never mind," said Feliz. "Never mind." He took a
deep breath and forced his voice to a calm level. "Kai," he
said, "I think it's time I began to fill you in on things. Do you
know where we are?" He amended that quickly. "Where
this ship is?"

"Certainly," Kai said. "In the woods north of town."

"No," he said. "We aren't. I can see I'm going to have to
educate you, Kai. We're actually not on the world you know
at all. We're thousands of miles above it and getting farther
away all the time. We're out in space."

"Oh!" said Kai. "That explains all that strapping-in and
what happened after I did. I know all about space."

"You do?" said Feliz with a sinking sensation inside him.
He glanced at the red dots, which were closing in toward the

center of the screen. They made a pretty pattern.

"Oh, yes. Our world is really one of millions of planets circling stars like our sun. Everybody knows that. Between these worlds and stars, there's no air."

"Oh," said Feliz. "Well, did you know that out among these stars there are other people?"

"Feliz!" said Kai. "Don't be silly. How could people be out where there isn't any air?"

"What if I showed you a picture of one?" he said. "Would you believe me then?"

"Certainly not," said Kai. "A picture doesn't prove anything."

"A picture that moved and talked?"

"People in book-films move and talk. Certainly not!"

Feliz crossed his fingers. He reached down and turned on the screen. The Malvar appeared on it, still repeating his demand for surrender.

"So," said Feliz sadly, "you don't believe that there exists—" He broke off suddenly. Kai was certainly not behaving as if the Malvar on the screen did not exist. She was staring at him as if her eyes would pop out of her head and her face was a study in horror. "Kai!" cried Feliz. "You mean you *see* him!"

"See it!" quavered Kai, still staring. "How could I help seeing it? I always thought they were j-just superstition."

Feliz felt himself turning cold inside. *It is not pleasant to gamble and lose*, he thought, *particularly with someone you—someone else*. He had been counting on the fact that the Malvar would be as ignorable as the people in black had been to Kai—and that somehow this ignorability would protect the ship during their escape even as it had protected Dunroamin all these years from the Malvar. He had, it seemed, guessed wrong.

"All right, honey," he said gently. His hand slipped quietly to the gun in his loincloth. The red dots were getting very close. "Never mind. I didn't know you knew about the Malvar."

"The—the what?" she looked over at him, then back at the screen. "That's not a—whatever you called it."

"It isn't?" Feliz stared at her.

"Of course not!" said Kai. "Don't you know anything? That's a goblin!"

"A goblin?" said Feliz unbelievingly.

"Of course."

"But you just said he was real!"

"I did not say it was real. I said, now that I can see it, it isn't just a superstition after all. Evidently there are such things as goblins. But goblins aren't *real*."

She stopped talking and glared at Feliz. Feliz looked back, and then became suddenly aware that there was silence in the cabin. He turned to the screen. The Malvar officer was still to be seen on it but he was no longer calling on them to surrender. Instead he was silent, staring straight ahead as if he could see right into the control room. Incredulously, Feliz glanced down at his transmitter button under the screen. But it was still in off position.

"Not real?" said Feliz.

"Of course not," said Kai. "They're just like things in nightmares. They don't have any real existence. They go out like a candle if you just pretend they aren't there any more. Want me to show you with this one?" Without waiting for an answer, she pointed a finger at the Malvar on the screen and chanted:

> *You're nothing but a nothing,*
> *You're hollow all clear through,*
> *To blow you out I point my finger,*
> *Bang! And out go you!"*

The image on the screen winked out as the Malvar abruptly stopped transmitting—actually, before Kai had finished her chant. But this minor discrepancy did not seem to bother her.

"See?" she said, turning to Feliz.

Feliz sat down heavily. He felt suddenly and inexplicably

weak. On the screen, he saw the red dots beginning to withdraw from the center. Their circle widened.

"I see," he said.

"I should think so." said Kai. "After all, I know a few things, you know. Oh, dear!" She frowned at him.

"What?" said Feliz groggily.

"I've got to get you some decent clothes. I know!" she said. "I'll make some out of bedsheets." She went back into the cabin, and he heard her break into humming, followed a second or so later by the sound of ripping cloth.

Why don't you make yourself clothes out of the sheets, and give me back my own clothes, he thought of saying. But it was too much effort after what he had been through to say it out loud; and besides, she would probably have a dozen good reasons against it.

He looked back at the withdrawing red dots on the screen and, to his new numb astonishment, saw the face of Psi-Man Verde framed in their midst.

"You?" said Feliz.

"Oh," said Psi-Man Verde, speaking through a receiver that Feliz had time to note was not turned on, "I'm not really here."

"Oh," said Feliz. "Well, of course. Naturally. That explains it.

The psi-man smiled. It lit up his lean face.

"I've been sort of riding piggy-back on your mind," he said. "Actually, I'm speaking in your mind right now. It's just that your imagination insists on finding a logical apparatus to supply my voice."

Feliz sat up suddenly.

"You've been in my head all this time?" he cried.

"Don't worry," said Verde. "Your private life and thoughts are under the strict seal of my professional confidence. We're like doctors and lawyers that way."

"It's not your telling people I mind!" muttered Feliz, suddenly remembering to keep his voice down for Kai's sake. "It's your knowing at all."

"I'm sorry. We couldn't miss the opportunity to send a mental link in with you."

"I'll sue!" growled Feliz. "There must be a law against it." He growled to himself for a second. "After I risked my neck, solving your problem for you too."

"Don't doubt we're grateful," said Psi-Man Verde, floating among the stars. "You and Kai are entitled to, and you'll get, just about anything it's possible to give you."

"Well," rumbled Feliz, slightly mollified. A technique trader, he reminded himself, is nothing if not a businessman. With a promise like that—he stopped thinking about it abruptly, remembering the psi-man would be listening in. Kai, after all, and her future, were the important things. "Something had to be holding back the Malvar. Do you know, though—" He stopped, remembering something. "There was a time when I even thought it might have more to do with the rabbits."

Verde laughed quietly.

"That occurred to me too," he said. "But I had a look at the mind of one of the rabbits and settled the matter. They're perfectly ordinary Terran-stock rabbits variformed to fit Dunroamin conditions."

"Yeah," said Feliz. Curiosity overcame him. "Tell me," he said, "I figured out that it was the disbelief the people on Dunroamin were broadcasting that was hard for those Malvar telepath receivers to take. But how come?"

Verde's face grew a little sad, where it floated on the screen.

"I don't know if you can understand," he answered. "To those of us who have talents, the universe is a larger place. A more complex place. We are moved by more than physical things. I myself am the spearpoint of human effort against the Malvar; but there are some things which I understand and the Malvar understand that plain humans like yourself don't."

"For example?" said Feliz.

"Things without substance to you have solidness for us—not a physical solidness, but solidness all the same.

Happiness radiated our way is as warm as sunshine. Hate, to us, can be as hard and heavy as a steel bar.''

"Yeah," said Feliz.

"So you see," said Psi-Man Verde. "You see the weapon that Dunroamin's people found for us against the Malvar.''

Feliz nodded. But his curiosity was still itching him.

"Tell me," he said. "To the people—to the Malvar— what does it feel like? I mean when somebody refuses to give you any points at all for existing?"

"It's something," said Verde, "like hate—only empty. Empty.''

"That bad, huh?" said Feliz.

"It's impossible to put in physical terms," said the psi-man. "But you might get an idea if I said it would be close to the sensation of having your guts scooped out by a garden trowel.''

Feliz felt the stomach muscles under his loincloth tighten.

"I see," he said, after a second.

"No," said Psi-Man Verde, "I don't think you do. But maybe that's just as well. The point is, the people of Dunroamin have survived all these years simply by effectively telling the Malvar—oh, not in so many words, but with a powerful emotion—that they *don't exist*. The Malvar may not understand, but they feel extremely uncomfortable in the vicinity of these people.''

He started to fade out on the screen. "I'll leave you now," he said. "The road home is clear for you and one of our heavy cruisers will intercept to pick you up at the edge of our spatial area and bring you in.''

"Hey!" said Feliz. "Just a moment. Are you coming back?"

Psi-Man Verde chuckled, as if from a long ways away.

"To your mind?" he said. "Only by special permission.''

Then he was gone.

Feliz blinked his eyes and sat up as if he had fallen asleep. From the cabin adjoining, he could hear the sound of Kai, still humming.

Domestic already, thought Feliz, with a sort of desperation. *And what do I really know about her? Nothing. Absolutely nothing.* The thought reminded him of something else he had meant to ask the psi-man.

"Kai!" he called.

"Yes—yes!" she caroled back.

"Want to ask you something."

There was a moment's pause.

"Yes?"

Now I'll find out, thought Feliz.

"Kai," he said. "Rabbits. The rabbits you had there around Shangri-La. Can you tell me why a rabbit should bark?"

There was a long moment of dead silence. Feliz opened his mouth to call again, but just at that moment Kai's features appeared around the edge of the cabin door. Her face was set in a mask of astonishment.

"Why not?" she said.

Gordon R. Dickson

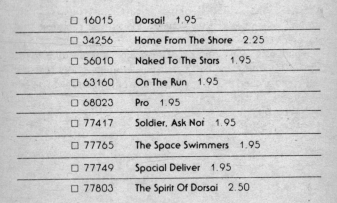

☐ 16015	Dorsai!	1.95
☐ 34256	Home From The Shore	2.25
☐ 56010	Naked To The Stars	1.95
☐ 63160	On The Run	1.95
☐ 68023	Pro	1.95
☐ 77417	Soldier, Ask Not	1.95
☐ 77765	The Space Swimmers	1.95
☐ 77749	Spacial Deliver	1.95
☐ 77803	The Spirit Of Dorsai	2.50

Available wherever paperbacks are sold or use this coupon.

Current and Recent Ace Science Fiction Releases of Special Interest, As Selected by the Editor of Destinies

Poul Anderson, ENSIGN FLANDRY	**$1.95**
FLANDRY OF TERRA	**$1.95**
THE MAN WHO COUNTS	**$1.95**
James Baen, THE BEST FROM GALAXY, VOL. IV	**$1.95**
Donald R. Bensen, AND HAVING WRIT	**$1.95**
Ben Bova, THE BEST FROM ANALOG	**$2.25**
Arsen Darnay, THE KARMA AFFAIR	**$2.25**
Gordon R. Dickson, PRO (illustrated)	**$1.95**
David Drake, HAMMER'S SLAMMERS	**$1.95**
Randall Garrett, MURDER AND MAGIC (fantasy)	**$1.95**
Harry Harrison, SKYFALL	**$1.95**
Keith Laumer, RETIEF AT LARGE	**$1.95**
RETIEF UNBOUND	**$1.95**
Philip Francis Nowlan, ARMAGEDDON 2419 A.D. (revised by Spider Robinson)	**$1.95**
Jerry Pournelle, EXILES TO GLORY	**$1.95**
Spider Robinson, CALLAHAN'S CROSSTIME SALOON	**$1.75**
Thomas J. Ryan, THE ADOLESCENCE OF P-1	**$2.25**
Fred Saberhagen, BERSERKER MAN	**$1.95**
THE HOLMES/DRACULA FILE (fantasy)	**$1.95**
LOVE CONQUERS ALL	**$1.95**
AN OLD FRIEND OF THE FAMILY (fantasy)	**$1.95**
THE ULTIMATE ENEMY	**$1.95**
Dennis Schmidt, WAY-FARER	**$1.75**
Bob Shaw, SHIP OF STRANGERS	**$1.95**
VERTIGO	**$1.95**
Charles Sheffield, SIGHT OF PROTEUS	**$1.75**
Norman Spinrad, THE STAR-SPANGLED FUTURE	**$2.25**
G. Harry Stine, THE THIRD INDUSTRIAL REVOLUTION (science fact)	**$2.25**
Ian Watson, MIRACLE VISITORS	**$1.95**